WHAT PEOPLE

BLOOD

I have long admired author Jim Patrick's imagination, knowledge of politics, and grasp of global affairs, a background that gives depth and breadth to his complex, wide-ranging plot. I am already looking forward to the next volume in the new series!
Patricia Feldman, Senior Associate Director, Altshuler Learning Enhancement Center, Southern Methodist University

Finally a true to life yet fictional account of the immense corruption at the highest levels of our government, political systems and business community. America is being sold to the highest bidder and *Blood Profit$* is the first novel I've read that gets it right. A great read. I felt I almost knew some of these characters. A call to arms for every American who is tired of those who disparage the US Constitution and the American way of life for their own profiteering!
Howard Putnam, Former Airline CEO, Speaker & Author of *The Winds of Turbulence*
www.howardputnam.com

Blood Profit$* is a fast-paced page-turner from beginning to end, and an all-too-believable tale of corruption at the highest levels of government. *Blood Profit$ would make a great story for a TV mini-series.
Randall Larsen, author *Our Own Worst Enemy* (Grand Central, 2007)

A superb "page turner". Grips you from page one and does not let go. Plenty of plot twists, but not convoluted. A MUST read!!
Stephen Hull, MS, PhD

Being a PHD scientist with over 40 years of work at high levels with both private business and government entities made *Blood Profit$* a very compelling and interesting account of how 'business as normal' is anything but normal.

I am very familiar with the work of Mr. Patrick and Mr. Tomaszek and their abilities to be visionaries and prophets of the social, political and economic challenges just ahead. When I reviewed *Blood Profit$*, and the unmasking of special agendas on Capitol Hill, shady business deals and outright collaboration with the mob, it seemed all too real.

Although *Blood Profit$* is a fictional account of how greed and corruption at all levels of the US extended enterprise by using mass deception, leads to the possible collapse of the American way of life; even killing innocent Americans being sent off to fight phony wars all for greed driven wealth.

The portrayal of a 'captured' Lithium market in the hands of a few working in conjunction with organized crime and even underwritten by our own tax dollars, puts chills down backs of thinking persons who follow the age old 'golden rule.'

Do we really live in a decaying society that is out of control and at the hands of organized corruption? That is something only you the reader can decide, but the story told on the pages of *Blood Profit$* could also be very real.

Blood Profit$ provides the reader with the age old story of good vs. evil. But, it also portrays the coming of age of Generation X who ultimately rid the country of decades of corruption by exposing every element of criminal activity no matter what the costs or what levels of those exposed are in American society.

John Ferrante PhD, Nationally recognized Scientist, and Professor

Blood Profit$

Blood Profit$

James N. Patrick Sr.

and

J. Victor Tomaszek

Winchester, UK
Washington, USA

First published by Roundfire Books, 2014
Roundfire Books is an imprint of John Hunt Publishing Ltd., Laurel House, Station Approach,
Alresford, Hants, SO24 9JH, UK
office1@jhpbooks.net
www.johnhuntpublishing.com
www.roundfire-books.com

For distributor details and how to order please visit the 'Ordering' section on our website.

Text copyright: James N. Patrick Sr. and J. Victor Tomaszek 2013

ISBN: 978 1 78279 483 7

A CIP catalogue record for this book is available from the British Library.

Design: Lee Nash

Printed in the USA by Edwards Brothers Malloy

We operate a distinctive and ethical publishing philosophy in all
areas of our business, from our global network of authors to
production and worldwide distribution.

This fictional account of corruption in war is dedicated to America's military men and women.

The authors are donating 15% of the royalties of Blood Profit$ to: http://www.woundedwarriorproject.org/

To our families who have had to endure the two years
of research and analysis it took to focus on and write
Blood Profit$

To Howard Putnam who believed in the project and
spearheaded publication

To those who reviewed the novel, especially those who lent
their names to it – John, Howard, Steve H, Pat, Steve P, David,
Rita, Billy, Stephanie, Kallie, Jay, Shelley.

"Fear not little darlin' of dying if the world is sovereign and free.
For we'll fight to the last for as long as liberty be."
'The Alamo' Donovan

Chapter 1

"A hundred grand," wide receiver AJ Morales repeated to himself yet again. "All debts erased in an instant." But his father's warm smile and glowing eyes invaded his mind. "Corruption killed my father and I will not slander his memory. I will not drop another pass."

AJ rose in pain and shuffled back to his teammates.

"Well, folks," the color commentator said to his television audience, "while we wait for a stretcher to transport an injured player off the field, we can recap a game that many of us are watching with a sense of disbelief. The UCLA Bruins, a team that has struggled all year, and often won ugly, has so far played an error-free game. Their opponent, the University of Texas Longhorns, a team that has crushed and sometimes even embarrassed all comers this season, has struggled with interceptions, missed field goals, and penalty upon penalty."

On a typical day in Pasadena, California – clear skies, upper seventies, not dry, not humid, no wind, the annual Rose Bowl parade was particularly colorful and now the venerable stadium was filled to the brim with football fans. UCLA Bruins fans were out in numbers to exhibit school spirit, expecting a bold showing. Texas Longhorn fans expected their team to crush the Bruins and salt the wounds from scored points with waves and chants to the rallying tune of 'Charge' from several horns from different sections and levels of the stadium.

"This game has to be a bitter disappointment for the University of Texas Longhorns. I'm Jack Fanning and with me is a former Heisman trophy winner and NFL great, Chuck 'the Barrel' Barrows who has been handling the play-by-play for you."

"Thanks, Jack. This re-energized UCLA team has shocked the Longhorns today, who came here with hopes of completing a perfect season."

"It seems the Bruins found their mojo a few weeks back and have turned a lackluster season well around. How does something like this happen, Chuck?"

"We can credit the UCLA offensive line with holding off the Texas defense. Palermo has been given all the time he needs to connect with his receivers. For me, the Bruins began to dominate after that brutal sack on Prendergast in the final minutes of the second quarter. While two linebackers were called for unnecessary roughness, the Longhorns' quarterback was slow to get up and hasn't been connecting with his receivers."

The sack was replayed several times, at normal speed, slo-mo twice and from various angles.

"Ouch!" Jack said.

"It almost looks personal," Chuck the 'Barrel' muttered. "Poor sportsmanship."

"And the Bruins have totally shut down AJ Morales. Zero completions today. Zero."

"Jack, the Texas defense has to be bone-tired. UCLA has kept them on the field with excellent ball control and play selection."

"And Texas was favored by ten. Maybe we could get a camera on the mascot, Joe Bruin and his best girl, Josephine. You can see the anticipation in their actions."

"Alright, they have waved off the stretcher. Caesar Sanchez is up and is being helped off the field. Now Texas has lost its best running back. Less than a minute left to play. A camera scan of the fans clearly shows who is rooting for whom. The spectators already leaving have to be fans of the Longhorns. The thrill of victory and the agony of defeat."

"The score is fourteen to nine," Chuck said. "A field goal won't do it for Texas and UCLA has them at their own five-yard line. For a pass play, quarterback Charlie Prendergast will have to fade into his own end zone. UCLA defense is lining up and showing a blitz. Talk about 'the whole ball of wax' resting on one play, this

Texas quarterback may end his college career buried in his own end zone."

* * *

Charlie Prendergast was nervous as he readied himself for the play. The hit he took just before halftime hurt his back and his head pounded. He had never been hit that hard before and knew he had not fully recovered; dots were still appearing in his peripheral vision. As the center hiked the ball on command, Charlie could see his burnt-orange front line immediately pushed backward, his safety pocket collapsed. A wall of UCLA blue and gold jerseys picked their way through gaps and accelerated at one target: him. Backpedaling, searching in desperation for an open receiver, Charlie knew a first down was a must. No one open, footsteps and grunts in his ears.

Sprinting to his right, evading a swarm of opponents reaching for him, his eyes locked on his go-to man, AJ Morales, moving at a full gallop along the left sideline, a one-step lead on three defenders. Feeling a slight tug on the back of his jersey Charlie cocked his shoulders and hips, uncoiled and let fly the pigskin, across the grain, from right to extreme left and long, as hard as he could throw. The simultaneous hits from behind and the side forced the air from his lungs as his body was flattened to the ground. He winced in agony, a stabbing pain in his knee, his left leg pinned at an unnatural angle.

A spontaneous roar from the stands.

Charlie cursed. *Had to be an interception. Must have thrown short. Sacked in my own end zone.*

But amid the thunder of the crowd and the smell of linebacker sweat, Charlie's ears filled with UCLA linebacker cursing as they pushed themselves up, using his pain-racked body for leverage. Rising to his knees with a grimace, he saw the scoreboard no longer read fourteen to nine. Now it said fourteen to fifteen. The roar was for his receiver, AJ, who despite all odds, had scored. Charlie's heart pounded in his ears, his stomach filled with butterflies, the euphoria of triumph only slightly deadening the pain. His bull-like center saw Charlie's dilemma. Everybody, refs included, were at the other end of the field with Morales. He put a muscled arm around Charlie's waist and helped him off the field. Charlie had missed seeing AJ's completion in real life but it would be played over and over across the entire country for years to come. Charlie would view it time after time, noting how he disappeared under a mountain of muscle as a football hurtled like a missile toward AJ, who running full out, leapt and turned for a one-handed catch, his forward momentum so forceful he was able to hop backwards the few yards needed to cross the goal line. The referee raised two arms to the sky and the crowd erupted. Touchdown!

Charles Prendergast III was in the record books; his dad, mom and mentor watching in the stands. Dad was Admiral Charles (Elmer) Prendergast, Head of the U.S. Joint Chiefs of Staff, one of many in a long line of Prendergast military brass dating back to the American Revolutionary War; his mentor, the Honorable Parker S. Cowel was the Senior United States Senator, a Republican from the 'Big Sky' state of Montana.

* * *

"Chuck, that has to be at the very limit of how far a quarterback can throw a ball."

"Given the luxury of time, the top dawgs can throw 100 yards in practice. But that's not the same as when a wall of linebacker is coming at you. Then we have velocity. Who can deliver a ball at top speed? Then there is accuracy, and running one way while throwing at an angle. All those factors had to line up perfectly for Charlie Prendergast to complete that mother of all Hail Mary's. I guess that ball flew maybe 130 yards."

"Chuck, right now the NFL owners are checking out how much is in their piggy banks. They'll all want this guy. Five will get you ten, Prendergast will probably be the number-one draft choice, and we know that Dallas has expressed a lot of interest. So while they have the number-three choice, they will have to put some sweet deal together to get him."

"Prendergast would fill the stadium in every time he plays. Just imagine the opposing defense and the threat of how fast and how far he can hurl that missile or how the fans would anticipate him throwing long."

His left knee throbbed, and shooting pains ripped through his leg muscles, but the drug of victory sedated Charlie. Lifted onto the shoulders of two gigantic linebackers and paraded around the field, he shook hands with out-of-control teammates, coaches, fellow students, rabid fans and complete strangers. This was what it was all about – taking victory out of the jaws of defeat. With chaos all around, a stationary vision caught his attention. Raven hair, an electric smile and bright green eyes looking at him. Antonia.

With camera lenses alert with hopes of snapping the definitive shot to capture the essence of today's game, the Texas homecoming queen and former Miss Texas, Antonia Scozzari pushed one hip to her right side and smiled and waved to the hero of the game in a more-than-subtle flirty pose. The media photographers lit her up like a firecracker and the Internet buzzed for a week with her image, bio, rumors and ambitions all told in bumper-sticker terseness and sound-bite succinctness. Antonia was the only thing on the planet that could have and did take Charlie's mind from his success on the field.

The linebackers brought Charlie off their shoulders and set him gently back on earth. Then AJ was at his side, supporting him just as he nearly collapsed while attempting to put weight on his left leg. Antonia ran up and embraced both of them. When a cameraman asked for a picture, Antonia stood between the two

Texan heroes and they smiled. Charlie collapsed with a shriek as his left knee gave out with mind-numbing agony. The crowd instinctively separated as he was helped into the locker room by AJ and the two linebackers. Wide-eyed smiles turned into concern.

"How the hell did you catch that pass, AJ?" Charlie whispered.

"Montesquieu just sprang into my head and reminded me that true liberty is the freedom to do as we ought to do."

Charlie winced, but not from his bodily pain. "Do me a favor, amigo, and don't share that on any interviews. They will burn you as a witch or have you committed. Help me to that cot."

"Your leg bone is broken, sticking out of your skin, you're sweating like a whore in church and you're cracking jokes. What is it with you?"

"My way of avoiding fear – make light of it all."

Someone opened the dam and the instant heroes were surrounded by newsmen and women who shouldered and elbowed, cut and weaved around Charlie's teammates and coaches to light up Charlie and AJ with lights and push microphones into their faces.

"What does it feel like to be a Texas hero?" one sports reporter said, reminding Charlie of a drooling dog hungry for his dinner.

"Damn," Charlie said in his maximum drawl. "AJ here runs down the field at the speed of light, eluding the best pass defenders on the planet to catch a poorly thrown wobbly ball and everyone in the damn stadium is all gaga over the now one-legged quarterback."

A big laugh from all and the lights and mikes attacked AJ. Despite his discomfort, Charlie rose at the waist and managed a smile. "You're the hero of this game, amigo. And we all know it."

The UT coach instructed his team to shoo the reports away and a wall of muscle complied, leaving only a few men in the room.

"You need some Makers, buddy," AJ said.

"This will do more for him," the team doctor said as he readied a syringe. "It's Novocain. Relief without the hangover. Let me work here, boys. This is not a good break, especially for an athlete."

"Doc?" Charlie pleaded. "My knee makes me moan in pain so ya' think I got KNEE-MOAN-IA?"

"Not funny, Charlie. What's the damage, Doc?" AJ asked.

"He broke his leg below the knee and the knee is cocked to the outside. Never saw one like this before. We need to get him to a hospital for an MRI immediately."

An all-business security detail preceded Charlie's mother and father into the locker room, followed by a man who changed AJ's feelings of euphoria for his incredible pass reception into one of cold hard hatred. AJ glared at Senator Parker Cowel, the man with whom he had a score to settle. It was only his extreme self-control keeping him from giving free rein to his growing rage and a vision of choking the red-faced fat man to death.

"Charlie, one minute I'm cheering for you and then I hear you are badly hurt," his mother said as she cradled Charlie's head in her hands.

Admiral Charles Prendergast, the reason for the security detail, stared at his son's smashed leg. "This isn't football, its carnage. What were those dame linebackers thinking, Son?"

"Dad, Mom, you've never met AJ Morales. He's the guy who caught my pass and won the game for the Longhorns."

AJ forced a smile and shook hands first with Mrs. Prendergast and then with the admiral. While Charlie was a good-looking man, AJ could see his eyes and mouth came from his still-beautiful mother.

"And this is U.S. Senator Parker Cowel," Charlie said.

AJ offered a firm grip and felt one in return as he stared down into the eyes of the man who had caused his father's death. AJ sensed the senator was not too happy shaking his hand. *So the hundred K check in the mail had to come from this son of a bitch. Doing the right thing is always rewarding. I never want to be beholden to this prick.*

"Morales? From around here, son?"

"AJ hails from Montana," Charlie said.

AJ noticed a tense jaw, a sense of masked anger coming from the senator. Was he connecting the dots between AJ and his father?

"That was an incredible catch and touchdown, son," the senator said to AJ, "I believe I will remember it my entire life"

"Thank you," AJ said. "I think it is good to always remember important things, you know, the life changers." AJ watched as the edges of the senator's lips drooped slightly from his polite smile.

"Well, Charlie," the senator said, turning from AJ's stare, "we need to get you to the best medical care we can and get this leg of yours back to playing status."

After Charlie's parents and Senator Cowel left, Charlie offered his hand to AJ, who took it.

"We did it, buddy. Despite this scrape on my knee, we can go back to school as heroes."

"You never told me you knew Senator Cowel."

"I keep that stuff quiet, AJ. Most people think I'm name dropping or I think I'm somehow special if I mention who I know. Mostly Dad's friends. I've met many of the big dawgs in Congress."

"But he's a personal family friend?"

"I call him Uncle Parker when we're in private. I've known him since I was a tike. He bought me my first pair of boots."

The celebration of the University of Texas winning in the Rose Bowl spilled out into the streets of Pasadena and lingered for two days. While the residents of the city were used to the victory parties and tolerated it, the merchants made a killing, especially on beer, wine and fast food. The two heroes of the game, the quarterback and his wide receiver spent those hours at Huntington Memorial hospital and then at a Pasadena sports clinic. AJ wheeled Charlie around from one test to another and, as results came in, they listened to an increasingly grim prognosis. On the third day, with the family, AJ and the head football coach assembled, the final verdict was laid on the table.

"Charlie," the orthopedic surgeon flown in from Michael Reese Hospital pointed to the MRI results said, "this knee has been too damaged to repair. It will have to be replaced."

"Will I have a guarantee I'll be 100 percent for the NFL?"

Charlie's military trained head coach broke the awkward silence.

"I'm afraid you've played your last game, Charlie. It's over."

AJ looked away as he saw his teammate turn pale, eyes focused a hundred miles away.

"Count yourself lucky you're going out in glory," the coach continued. "A Longhorns' legend. And there is always coaching. UT will always hold a spot on our staff open for you."

Charlie looked to his father.

"Son, you made your terrific football play. Now you'll graduate and it's on to better things. We will talk more in the next few weeks."

"Guess I'm not meant to follow in our family's military tradition," Charlie said, staring at his cast leg, sans his typical wry humor.

AJ leaned against the wall as Charlie's parents said their goodbyes and the doctor and coach left with them.

Charlie broke the awkward silence in a choked voice. "We'll both be at the same football games as we hoped, except you'll be on the field and I'll be in the stands."

AJ bit his lip, struggling to think of something positive to say. "Remember when you used to compare us elite athletes to expensive horses and not human beings?"

"Yeah. Our job was to make money for our owners."

"Well you are living proof that is not true."

"How so, amigo?"

"When a racehorse breaks its leg they shoot it."

Chapter 2

The American dream of freedom and justice was built on the back of the horse. Lexington, Kentucky is perhaps the quintessential place you can still hear the hoof beats of the nickering giants. You can lean over the split-rail fences and experience these once-critical implements of transportation, war and commerce as they graze and gallop over sweet-smelling manicured pastures. Now relegated to pets for racing and hobbies, they are all but forgotten as having served us loyally in our quest for freedom from slavery of body and soul.

Equines provided a critical asset in the American Revolutionary Army – the cavalry. They served as the engine of our westward movement, hauling those rickety-looking but durable covered wagons across the country where no foot or hoof ever trod. With cowboys on their backs, horses charged fearlessly into herds of driven beef cattle, ripe for market, food to sustain an always growing and hungry people. They pulled raw materials and finished goods along the Erie Canal. Horses were there for every leg of America's thirst for individual freedom. The horse was part of the spirit that forged an *E Pluribus Unum* country, unique in the history of our world.

As individual and collective success and wealth grew, 'El Diablo,' the fiery steed was relegated to the curio of 'Old Dobbin,' the pony for children to ride. The age and value of the American horse had passed, abandoned and forgotten for her gallant service to her country, her willingness to serve and for her indomitable constitution. She had faded as had the American meritocracy fueled by the beliefs that each soul has merit and eternal truths.

Amid lush green pastures where mares grazed, stallions threatened, and colts frolicked, three elderly American statesmen – traitorous oligarchs profiteering on the blood of young American patriots – sat leisurely around a table in the heavily wooded study of a Lexington hunting lodge with their host, an American Mafioso, 'Don' Nicola Scozzari, the financial mind of the Boston Mob and a graduate of the Wharton School of Finance; a true genius in money laundering. Together, at their regular quarterly meeting, in the guise of a corporate executive committee of their board of directors, and thereby tax deductible, they discussed the state of their mutual business, revenue and expenses. They also discussed funding a South American war to boost the profits of the Mob backers. Theirs was a ten-year plan, carefully guided through recruitment of the brightest and best U.S. talent assembled from pedigreed universities. These protégés were developed to gather the appropriate metrics, analyze, plan, control and ensure quality implementations – on time and under budget. They were tutored by Machiavelli and mentored by the likes of these oligarch fathers who now sat in this ornate office, men who had built personal financial empires committing America to warring in Asia and the Middle East, reaping unimaginable profits, and always maintaining an iron grip on their oligarchy.

These men knew how to leverage the modern American horse – high technology, to better impress their wills upon reality, cut costs and reap profits. Their enormous political power echoed through the halls of the U.S. Congress. Their tentacles reached into every corner of society. Their influence spanned the globe. Hegemony reigned as America became an empire like so many in the past, her people generally oblivious or purposely blind to it, the Land of the Free and Home of the Brave now a transparent and shriveled collective soul. Sipping bourbon with branch water from leaded crystal tumblers they formed a cartel of powerful men who did not necessarily like or trust one other, but came together in individual self-interest. It was business.

"We have ten states now with more people on welfare than not," Senator Parker Cowel, the five-term Republican elder statesman from Montana, noted. A portly man, pale complexion, balding, his belly pushing against his buttoned suit jacket, he sat in his high-backed red upholstered chair as if it were a throne. "That's 163 electoral votes guaranteed to vote for big government since those on the dole will always feather their own nests."

A fellow U.S. senator cleared his throat then took a sip of bourbon. "California and Illinois represent nearly half. What can we do there?"

"Lost causes," Cowel replied. "Multi-generational parasites are in the majority. Nothing short of another financial collapse followed by an all-out war would change them."

"So it is time to move on the lithium interests?" the Mafioso asked in a matter-of-fact tone.

Cowel nodded to his host. "The Chinese must be found to be infringing on the Monroe Doctrine by supplying the rebels in Bolivia with tactical weapons in exchange for in-country missile bases and control of the largest lithium deposit on earth."

"It will be like JFK and the Russians going head to head in Cuba in 63!" Retired US Senator and Majority Leader Billy Kiddenly said, suddenly alive and animated.

"That fiasco nearly ended to our detriment," current Senate Majority Leader, Buford Ebers (R – IN) said, his constant glare legendary. "The damn Russians pushed too hard, and that damn Jack Kennedy held his cards too long. And tell me we can't successfully attach a Chinese oil shortage to this scenario; damn right we can and the American people will eat it up and demand we stop those Chinks right there in Bolivia!"

"The media will reiterate that China has adequate oil reserves," Cowel replied, sitting arrow straight in his chair with arms crossed. "We will justify the Chinese urgency for weaning themselves off of fossil fuels because their god damn air is near lethal in Beijing. The story will read the Red Party does not need a billion Asians up in rebellion. They want lithium. They will want to protect their investment in the U.S. with missile bases in

Bolivia to corner the world's lithium deposits; a true monopoly if they can take down our interests in Afghanistan. We can sell this uncertainty and doubt to the American people hook, line and sinker and inject fear into the veins of anyone in Congress that might speak against us as not looking out for American interests. The President is a lame duck now, and the people disillusioned with him."

Kiddenly fiddled with his tie as he spoke. "That will keep our war mongers itching to invade Bolivia, the peaceniks will rag on the importance of the Green issues and our private military contractors will make a killing and possibly jump start this crappy economy."

"A downturned economy is a good thing, Billy," Ebers said. "It keeps the Mob bellyaching about jobs and voting more power to Congress every year. A nation in debt is a good nation."

Cowel summed up the new war strategy for his fellow senior board members. "Then we agree the story will be leaked that the Bolivians have the largest lithium deposits in the world. They lack the knowhow and the infrastructure to mine the product or manufacture lithium-ion batteries. They are in preliminary talks with the Chinese who want to risk the entire future of the world economy on the pipe dream of clean and reliable power. We all know electric cars, faster computers, boutique cell phones and that kind of crap all have one shortcoming – a lack of long-lasting and efficient power. That's the long suit of lithium-ion technology. I smell profit. If we dump venture capital into the hands of the right R&D entrepreneurs, lithium will become pure gold for us."

"Left to their own devices the Bolivians would drive this opportunity into the ground. Have we looked at a plan to buy off their government ourselves?" Cowel asked. "Bribery is a way of life with the Latinos down there. We sell them the equipment they need to mine it, we build the infrastructure, and everybody makes out with maximum financial gain and minimal effort. For them it's an extra taco in every pot."

"Let me make it clear I have no intentions to help develop South America," Ebers stated, cleaning his glasses with a handkerchief. "Too much of a threat. They will remain third world. Period. With no weapons left behind to come back to haunt our interests later, none!"

"So," the Mafia host whispered as he studied his drink, "how do we guarantee the sale of this to the oral majority and do-gooders on this proposed threat from Bolivia?"

"Our intelligence will leak to the media that a mad Bolivian dictator is working with the Chinese to develop WMDs in exchange for access to lithium deposits," Cowel said. "As we have already discussed, I'll guran-damn-tee we can sell this to Congress and the American people if we can get people to believe that these nut cases are setting up shop in our own backyard. Lot of flag waving, patriotism and regurgitation of the Kennedy Cuban Missile Crisis BS!"

"I like it," Kiddenly nodded. "An invasion is relatively straightforward to protect U.S. security. Imagine our Pacific fleet sitting off the western coast of South America. Some powerful media images there. Some saber rattling could make the nation proud of our warriors again. We'll need to improve relations with Peru and Chile anyway. We can ship product out by cargo aircraft or large tankers to some of our Central American sites."

"Our men know desert warfare well," Cowel said. "We'll need to include deep jungle training if memory serves on the Bolivian climate."

"Who's the dictator?" Nicola asked.

"It's a stable centrist government," Ebers replied. "But there is a socialist element there. If we can find the right political and military types, label them freedom fighters and offer them a loaded Cayman Islands account, we can manufacture a coup." Ebers leaned elbows on the table. "We certainly have experience with this. Tip the scales from a balance to an out-of-whack left or right government and offer to free the workers from tyranny. Send a team in now. Identify some military fanatic type who's second or third in command, someone like Colonel Diego Voctoiar Tomas who heads the Eagle Corp. Buy him. Dispatch a group of our phantom mercenaries from Afghanistan to eliminate his superior officers. Drones are under scrutiny domestically, but no one will give a rat's ass if we take out some south-of-the-border Commie Spicks."

"Then it's settled. We'll need to finalize a plan, a budget."

"And profits," the Mafioso raised his voice. "The New York and Boston families are both bitching about decreasing profits. Those Wall Street ass wipes hurt our bottom line, also."

"Profits will come like a tsunami once we pull the trigger on South America," Kiddenly promised.

"How will the demographics play out?" Cowel demanded.

"Like always, the majority is city dwellers," Kiddenly replied. "The high-density apartment building and tenement dwellers, multi-generational welfare recipients are easy to sway. We preach class war, race war, and ensure drugs are readily available. We issue food stamps so they can get their iPhones and iPods, big-ticket gym shoes, supersize their Whoppers and tattoos. We'll help them project frustration and fear somewhere other than at themselves. As for the better-off city dwellers, they are mostly lifelong Democrats with a smattering of independents and an ever-growing cache of those with no political identity who just run their mouths."

"They are like sheep," the Mafioso said, "and easy marks. The bulk of the suburbs hold the white flight, well-off commuters who live off the city but don't like its dirt or crime; small business owners, technocrats, 'maintenance of the world' types. Politically they range from liberals, to independents and conservatives – the South being the only exception, where they are mostly conservative to ultra conservative Evangelicals. We have some Neo Nazis, KKKs, anarchists, hardcore Communists but they don't vote, tend to pitch their piss to the media or blow up a candy store or something."

"We can do some saber rattling for the rural and Southern types," Cowel added. "Invoke some of that 'thou' and 'thee' Bible crap; tell them South America is a communist threat. Show some shots of Rio's Carnival – all those sweaty, hefty black girls shaking their T&A to fertility rites dance steps at it will rile up the Christians."

"So," Ebers said, gathering his phone and papers off the table, "we fill the airwaves with shit about how the flow of drugs into the U.S. will finally end if we move on Bolivia."

"That's good." The Mafioso stood and nodded. "They'd vote for Joseph Stalin if he could guarantee legalized marijuana and cuts the cost of cocaine and we've got a solid flow of opium from the poppy fields we manage in Afghanistan."

"Any new business?" the elder statesman Kiddenly asked, before draining his glass.

"What the hell happened at the Rose Bowl last weekend?" Ebers demanded of Cowel. "You cost some of us a pretty penny, Parker."

"I had the fix in on two UCLA linemen to take out the Texas quarterback."

"I looked like a fool," Kiddenly complained. "I was on my yacht with two young girls and they bet on UCLA and me on Texas. It was a winner says and loser does bet. Still fun, but I don't like surprises."

"Parker, why didn't you buy the quarterback from Texas?" Ebers snarled.

"He's one of my protégés. I'll turn him when the time is right and for bigger things than a football game. And remember his daddy is an Admiral who we do not have in the proper key position yet."

"My people were upset over the game, too," the Mafioso added, his eye glaring, cold as ice.

"Did you see that throw? That catch?" Cowel pleaded. "We offered that damn Morales punk one hundred grand to drop every key pass. He did his job until the last few seconds of the game. Then he pulls that damn pigskin out of the air with one hand. I'll get him. His time is coming."

Chapter 3

"Word has it a U.S. senator is on base primarily to see you, Major Abbott, ma'am."

"Loose lips sink ships, Sergeant Kelly. And knock off the ma'am crap."

"Yes, ma—sir," Sergeant Kelly replied as he steered the armored truck around a pit in the road, surrounding it in a cloud of dust. "I heard the senator got off a C-130 with a crowd of journalists. It was their loose lips."

"And that bothers you?"

"Hell, yes. Those idiots think they can do anything and go anywhere they want. Last tour, we got tagged to let some arrogant reporter and his camera crew go out with us looking for a fire fight or some dead bodies. It was as if what they did was vital, and we were just their bodyguards."

"And that can get you killed."

"Amen. We were taking fire from a small ridge, firing back just to keep them off guard while we called in an air strike. Then I see this stupid cameramen stand up and point his video camera at the ridge. I shouted to him, but he just kept filming until he got his head blown off. Then the reporter—"

"They call them journalists."

"We call them dumb pricks. The reporter shit his pants when he sees the camera guy's brains mixed with video-camera parts and he started crying and gagging. So one of our guys has to babysit him while we're under attack. When we call in that a reporter is down, we get the air support in half the typical time it takes. They level the cliff. That means the soldiers are just meat out there. Then, when a chopper lands to take the cameraman's body, the reporter starts whining to the crew how inept we were and unable to protect a news crew. I end up spending two hours in debriefing with big brass, not just the 2nd lewies we usually get."

"Are you kidding me?"

"So that's why I don't want to be part of any reality TV. They don't like reality."

"Senator Cowel is the reason I got into West Point, and I admire him enormously. I am sure his reason for being here is in full support of our mission and on orders from our Commander and Chief."

"Whoa. If you are someone special, I take back what I just said."

"Kelly, how long have we worked together here?"

"Don't get me wrong, Major. I just got enough shit to deal with here. How do you get a senator to visit you?"

"I won the sharpshooter competition last month."

"And he's here to give you a medal?"

"Among other things. And yes, the politicians and the journalists love to single out minorities for Boy and Girl Scout badges. Makes the viewers back home see the war as politically correct, just and fair."

"At least this is a better gig than guarding the poppy fields in Afghanistan from getting torched. But I still don't understand who is burning them."

A dust devil at 2 o'clock caught Major Abbot's eyes. From the Humvee's shotgun position she scanned the faded and desolate war-pocked landscape, this area of Northern Iraq ravaged after ten years of continuous conflict, looking for quick movements, potential rooftops for possible snipers, obstacles in the road, approaching cars, trucks and wagons for any threats, the people for any sign of aggression; everything moving or still was held in suspicion. She was leading a 'ride along review' inspection tour of the immediate area to assess more the mood of the locals rather than the threat of insurgent violence. Spitting, rock throwing or angry gestures were not on display. The heat reflecting from the sand rose and rippled, making everything shimmer, seem unreal.

Army Lt. Mansfield Cooper wiped his forehead with the sleeve of his fatigue shirt, constantly watched the road, avoiding any debris that could hide an IED, landmine, or anything that would slow their truck to give a sniper a better shot at them.

"Where did you learn to shoot, sir?"

"You mean with a nickname like 'Hawk Eye?'"

The driver smiled.

"Home. Montana. Coyote, wolf, mountain lion, duck, pheasant, turkey, deer."

"I could use some of that turkey."

"Even I am not that good a hunter to find turkey in the desert."

"Glad anyway that you can handle your rifle. This Sunni Triangle is almost as dangerous as Harlem."

"You're from Harlem?"

"Queens. But as kids we drove through Harlem at night."

"Almost anything could happen there, too?"

"I thought war would be like a fire fight with the enemy out there and us here. Instead, they are all around us. That preys on me big time."

"An old tactic to elicit fear."

As the camouflaged Humvee approached the territory border of Mosul, U.S. Army Major Julia 'Hawk Eye' Abbott relaxed, allowing herself a respite from her catlike surveillance. The temperature gauge read 112 degrees outside. Looking out over a landscape so different from the familiar nourishing green and blue colors of home, she wondered how she had ended up here. A collage of fond childhood memories growing up in Bozeman, Montana returned. Her mind filled with images and impressions of hiking and rock climbing in the Sourdough Canyon, boating on the Gallatin River, rafting in the frigid streams, and fishing in the Bozeman Creek near Main Street. The smell of thickly cut bacon, sizzling at the 4 Bs Restaurant, prickled her senses. Back to reality; first a meeting with her mentor, U.S. Senator, Parker

Cowel (R, MT), who had somehow plucked her out of Big Sky Country in her early teens and into the chalky rock and wreckage strewn world of Iraq – then back to base, a quick soapy hot shower and—

A deafening roar. Her ear drums popped. A bone-jarring jolt to her right side. A cry of pain through a grimace as her body jerked upward and to her left. An explosion forced everything but her survival instincts from her thoughts, as she felt the armored truck catapult into the air, landing hard on its side. Sand pushed into her nostrils and down her throat, her ears rang with pain. IED. Hanging upside down, blood rushing to her head, she released her seat belt then kicked open the crumpled door, with the business end of her M16 leading the way out of the crippled truck. She squinted from the smoke and dust, her eyes watering. She struggled to reorient herself. Where were her Recon teammates? What was the damage? Where was the enemy? Pftt. Pfft. Pfft, she heard over the ringing in her ears. *We're taking fire. Small caliber. One soldier down. Get him to safety. My responsibility.* While struggling to put the wrecked Humvee between herself and the gunfire, a blow to her left temple wrenched her head forward, flattening her to the rocky ground. A warm liquid spread over her face. The hollow sound of automatic fire from around her was a sound of hope. Two of her men were engaging the enemy.

Struggling to rise, coughing dust, a strong arm grabbed her at the waist, lifting her to the protection of the destroyed truck. Wiping blood from her face with her sleeve, she realized the left side of her head was numb on the outside, with daggers of pain on the inside, flashing shimmers of light behind her eye. She wiped blood from her right eye. A blurry face above, then focus. A familiar face. A second face behind his. "*Three hit, including herself,*" she heard. She rose to her knees. Lopez was returning fire and shouting something. Julia made out "*Snipers at 2 o'clock. Two, possibly three. Together. In a makeshift rubble nest.*" A puff of smoke at Lopez's left shoulder; he cursed as he crumpled to the ground, his face lay half in mud made from the Humvee's ruptured radiator and the dust.

Three men down. The radio unreachable. Three snipers. If only I could see better. As if in answer to a prayer she spotted the team's M249 machine gun, thrown from the truck in the explosion. It lay a few meters in front of her, on the road, in a direct line with the sniper fire. Without thought, she left the protection of the derelict truck, running in a zigzag pattern toward the machine gun, her M16 on rock and roll, the ground around her peppered with tiny dust clouds as bullets zinged as they ricocheted off the stony road. Dropping her spent rifle, she snatched and shouldered the machine gun, its barrel spitting death as she accelerated her full frontal assault. Her charge caught the snipers off guard. She fired into the pit until all movement stopped. She reloaded, and her rifle spit fire again.

Popping her head out of the hole she saw her team secure behind the truck, helping each other with their wounds. Ahead she noticed two old men in white cotton thawbs. They struggled to wheel a decrepit wooden cart from an open area on the left side of the road to the right side of the road, toward the three-story Iraqi police station, where a crowd was gathering. She yelled, *Vaaisaw! Vaaisaw!* Halt! to the men pulling the wagon. When they started to lean forward to pull the cart faster toward the police station and the crowd she began firing her rifle at the cart. The truck bombing had been a diversion. The explosion pushed her back into the hole, a crippling pain in her stomach, and then she landed atop the bloody messes who were once teenage boys.

Unreal twilight of half awake-half not, of sweating and chills together, of a thick wetness and pain, of groaning that somehow made her feel a bit better; the whirr of rotor blades, static mixed with radio chatter, retching with nothing left to expel, sleep, pain, the medicinal odors, bright lights, eyes behind white masks peering down at her. Senator Cowel's ruddy face slowly coming into focus, a mop of unkempt gray hair, the persona aura-like, above her.

"There's my girl. Julia Abbott, winner of the Purple Heart."

An encouraging squeeze of her cold hand coaxed a smile.

"Senator Cowel, where am I?"

"You're safe, and I'll guran-damn-tee it. You're on base and in good hands."

"My team?"

"All on the heal. Alive because of you. I'd give anything to have watched you rush that sniper ambush, face splattered with blood, spitting lead, always forward. All strawberry blonde five-foot-two of you. You dragged a six-foot-two sergeant to safety. That's when they shot you. You got up, rushed the snipers, and then foiled a well-planned attack on an Iraqi police station. You saved twenty some men and most of the crowd."

"Most?"

"Five casualties. Collateral damage. I couldn't be prouder of you."

Julia suddenly remembered running up a small pile of rubble, spraying bullets down into it to where the return fire came from. Two boys – shrinking, cringing, bloody. Her head pounded. Her stomach was numb.

"They were boys, sir."

"That's always the case, Julia. Something we don't speak of. We put evil faces on them in the movies. Make 'em ten feet tall, leather-faced and dirty. But they are boys who can kill and do. This is your third tour since West Point. If anyone should know the story of kill or be killed, it's you."

"Shooting at yardage didn't bother me. I was doing my duty as a soldier. But this—"

"They disabled your truck with an improvised explosive device, an IED, Julia. They planned on finishing you off with their AK 47s as a spectacle for the crowd then probably sell your weapons to the insurgents. Life is cheap here."

"Did you ever kill anyone, sir?"

"You aren't that baby-face prom queen, valedictorian I met 16 years ago. You have become a seasoned soldier. And an All-American war hero!"

"I saw their anger and hatred turn to fear. I killed boys. Why is my face bandaged?"

"Julia, you've risked all for your country. The surgeons tell me a bullet nicked your left eye. They might be able to save it. But you recovered and attacked with only one good eye. Then a fragment of metal from the explosion you set off hit you full in your midsection, under your bulletproof vest. Bad luck there."

The senator's measured response sent Julia back to the explosion: the blow to the left temple, the blood, the dizziness. It had been a bullet and not a blow to the head. A bullet. An inch to the left and she'd have been fine. An inch to the right, death. Shrapnel to her gut, *OH God* . . .

"My nickname, 'Hawk Eye,' now seems to be a cruel joke. I never saw any of it coming." By habit, she tried to grit her teeth, but her face hurt too much. *I just went from a pretty, and thought to be naive and defenseless girl to an ugly, naive and defenseless girl. Blind and hunched over for the rest of my life.*

"I bet if you returned to your unit you would still outshoot all of them. But there's no going back now, soldier."

"When can I get out of here, Senator?"

"Soon. I approved the funds five years ago to have this hospital built by one of our independent contractor firms. Good friends of mine. SMS. This is the best place for combat-related emergencies, and you are lucky to be alive, but we need to get you stateside for specific expertise."

"My parents—"

"Notified. Fully debriefed. Concerned, but proud, and en route to meet you at Landstuhl Regional Medical Center, about an hour away from Frankfurt, Germany, with the world media on their heels. My PR gal, Lo Stewart, will handle it all. Your parents are arriving first class, at government expense from Dallas to Frankfurt. They should arrive around 8:30am and a military Limo will be awaiting them. You will be airlifted out of here tonight and should arrive at the hospital about an hour before they get there. I know they are proud of you just like the whole nation is; you are a hero at home and a reoccurring topic of every news bureau."

"Thank you. Can I see my men?"

"It is on our agenda. And prepare yourself for being quite a celebrity back home. The media has dubbed you 'Ramboette.' And I'm feeding them from the sidelines. Once cheerleader, Army major, prom queen and now a spitfire, knocking out a sniper nest on her own. I know the potential loss of an eye is a shocker, but your career has blossomed. I've formally recommended you for the CMA."

"The Congressional Medal of Honor. Me? I rode into an ambush. Got my men shot. Killed two Iraqi boys."

"You could not have anticipated the elaborate trap they set. The explosive charge was minimal so the crowd would watch your firefight while the insurgents wheeled the deadly bomb to its intended location. Your men are alive because of you. The enemy now knows our young female soldiers can be blown out of a truck, shot in an ambush and are still capable of swift and deadly retaliation. Reads like a fairy tale. Julia Abbott, patriot."

"Patriot," she whispered, squirming to find a comfortable position in her hospital bed. "Sounds undeserved. And, my career is over."

"It's just beginning, Julia. Even though lately I've been busier than a one-legged man in an ass kicking contest, I've been singing your praises to Washington. We need women like you front and center in the Grand Ole Party. I need you to help us save this country from the Doves and war haters."

"How can a one-eyed Montana cowgirl help you with Congress?"

"As of now you are Colonel Julia Abbott; a fitting promotion. As a West Point top-of-her-class graduate, a three-tour Iraq war hero, you will retire at a full colonel's pension. You'll soon see things clearer with one eye than you ever have with two. You are going to help me fight in Congress, where most have long noses and burnt buttocks."

"I know nothing about Congress, sir."

"Neither do most of them in office."

"We need to get you prepped as to what to say and how because there will be hordes of free-world news bureaus awaiting you in Germany, even the Ruskies will take notice; given they got their ass handed to them in Afghanistan. You have a whole new life ahead of you as soon as you mend. Book contract, movie rights – you will be set financially for life. You can become a regular talking head for the media, but I have ambitious plans for you, uncommonly lofty plans my dear. We will talk about that more a ways down the line!"

After only a night and a full day spent in a sleepy dreamlike world of combat nightmares mixed with a fear of blindness, Julia suddenly realized she was the first down the stairs to the press-conference area, covering her one eye to shield it from the bright lights and flashes with Senator Cowel behind her, whispering, "Wave, but not too energetically. Look like you've been through hell, smile, nod to the press. No chatty Kathy stuff. Remember, these photos and videos will find their way onto global airwaves."

Colonel Julia Abbott may have picked off snipers in an arid war zone, but the press hit her like an avalanche.

Chapter 4

Antonia Scozzari stood dutifully across the desk from her father. "Morales?" Nicola Scozzari growled. "Did you check his green card? Yet another illegal Mexican immigrant. I've got enough landscapers here."

"For starters, Daddy, AJ is a shoo-in for the number three draft pick for the NFL. That's millions, Dad, millions. Didn't you see him on TV last month at the Rose Bowl?"

"I hate sports, *figlia mia*. But I did get a report on the quarterback, Prendergast. Know him?"

"Charlie? Sure. AJ and he are best friends."

"Listen, Antonia. The quarterback is the son of blue-blood Houston and Connecticut money and power. He's the one whose ring you should be wearing. A merger like that would bring a lot of useful contacts to both families."

"Is it always business with you?" Antonia couldn't help shaking her head.

"You are here because of business."

"Momma told me—"

"That whore, Benedetta, took a lot of cash with her when she deserted me. Had some safecracker rifle my vault. Then tried to take my best stallion, but we caught the two guys. They're helping my flower bed on the south side bloom like mad."

"Why not buy the Cincinnati franchise? They're right across the river from your company. Hire AJ with a huge contract. Give us a few hundred acres and we'll build our dream home right here on the property."

"One thing you got from your mother was your ears. She only hears what she wants to. I said I hate sports. Football careers are measured in months. He'll piss away the money on booze and broads and end up selling used cars on a 'tote your note' lot in El Paso to his illegal Mexican cousins. Great future, you got planned."

"AJ's father was born in America. He was a Governor of Montana. AJ's a University of Texas football hero. He's a tall, dark and handsome Latin-lover type."

"His father died in shame, a corrupt politician. The apple never falls far from the tree. And his buddy is the son of one of the Joint Chiefs of Staff. An Admiral. You don't even know what that is, do you?"

"Someone who drives a boat," she replied in frustration. "I was never good in school. The other girls—"

"So you become adept at making babies. I don't want no Latino litter. Make me some well-connected grandsons."

"But AJ—"

"If you and the quarterback don't make sparks in bed, get yourself a lover. Get ten of them. That's what pissed your mother off, but I think you're different."

"So what do you want me to—"

"Antonia!" Nicola raised his voice and stood.

Antonia's head dropped and her shoulders sagged. "Yes, Father?"

"Mention this man one more time and I'll send some of my men after him. Got it?"

"Yes, Father."

"I will not have spick grandkids running around here wearing *sombreros* and singing Mexican horse-shit music. Think with your head, not your damn hormones."

"What do you want me to do with Charlie?"

"Marry him."

"But I don't love him."

"The elephant and the ant meet for one wild night of passion. The ant awakens to find the elephant has died. The ant puts its arms on its hips, shakes its head and says, 'One wild night of passion and I spend the rest of my life digging a grave.' That's marriage. Before you know it those headlights of yours will dim, and your boyfriend will look like Pancho Villa. Are you my daughter or about twenty some years ago was your mama out slumming one night?"

"No, sir. I'm your daughter, Father."

"The quarterback has a gimp leg now. There's no sports career ahead for him. He needs consoling. Do what you women do best. Get him in bed. Make him marry you. I'll give you a princess wedding and that new red Ferrari you have been hounding me about. If you fail to do this, I will also buy you a Ferrari; a black one to drive to your boyfriend's funeral if you don't drop him now."

"Can I—"

"Antonia, you know what happens to little girls who try to defy their father."

"Yes, Father."

Chapter 5

A morose Charlie Prendergast III recovered from surgery at his parents' home, the official residence of Admiral Charles Prendergast and his wife, Yvette. One reason Charlie was in no hurry to move out and settle down was because he thought of this boyhood home as a paradise and always felt recharged when he returned.

They lived in the Woodlands, a meticulously planned upscale community in the far northern suburbs of Houston, Texas. Charlie believed the Prendergast Spanish-mission-style estate stood in contrast to the McMansions, starter castles and often ostentatious paeans to the wealth of their neighbors. Three acres had been cut from the secluded seven of the estate and surrounded by an eight-foot-high, light-brown adobe rectangular wall, topped with red clay tiles and a government-installed gate and security shack with armed guards.

Tasteful shrubs, magnolia trees, willows and vines hid much of the wall and thereby what was behind it. The one opening, an arched entrance, was protected by two weathered ten-foot-tall and eight-inch-thick wooden doors. Visitors for whom the gates swung wide were treated to a spectrum of vibrant greens, bold reds, soft yellows and blue trims. Sitting adjacent to a golf course and ringed with southern Texas spruce the air always smelled fresh. Birds sang from the trees, bees buzzed and darted from one flowering shrub to the next and butterflies alit atop blooms. The smell of the always freshly cultivated soil serenaded by the peep-peep-peep-peep of underground sprinklers as well as the myriad of fruit trees, shrubs, rose bushes and regional plants all whispered "welcome to paradise."

Charlie's mother brought her love for nature, especially flowers and lush, leafy hedges from her native France as if to transport a piece of her homeland's beauty to South Texas. A faded yellow cobblestone driveway, split by an immense garden, ringed both pathways with red and yellow blooms, each anchored by a mighty red-fruit-bearing tree. The path to their Spanish-mission house led to an arched stone portico, the splashes of color from window sills and roadside pots a calculated scene orchestrated by a master. Yvette and her husband, Head of the Joint Chiefs of Staff, lived with their four children, Charles 3rd and three younger daughters amid elegance and beauty in form and function.

Today, U.S. Senator Parker Cowel joined the family to "strategize" on Charlie's future. Charlie watched his mother, her jet black hair streaked with gray, speaking of Houston's mild winters, but the sparkle of her eyes and inviting smile was pure spring. She spent some dutiful minutes in pleasantries with the senator then excused herself politely. Changing from a yellow sun dress into jeans and a tee shirt, she disappeared into one of her many gardens to nurture the soil and flora while the men talked.

Charlie and his father sat leisurely on the veranda sipping sweet tea served by a Mexican attendant replete with a security ID badge, facing the venerable senator, a family friend and frequent guest. The Admiral, dressed in white cotton pants, a royal blue short-sleeve shirt, leather sandals, and black sunglasses, watched the ice twirl in his tumbler. The March early afternoon was temperate and windless, in the mid-seventies, a hazy blue sky with typical Gulf Coast humidity. Goldfinch, wrens and waxwings chirped and darted from once choice bush or tree to another. A hawk circled lazily, and there was a trace of salt in the air from Trinity Bay to the south. The senator sat in a wrought-iron chair on a pink cushion, his trademark blue sport coat, white shirt and red tie, a bit wrinkled, gray slacks, his face red as a chapped baby butt. Charlie chose long jeans, a polo shirt and sandals. All three men wore white Stetsons. While Charlie's Rose Bowl touchdown pass was now the stuff of legends, its replay aired over and over on the sports channels from every angle, and in real time, slow-mo and fast time was instantly relived. But Charlie's future was the topic this afternoon.

"So your last great football pass cost you a career in the Pros," the Admiral sighed and took a long drink of tea.

"Pop, you've heard all the guru experts, seen all of the pictures. This is a new knee. A replacement. Plastic or some polymer shit. I limp. I don't even wear shorts anymore. The scars sicken me."

"They will fade."

"Much slower than my career in professional sports did."

"What about owning a team?" the senator asked.

Charlie looked at him with wide eyes. "Only you, Uncle Parker, could come up with a plan like that. I'm a few mill short right now."

"Money is no problem with us. I guaran-damn-tee it. I'm just toying with you to see what you have in mind."

"I loved to play the game. Don't wanna teach or manage. To tell ya the truth, being around the game now as a spectator annoys me."

"We had hoped you could spend a few years in pro football to get more name recognition and then attend Harvard law school, before running for a congressional seat here in Texas. So we adjust our plans." The senator shrugged.

"I'd rather go to the dentist every day than law school."

"It's the road to Washington," the senator fired back.

"If memory serves, Uncle Parker, America has four percent of the world population and seventy-five percent of the world's lawyers. That cannot be a good thing. Therefore Washington cannot be the cat's meow."

"There are so many lawyers on Capitol Hill," the admiral added, "that each one is no more than a fart in a windstorm, Charlie. But it's the usual way through the political door."

"Son, what did you favor in college?" the senator asked.

"Doggy style, sir."

"Charlie majored in philosophy, Parker. Political science was a minor."

"I liked wondering about just who the hell we are and why we were here," Charlie offered, without the hostile undercurrent. "Never did get it answered."

"What about an MBA and then on to a captainship in business?" the Admiral suggested.

"That's an excellent idea," Senator Cowel said. "I need men I can groom to rely on at my company. SMS. Let's send you off to Harvard business school for an MBA. Charles Prendergast III, captain of American Business."

"How can I go to Harvard, Uncle Parker? I was a good student, but I sure the hell was not great. I ain't no East Coast blue blood, like Pop. I was born in Texas and I am Texas Burnt Orange through and through. Harvard would laugh at my transcripts."

"What do you think I am, Charlie, a logging train hobo from Great Falls? I'm a five term, sitting U.S. senator and can damn well bring my goals to fruition. I donate to both Harvard and Yale. I golf with the chancellors and their cronies. It'll take you a couple or three years and you will come out polished and prepared to assume a leadership role at SMS. We need your leadership Son, just as you captained the winning Longhorns to victory, so too will you captain SMS to greatness; we need you Son!"

"Don't know if I could pull good grades there, Pop. I'd hate to fail out."

"Charlie," the senator explained, "boys and girls we send to Harvard do not fail out. We have our own tutors and the professors all know us, especially at bonus time. I think we are barkin' up the right tree here." The senator wiped his dripping brow with his suit coat sleeve. "Any more tea?"

Charlie dutifully rose and limped into the house to tell the maid to bring more sweet tea.

"He does not seem particularly motivated here, Charles," Cowel said to the Admiral. "We'll need more than a great college football career to make him useful."

"He understands politics at a very human level, Parker. He has a fine head on his shoulders."

"That's all rat's ass theory. He's not motivated for anything but football. With that option in the past now he's pouting."

"I agree with you about Harvard business school. That will inspire his competitive nature. It will take time to bring him onto your team, but it will give the Texas boy, the polish of a Harvard man."

"Job one is business. We've invested in him. You can wave the U.S. flag all you want, but we need to keep filling the coffers. He has to deliver as do all of us."

"I get your meaning. I do my job in spite of all your back-alley intrigue, and he will do his."

"That back-alley intrigue keeps America strong. If your son is not one of us he—"

"Don't ever threaten me with my family. Come for me first, Parker, but don't miss. I know where you live, too."

"You hold a prominent position in the greatest nation on earth and—"

"And I do my job, which is a ceaseless devotion to protecting us from our foreign enemies."

"And to do that you must work as part of a united team of—"

"International businessmen. Where does 'For the People' meet with profits *uber alles*?"

"Enough for now," Parker said as the maid appeared with a full pitcher. "But I'll guaran-damn-tee you we will speak more on this subject."

Charlie returned, dutifully sipping tea for a time as the Harvard plan was sanctioned and the conversation inevitably turned to local D.C. "inside the Beltway" gossip. Charlie skillfully excused himself at a fitting moment, walking out through the back of the estate to the blue ceramic-tiled private terrace and the Spanish fountain. Its water, an inviting cobalt blue, sent a refreshing spray against Charlie's body. The patio opened to nature in bloom. Even in mid-March, his mother could capture and retain color. He waved to her, and she rose from among a splash of azaleas, knees and elbows muddied. As she walked to him, her face sporting a contented and sincere smile, he wondered how she had so much energy, so many facets. How she could dig and plant in the hot sun, take time to read, listen to music, workout and then show up in the early evening, dressed to kill, to greet guests.

As he stood at the top of the patio looking down at the spread of flora a glint of light caught his eye from somewhere high in the pines, beyond the manicured golf course.

"Another sniper scope caught the light," he said, looking down at his mother.

"Senator Cowel is an important man. He always travels with protection."

"I see this stuff occasionally when the senator is not here."

"Your father is an important man, also."

"It bothers me that right now some nut is looking at me through crosshairs superimposed over my body."

"An occupational hazard of being the son of an Admiral."

Charlie walked down several steps so the wall of the estate blocked where he saw the flash of light appear.

"I see a hint of frustration, Charles," she said, kissing him on his forehead as she sat next to him. "How can my favorite son have such a 'poor me' expression on such a day?"

"I am your only son."

"That does not preclude favorite, does it?"

"Semantics."

Up until Charlie was ten these mother-son private conversations were in French, but after that English became the mutual choice.

"Your thoughts are disturbing you more than your knee."

This brought a smile. "The knee is simply a combination of sore, numb, occasional shooting pains and ugly red, yellow and purple swelling. While those colors blend well in your flower beds, they look like crap on my body. I feel like hurdling that fence and running somewhere."

"And your mind is in the dark with no visible path to gallop away."

"My future has just been decided for me on the veranda. All I need to do is hang on for dear life."

"Preferable to aimless wandering, isn't it?"

"Does Pop love me?"

"You are really asking me if he ever gives thought to your wishes."

"Maybe."

"You are part of your generation. Possessions, popularity, instant gratification, the pursuit of pleasure."

"That pretty much sums it up."

"Are you happy?"

"Are you, Mom?"

"Yes. Because I know there can be no happiness without love, no love without freedom and no freedom without choice."

"Say it in French. Maybe I'll understand that better."

"Your father and I have never seen you seize upon something with an unquenchable passion."

"That weighs on me, too. I can't suck up the prestige from being an athletic hero anymore. So I ain't popular. The military won't have me cuz of my knee. So that leaves out following in Pop's footsteps. And I don't much care for Uncle Parker's line of bullcrap, that opportunist pitchin' positive attitude stuff day and night. Dad wants me to be a financial guy now. ROI, compound interest and capital gains."

"Those are terms for things that make wealth possible. And not all old people are simply young people with wrinkles and gray hair. Today's world is about finding temporary solutions to an unsolvable problem. Your father knows this."

"So Pop is just biding his time for some reason?"

"Charles, we may be the first species ever known to devolve back into the trees. My point is that much of what we deem important today is not."

"Mother's famous riddles."

"Your father is a good man, and a strong man. It is an often-at-odds combination. His military responsibilities are enormous. And he is forced to compromise, turn a blind eye. I think he is at wit's end and has been remote to both of us for some time."

"So how do I help him?"

"Become a financial wiz. Win a prestigious sheepskin. Think of it as a tool in your ever-growing toolkit."

"I suppose I can live with that," Charlie said, stretching his legs out on the lower stairs, one leg crossed over the other. "So that's what you saw in Pop – goodness and strength. And you left France."

"I met a sexy, handsome and ambitious American Navy captain. He was in love with his country and willing to give all for it. I on the other hand came from a once-great country whose people now only use it for personal gain; drain its very life blood like vampires, seeking entitlements and comforts. I wanted that feeling of living with a just man in a just culture. It was true for a time, but America inevitably contracted the European disease like France. But I still have a loving and true husband who serves his country with honor, three playful and naive daughters who have not yet been infected by an evil world, and a beautiful son." Wrapping his head in her arms she kissed his forehead. "There is that precious smile."

"So you and Pop still love each other."

"Your father is always upset when the senator is here. Tonight we'll drive out to our beach house. He'll float targets into the surf and wait until the currents take them. Once they are so far out I can hardly see him, he'll prep his rifle and shoot at them – one shot – then up come his binoculars. Then he'll sit alone on the porch and hit the whiskey. On his third glass he'll blast that damn 'Do not forsake me, oh my Darling' song."

Charlie laughed knowingly. "*High Noon*. Heard that many a time."

"Then that damn sleazy violin tune starts up."

"*The Man Who Shot Liberty Valance*. Both songs are about standing up to evil."

"But the rifle, coupled with the whiskey and those tunes always scare me."

"Something bothering him deep down?"

"Yes. It took me a while to catch on, but he was playing them for me. Now I come downstairs, hug him, run my fingers through his hair and bring him up to bed."

"Aw, a love story."

Yvette pinched her son's cheek. "You males are always a challenge when it comes to communicating deep feelings."

Charlie nodded with a righteous jerk. "Better than being buried as a craven coward."

"Do you believe man was made for the earth or that the earth was made for man?"

"Is this a trick question, Mother?"

"Use your intuition."

"Judging by how intensely you work the earth and enjoy growing and cultivating things, I believe the earth was made for man."

"Good boy. But there are others, many in power, who believe man was made for this earth, that we are just another species. We are no longer special and believe we have wrested control of our fate from God and can do a better job."

"And that's what Pop deals with while he sails around on his boats and is obsessed with our nation's security."

"Your father grapples with love of his country, personal

integrity and the egos, greed and lust for power of hollow men."

"Who would wish for that kind of job? Even MBA crap sounds better than that."

"Yes. I suspect his work is lonely, frustrating and he questions the meaning of this life."

"Me, too. We didn't cover it much in school but near as I can see, other than not knowing what we are, where we came from, what we are supposed to do while we're here or where we are going, we know pretty much everything."

"You have inherited the gift of irony from your Gallic ancestors. This mantra of man is king of his own destiny is how Hitler was able to proclaim his race the greatest race and eliminate or enslave much of Europe. This is how Stalin was able to make class war, kill millions and force millions of others to live in fear for half a century. This one idea of man without God is how my country lost several generations of males in war."

"How do I fit into all of this?"

"America is quickly losing its spirit. You do not realize that this country has caught this European disease. We vote to entrust our entire beings to our politicians, expecting happiness from material things only. What is best of your culture is no longer valued, it thirsts and withers on the vine. John Wayne rides off into the sunset, atop his horse, holding a crumpled and stained U.S. Constitution. All the while you concentrate on appetites."

"Damn. I think I was enjoying Uncle Parker and Pop's conversation more than this. So why doesn't this mysterious disease affect you?"

"For me it is not about surviving the storm, but dancing in the rain."

"Right now I feel like the south end of a northbound horse."

"You know the names of the families that controlled Europe. Plantagenet, Lancaster, York, Tudor and such from England. Valois, Bourbon, Bonaparte in France, and the mighty Habsburgs in Central Europe. The Medici in Italy. The names are still familiar. They interbred to keep power in the hands of a few. Even in the Great War it was cousin king against cousin czar against cousin emperor. The people who died for their causes in war, died for elite pride, wealth and aristocratic bragging rights. It was business. An incestuous lot. They gave lip service to God. The people suffered – yet again."

"So our ancestors came here and built a great nation."

"In Europe, the Caesars cried, 'Might makes Right.' Here, the cry is, 'Might for Right.' Here, the people own the government and not the reverse. If a Caesar rose here, your U.S. Constitution would impale him on those deadly American Eagle talons. This is freedom. This, to me, is the American Dream and why you have prospered so and spared yourselves the deaths of countless sons."

"So for me, that means I am free to do nothing. Something's not right. I'll fess up to that for sure."

"You've changed as a nation. A president was killed in my lifetime here and nobody was brought to justice for it. Americans realized a new gang of Caesars are here who are controlling America as they did Europe. Camelot fell. So what? The living here is too good to care. It will not be so for my grandchildren, my Charles. Our constitution promises equal opportunity. Only fools and liars promise guaranteed outcomes. Only the spoiled listen and believe. The Caesars are offering the people trinkets and destroying your American dream."

"What are the names of this gang of dawgs?"

"You've sipped sweet tea with some of them."

"What are you saying, *Ma mere*?"

"You are no longer proud of your country. You no longer have the freedoms to do what is right, but the right to do whatever you please that your whims and fashion dictate. You must serve the America of your Pledge of Allegiance, which I do not hear anymore. Truth, Justice and the American way."

"That's what is said about Superman, Mom. Do you mean,

'One nation, under God, indivisible, with Liberty and Justice for all'?"

"Oui, c'est ça. *Même chose.*"

"I suppose so."

Charlie shook his head and sighed.

"Charles, you are not going to find yourself in this life. You are going to have to make yourself. Go to your iconic school; learn about the magic of business while opportunity knocks. Perhaps you will find your passion there. Your country is under attack. The foxes are in the hen house dressed like the chickens. The chickens squawk for more food, more leisure. The masked foxes offer empty promises while they fatten up the chickens. Fear the fox, but also the chickens. Trust your Founding Fathers."

Chapter 6

Weeks later, two former gridiron heroes sat in AJ's efficiency apartment in Austin, chosen solely for its convenience – walking distance from the University of Texas campus and a nice view of a manicured lawn with shade trees and a small pond from their 3rd-floor vantage point. University and its bohemian lifestyle was over and done with, both had graduated with respectable grades and were now forced to come to grips with choosing one of the many forks in the road ahead. AJ and Charlie sat staring out the picture window, contemplating their polarized view of UTs Dome as something soon to be in their past.

Austin, Texas served as state capital, seat of Travis County and home of the University of Texas. Its city and surrounding suburbs comprised an eclectic mix of state government employees and political staffers, university faculty and foreign and domestic college students and high-tech and blue-collar workers. The "Texas-style" sense of independence grew strong in Austin residents, with a desire to remain small and unique, protecting local businesses from being overrun by large corporations. While Austin lifestyle felt liberal, big business remained conservative. In the late 1800s, The "Violet Crown" name of many local businesses came from the unique violet glow spreading across the hills just after sunset.

AJ's tiny condo was mostly empty: a few heavily duct-taped brown boxes stacked in a corner; a 55" widescreen TV; the shabby sofa on which they sat; a plywood and cinder-block coffee table, filled with snacks and bottles of wine, champagne and beer; and three chairs were all that was left from the garage sale.

AJ took a healthy swig of champagne directly from the bottle. "I kind of expected us to meet on the gridiron, Charlie. Even playing against each other would have been a gas."

Charlie sighed. "My leg is so messed up I will always limp until some star-wars technology turns up. Maybe an iKnee."

"Easier to get email then too."

"I told the orthopedic expert to give me two knee replacements with both of them turned backwards. Then I could walk and bend like a stork."

"That would draw more attention than a 'hey look at me' tattoo."

"I heard the NFL scratched me as a potential draft pick after talking to the surgeons."

"What now?"

"Bubba AJ, I'm off to Harvard business school."

"Just like that?"

"Yep."

"Cold weather, snooty and clannish people."

"Hell, they're all cold after you get to know Antonia," Charlie said. "What a live wire. What is her story anyway?"

"Kind of sad, actually. She went to school here because her mother owns a vineyard in the hill country."

"A vineyard?"

"Gets even more interesting. She is the granddaughter of two Mafia dons."

"Come on. You're not gonna try and pull the leg of a born-and-bred Texas boy, are you?"

"Antonia Cortese Scozzari. Her father is Nicola Scozzari. She says he's a big player in the Boston Mob. Her mother, Benedetta Cortese, is the daughter of Ruffo Cortese, head of the New York Mob."

"Damn. Better have her home on time while you two are an item. Missing the curfew could be life-threatening."

"It's true. She says her mother's family ran a wine-importing business on the New York docks and owned the rackets, prostitution and gambling. In 1988, in a deal with the Boston Mob, known for their money-laundering abilities, they talked about an alliance of the families to thwart the expansion of the Chicago, Detroit and Vegas Mobs influence on the gambling, tobacco and distilling business in Kentucky and Tennessee. So the Boston son and crook, Nicola, was married to the New York girl and crook, Benedetta. The offspring is Antonia."

"Amigo, I hope you don't end up sleeping with the fishes, wearing cement shoes or something."

"Right now we're just playing it by ear. She will not let me meet her parents and my mom and sisters say I could do better with a girl I could hire by the hour."

"Love is blind."

The two men toasted.

"What's next for you, AJ?"

"Pro football, make a few bucks. Some name recognition. Then politics. I have a promise to keep."

Before Charlie could question the reply, the scantily clad Antonia burst through the door and plopped her curvy, tanned body on the sofa between each guy. She immediately swiveled her hips and put her arms around Charlie.

"I don't see you enough and now I'm leaving for Montana with AJ. Will you come visit?"

"It's off to Boston, for me," Charlie said as she leaned back against AJ, resting her long and tan legs across Charlie.

"Toni, pop a cold bottle of the Moet, will you?" AJ asked while rolling his eyes at his girlfriend's antics.

Antonia dutifully opened a bottle, handed it to AJ and popped another for herself.

"So today's the day we each go our own way," AJ said before chugging. The others did the same. Antonia leaned over and refilled, her full breasts protruding precariously against the bikini bra covering her suntanned chest. A silent clink of three bottles sealed the farewell.

"Some day those girls are going to pop right out of your bra, Toni," AJ said.

"I'd be okay with that. Don't think I haven't had offers to show them off, and for some real money," she replied, leaning back into her seat. "Miss Texas is not easy to win," she said with an obvious wink.

"Don't tell me," AJ said. "I don't want to know about payoffs, threats or sexual favors."

"AJ," Antonia said after taking a big gulp. "That was yesterday. Today is today."

"Is that Homer you're quoting?" Charlie asked.

"No, but I do love *The Simpsons*," she replied.

"I meant...never mind," Charlie replied.

"What are your plans?" Antonia asked Charlie.

"Well, my father and a couple of U.S. senators decided I will go get my MBA at Harvard."

"I hear Boston girls are stuck-up and clannish."

"I'll be watching AJ on TV in a pro game and looking for you in the stands."

"Here's a going-away present," she raised her top and bra to expose her breasts. "Nothing AJ hasn't seen before."

The men just looked at each other shaking their heads.

"Charlie, how come you don't have a girl?" Antonia asked.

"A few hot college romances fizzled out. A missed period that turned out to be only late caused a scare, a wakeup call and that relationship quickly fizzled. While her body was primo, being chained to her for the rest of my life was sobering. I tend to attract gold diggers. But I always have an eye out for Miss Right."

"I can't see how you lasted this long. You look like that first guy who played Superman. What was his name, AJ?"

"Keith Richards?" AJ said.

"No, stupid."

"Christopher Reeve," Charlie said and Antonia nodded. "I get that a lot. But I don't think blue tights and a red cape will work in Boston."

"So off to Harvard business school to get your brain expanded in classes with a bunch of anal-retentive girls with thick glasses and calculators," Antonia said.

"Let's not go there," AJ said. "We'd better be leaving soon. My flight to Helena leaves at three with a stopover in Denver. My family expects me at home to watch all the NFL draft hoo-hah tomorrow. And you and I, Toni, will be sleeping in separate rooms."

On the drive to the Austin-Bergstrom airport, Charlie and AJ promised to keep in touch. Antonia sat quietly in the back seat.

"My cell is dead," AJ said. "Toni, do you have the charger in your purse?"

"I'll check, but I thought it was on the bed when we left. You should have gotten one like mine with those lithium-iron batteries."

"It's just another high-tech toy. And it's ion not iron."

The ride to the airport was somehow nostalgic to both men as their eyes lingered on familiar sights as if to say goodbye.

Charlie and AJ shook hands at the drop-off point. Antonia made a show of herself kissing AJ goodbye, standing on her tiptoes to hug him. Charlie admired her beautifully muscled legs. She would follow AJ to Helena the next afternoon. As AJ looked back before entering the airport, Charlie threw an invisible football which AJ pretended to bobble and drop.

As Charlie drove Antonia back to the condo, she began to cry as she sat next to him.

"Hey, Miss Texas, turn off the water works, you'll run your mascara."

"I just am so emotional lately with the three of us changing just about everything."

"I feel the same way."

"I'm just realizing what you mean to me, Charlie."

"Me, too. I'll think of you every time a pair of naked breasts show up on TV. Here we are. I'll pick you up and drive you to the airport tomorrow. Okay?"

"Could you come in for a while? I don't want to face an empty condo. Please?"

Charlie sank into the sofa as Antonia popped the cork on the last bottle of champagne. She looked up at him, batting her eyelashes for longer than usual. After handing a cup to Charlie, she took a quick sip then fiddled with the TV remote to find a movie.

"I'm worried about you, Charlie," she said as she sat next to him.

"I'll be fine, Toni. You set a direction, work hard, and things tend to work out."

The movie was in French, with English subtitles. His fluency in French kept his eyes on the action and not on the subtitles. It was sensual and explicit. Charlie and Antonia drank, made faces at each other as the scene became more explicit and drank some more. Soon an awkward silence turned to a hint of expectation.

"What if they don't work out?"

"What if what doesn't work out?"

"Plans. What if after all your hard work and expectations your plans just don't work out?"

"Simple. Then you just put a sawed-off shotgun in your mouth and shout 'Geronimo!'"

"Oh, that's what I mean," Antonia said, her head resting on his chest. "I'm afraid for you."

"Hey, there's no need for tears. I was only kidding. I'm looking forward to something new. Come on, let's wipe those tears away, and I'll be on my way. This movie warrants a cold shower." The goodbye kiss and Antonia's knee rising slowly between Charlie's legs brought nature to a head. In the heat of sudden, impulsive desire, the point of no return came quickly. The bed was much too far, so the entranceway floor had to do. Time stopped. Ecstasy reigned as each body gave in to nature magnified tenfold by both alcohol and the forbidden.

The front door swung wide. AJ nearly stumbled over the

writhing bodies. The three friends froze.

"The flight was canceled due to weather in Denver," AJ whispered from above, his eyes averted. "Nothing until tomorrow. My cell was dead, so I took a taxi. Sorry."

He stepped back out of the condo and closed the door without a sound.

Chapter 7

He walked aimlessly at first, almost at a jog, in the warm March Austin air, every fiber of his being enraged.

While AJ somehow sensed he was a bit special as a child, this feeling in his gut was not that type of special. As a boy he felt everyone knew his father and showed great respect to his mother. The more he grew and learned of the world he realized this specialness was because his father, Jaime, from whom AJ got his middle name, was a prominent man. Sometimes AJ was allowed to stay up later than usual and watch his father on the television, the local news. AJ sometimes visited the enormous building where his father had the largest of offices. At Helena Elementary, teachers would always single out AJ and explain to the class that his father was the leader of the state of Montana. AJ pretended to know all about what that meant. On one of the proudest days of AJ's life, Father came to the school and spoke about America in the assembly hall. AJ pretended he knew all about that, also.

Over the years, he realized those who treated him specially did so because his father was Governor of the state of Montana. In high school, some made fun of his father, saying he belonged to the wrong political party or was a crook; some asked him for his father to do them favors. AJ knew he was treated special because of his father and not for himself. In high school, AJ excelled at football, and as a sophomore was brought up to play on the varsity team, a rare honor. But his new teammates resented him, teasing that he was there because of his father's authority. So he worked harder, ran farther, lifted more weights, and confided in nobody. He wanted to excel on his own skills, to prove he deserved his slot on the team. His family's religious practices and Sunday church made him accept that God sees everything. He always thought before acting to weigh the consequences of a decision and the related action. What time he did spend with his busy father was a good time; they'd talk about father and son things and how it was when his father was a boy and how they were both lucky to be Americans. AJ committed to his homework, improving his test scores, studying for college entrance exams, as well as honing his football skills. Soon he and his fellow students had to choose a direction in life, whether to get a job, choose a career, go to college, marry and begin a family, all sorts of changes – all so sudden for AJ. College was a given, per family values. But he always hemmed and hawed when asked what he wanted to do with his life.

One day after football practice his mother picked him up in the family car and on the ride home a pickup truck smashed into them. While the car was totaled, neither he, nor his mother, was injured, but Father reacted strangely. He took the incident to heart, to be more than AJ felt it warranted. Father sat, hunched over in the living room for hours at a time, staring out the window. He started attending church every day and prayed often. AJ remembered Father telling him that a few like-minded political opportunists could influence and maybe even take over an organization, perhaps even a country for their own benefit. While most people went about their own business and paid little attention, no more than lip service, these thieves could prosper. Shepherds were needed to stand up to and protect others from these self-serving wolves.

About this same time, Father ran for the position of Junior U.S. Senator from Montana. The entire family – cousins, aunts, uncles, and close friends were always at the house now, laughing and cheering, saluting, enjoying festive meals. The newspapers and television news shows proclaimed Father ahead in the polls. Expectations ran high for Father to become a Democratic U.S. Senator from the state of Montana. The optimism turned to shame within the span of a single day. The same newspapers and television reporters that once spoke highly of Father now condemned him. The television, AJ's relationship to the outside world, was telling the whole world that Father was having an affair with a young Mexican girl, an illegal immigrant. This was a terrible shame for the family, and AJ's face turned red and burned as he ran to his bedroom, slamming the door.

That night Father knocked and entered his room. Sitting on the edge of the bed, Father looked older, tired and deflated. The rumors were untrue. It was politics, Father said; dirty politics. And the media liked dirt because its viewers did. It was the work of others who held public office who did not want Father elected as a U.S. senator. It was about power. The senior senator from Montana, it seemed, Republican Senator Parker Cowel, did not want the Democrat Jaime Morales elected to the junior senate position. Father begged to be believed, and his son did believe, and so did Mother and his sisters and uncles and aunts, and close friends, but few came around the house like before the scandal.

Soon the television and the newspapers showed pictures of the young Mexican girl. She told of clandestine meetings at motels and said she could prove it with pictures and documents of sums of money transferred so as to create fake identification to bring her across the border to America. Soon Father was behind in the polls. He was called the "Beleaguered Senate Candidate," said to be unfit to remain governor much less run for a national office, an embarrassment to his state and country. At school AJ noticed his teammates and close friends became suddenly remote, some ignoring him completely. Even the football coach put him on the bench for a time, telling him not to show up for games or practice. There was too much shame.

Father changed. His face turned to wrinkled leather, seemingly overnight. He lost weight, looked shriveled in his clothes. He no longer went to work. He never picked up the phone or answered the door.

"I have not lost my personal integrity, Son," AJ remembered him saying, "and I have never been unfaithful to your mother, but I am so ashamed of how I have embarrassed my family, my friends, the people of Montana and America. It was not my doing, but these people who will slander a man, fabricate lies and pay others to lie to maintain their power says much about them. Always remember, Alejandro that this is our country and not one of corrupt officials. We must be ever-vigilant."

Of everything his father told him those many years ago, one concept was seared into AJ's memory. It whispered to him in his father's voice. "I call myself a man of integrity, of good character, and this means I must control my desires with reason and will. For the moral road is etched onto my very soul. I must not stray." From this fatherly admission of the meaning of life, AJ learned that his own life would also be a constant tug of war between intellect, reason, logic and soul against his imagination of physical desires, perceptions, and judgments. Once he willed his being through this portal there was no returning from whence he came. This habit of will made AJ appear different from his herd; aloof to some, distant to others.

From the time of the accident onward Father stooped and shuffled rather than walked. His face color turned ashen. His ever-welcoming smile collapsed into a scowl. The medicine cabinet filled with drugs labeled with unpronounceable names. Doctor Carrillo said the stress of the campaign had caused the massive stroke. Father's funeral was heralded by a circus of reporters who cared nothing for the family's loss or the truth, but only for more news; news skewed to filth. A once-prominent family, suddenly left without its prominent head, faced an uncertain future, viewed by former friends as corrupt; deserving their fate.

On one bright note, a University of Texas offensive football coach, who happened to be from Helena, had kept an eye on AJ the athlete. He offered AJ a scholarship to play football at the University of Texas. Given the new family financial situation and at the urging of his mother, he jumped at it, packed his bags and went off to play for the Longhorns. Somehow he had gone from a young man feeling unique and embraced to an outsider, a product of corruption, somehow less than a true American. But now, on the occasion of being asked what he wanted to do with his life, his answer was, "I want to be like my father."

The image of his best friend Charlie, naked, rocking up and down atop a woman cast the old memories out of his head. His stomach turned as he prayed it was not his Antonia. But there was her face, her mouth contorted in ecstasy. Now there was no rage in AJ, only hurt; a betrayal, as his father was betrayed by a corrupt political system, by the snake, Senator Parker Cowel.

AJ found himself in the middle of yet another nondescript strip mall near downtown Austin, just off I-35. Traffic flew by, everyone in a hurry to get somewhere special; except for him. Sandwiched between a Chinese takeout restaurant and a hardware store, a picture of an American eagle hanging in a window caught his eye. Only as he pushed through the door did he consider this possible fork in life's road.

"Is this from a wild pitch or are you disliked in this area?" AJ asked, as he walked into the hole-in-the-wall Austin recruitment office. His thumb pointed to a duct-taped hole in the window.

"Lots of folks are against the wars in Iraq and Afghanistan," the forty-something, shaved-head recruiting master sergeant replied. "Mostly they just run their mouths and parade around, but sometimes they do some damage late at night. Coward's way of doin' things."

"I want to enlist," he stated.

"Hey, aren't you AJ Morales?"

"So what?"

"The sports media is taking bets on how quickly you'll go in the NFL draft."

"They will all be wrong. I want nothing to do with football. Sign me up or do I go to another recruiter."

"No. I'll sign you up. I just feel like a traitor to college football. A leaping one-handed catch and then a backpedal into the end zone ain't never gonna be forgot. What gives?"

"I discovered I'm not an entertainer. No friends and not much of a lover either. There's a war on, isn't there?"

"Always. Have you thought about the Army, Air Force, Navy, or Marines?"

"What group does the most to help others? One that doesn't brag? One that gets killed more than kills?"

"That would be U.S. Air Force Para-rescue. The PJs."

"PJs, as in pajamas?"

"Para Jumpers."

"What do they do?"

"They recover downed and injured aircrew members – wherever they go down; mountains, desert, oceans, jungles, forests, para-scuba-diving, you name it. They get the toughest assignments and are the most highly trained. There are about 500 of them and hold several Congressional Medal of Honor, 12 Air Force Crosses and 100 plus Silver Stars."

"Sign me up."

"It's tough to qualify—"

"Do I look like I'm out of shape or a quitter?"

* * *

More than once during basic training AJ felt his body betray him, even after the superb conditioning required to play college football at the elite level. And later, at Superman School, as the PJs nicknamed their special-operations training, he had to force the idea of just giving up and relaxing out of his mind. The two-year training course, "the Pipeline" was intense physically and mentally, exhausting body and mind. It changed each man who triumphed over the challenge for life, and had a 90% dropout rate. The indoctrination course consisted of running, training with weights, swimming, beating obstacle courses, marching with heavily loaded rucksacks, as well as learning to scuba dive.

AJ learned medical terminology, CPR, weapons usage, and how to react in dangerous situations. The trainees did all this under the scrutiny of senior PJs who evaluated each candidate for fitness before passing them on to more difficult training and assessments.

Next up was jump school at Fort Benning, Georgia, where AJ learned parachute landing falls and then jumping from a C-130. But first he had to wait in line to board the aircraft while listening to the nerve-racking "Blood on the Risers." This was song about a paratrooper's worst nightmare. Sung to the tune of the "Battle Hymn of the Republic," the refrain of "Gory, gory, what a hell of a way to die" drilled into the heads of the newbies. Then came Navy Diving School in Panama City, Florida. Here, half his class failed out, the fear of drowning too much. This was followed by egress training at Pensacola Naval Air Station in Florida. Being stuck underwater in a sunken ship pushed AJ to the limit. But he surfaced, asking for another go at it. Survival training initially landed him in Washington. Then, whether in the desert, the jungle, adrift at sea, or in the Arctic he was shown how to survive by the best.

At each camp, as AJ progressed in his training, always humble and expecting no better treatment due to his celebrity status, he placed a little more distance between himself and the heartbreak that had sent him into the Air Force. A bit of the emptiness remained, but his pride in his new career and identity made him feel closer to his father, to his heritage.

Back to the South, at Fort Bragg, NC and then to Yuma Arizona for freefall jumping, sometimes so high oxygen was required. Next door, in New Mexico, came some of the best emergency-medical-technician training in the world. Many American combat soldiers, native civilians and even enemy soldiers benefited from the PG in the field. Then came the elite Pararescue Recovery Specialist Course at Kirtland, New Mexico. This covered field medical care and tactics (as in patching up a bleeding soldier with enemy bullets zipping past your head), mountaineering, combat tactics, and "hot dog" parachuting with helicopter insertion and extraction methods. Many times in Vietnam they lowered a PJ to the ground from a hovering helicopter to assist a downed soldier on the ground and then winch back up the wounded soldier. But often the PJ was lost to enemy fire. During the Vietnam War, only 19 Airmen were awarded the Air Force Cross. Ten went to PJs.

At the completion of these training courses, in one of the proudest moments of his life, AJ and his remaining teammates were formally awarded the maroon beret. He wore the beret as a symbol of his elite status, and to symbolize the bloodshed by former PJs, as well as the blood current PJs were willing to shed to save lives. The cost of training these men was enormous, but one could not put a price on the life of an American soldier.

"It is my duty as a Pararescueman to save lives and to aid the injured. I will be prepared at all times to perform my assigned duties quickly and efficiently, placing these duties before personal desires and comforts. These things I do, that others may live."

Chapter 8

Only four weeks after being shot, Julia Abbott found herself
flying into Bozeman Yellowstone International Airport. In that
time, she had been discharged from the U.S. Army and was
returning home with a still-bruised and off-colored left temple
and a bandaged eye, an ugly scar just above her bikini line and a
handful of brass medals. The military surgeons were just able to
save her eye. It was the wound to her midsection that most
troubled her. Taxiing to her gate, Julia wondered what the crowd
of people waving American flags, the "Welcome Home" banner
and the police and fire engines with red lights flashing was all
about. When the cabin steward handed her a bunch of red roses
her stomach turned, and she realized Bozeman, Montana was
welcoming home a war-hero daughter.

She walked down the exit hallway and was met by a tall
distinguished man in a suit who turned out to be the honorable
Richard A. Bowie, Governor of Montana. Video-camera lenses
traced her every move, she was forced to squint to compensate
for the fury of the camera flashes. Microphones were pushed
right under her nose. She learned later the other passengers were
held back from deplaning until the media feeding frenzy was
complete. Governor Bowie rescued her from a staccato series of
questions. Guided to a place set up with lights and boom microphones, she stood next to the governor as he gave a cliché-
riddled speech that had something to do with her service to our
country, the fine citizens of Montana and His Honor's numerous
contributions to all of them. He ended with a curt thank you to
sourpuss but well-spoken Senator Parker Cowel, Montana's
"legendary" senator for his help in getting Julia into West Point,
through the War College and the Congressional Medal of Honor.
She silently cursed when the governor mentioned her damaged
eye and noted the scarring and bruising still visible on the left

side of her face.

It was only then she was able to embrace her parents and brother. In that time she had two months of hospital stays, ocular-related operations to repair damage to the area around her left eye. But basically she felt back to normal and gave ample sparkly smiles to each camera or mike pushed under her nose. She retained that certain *je ne sais quoi* stately elegance that often went with a description of her.

The ride from Gallatin Field airport in Belgrade, Montana to Bozeman was spent sitting next to Governor Bowie in an open-top limo. Dozens of people along the 15-minute drive waved small American flags, which made even her sore recovering eye water. Another "Welcome Home" banner spanned Main Street and literally hundreds of people crowded the sidewalk with American flags of all sizes, waving wildly. Reps from the three local news stations and several of the national cable news networks vied for her attention. Several VFW and American Legion posts were there in numbers, the veterans fully decked out in uniforms and medals won from numerous wars and on behalf of our precious freedom. Some were setting up a buffet in her honor, and the local Chamber of Commerce announced a gala dinner to raise money for wounded Montana vets. In spite of her tough training, Julia shivered with pride. These were the men and women who knew war, understood her sacrifice and how embarrassed she was to be singled out as a hero. All who served were patriots. They showed up. But the ones who gave all were true heroes.

At a slow part in the agenda, Governor Bowie waved her over to a quiet spot. "I apologize, Julia, for this bombast, and for my part with these clichéd political speeches. When we celebrate in public, it seems the politicians take over. We all want to be reelected. But this is your day. You veterans' efforts are what allow us to assemble here freely and say whatever the hell we want."

"Thank you, sir. Montana has always given more than its share to our nation's freedom."

"Spoken like a politician in the making. Perhaps we can talk about your future before you fly off to your next challenge."

"I'd like that, sir."

"A Congressional Medal of Honor can open more doors than you may think. It can jumpstart a political career. I know Senator Cowel has plans for you."

"Yes, sir."

"Here's my card. Please call."

Though Julia smiled like a clueless girl as she accepted the governor's card, the request for a chat bothered her; sounded like a veiled warning of sorts.

The greater part of the afternoon was spent in a whirlwind of more speeches, innumerable handshakes, renewed teary relationships with old school friends and teachers and the relentless repetition of answers to "What was it like over there?" and "What's it like getting shot?" or "Were you scared?" Downtown looked somehow smaller and less congested, and she felt less associated with home. She knew of a bigger and darker world now.

When she dutifully completed the assigned schedule set by the governor's PR team, and promised twice to visit the Governor's Mansion for a day of honoring Montana's finest, Julia was discharged to her parents and brother Chet, all packing in to the same car she rode in as a young girl, a 1993 dual-cab Dodge pickup kept in meticulous condition by her father.

"It is so good to have you home," her mother Martha said, wiping a tear and looking back from the front passenger seat. "Every phone call we got scared me. Every one. Especially at night."

"Oh, Martha," father Norman said. "Don't make her feel guilty for what we go through. She's been through a hell of a lot more. You're safe now, Julia girl, this is a steel cab. Could probably lock horns with an 18 wheeler and we'd come out ok."

Chet, a week shy of his twenty-eighth birthday, seated next to Julia in the back just smiled at his sister, palms to the sky with an 'Is Dad nuts or what' expression on his face.

"It's good to be home, to be with familiar people and things."

"Do you have that PSDT stuff, Jule?" her brother asked.

"If you mean post-traumatic stress, no."

"Did you shoot any terrorists from like a mile away?"

"I was an expert shot, a marksman, but not a sniper. I engaged close up, with an assault rifle. Not long range."

"It seems cowardly to shoot someone from real far anyway."

"If you can save your own team by eliminating enemy snipers or top enemy commanders who are dangerous to your mission, you do it. Or they do it to you."

"I guess so. But I wouldn't like to shoot a puppy dog if it turned up in the crosshairs."

Julia winced, her mind immediately filled with the image of the two Iraqi boys she killed during the ambush. *Puppy dogs. Innocent puppy dogs.*

"Chet, will you stop with the war talk," his father said. "You won't even kill the damn foxes or pesky raccoons I send you after. Julia, he traps them and lets them flee in Yellowstone. Waste of time."

"I'd shoot a wolf, coyote or cougar in a minute if it attacked our herds, Dad. Did you bring any new-wave weapons home, Jule? I'm high on those Barrets. Tell me you smuggled one out."

"At five feet long and thirty some pounds I just couldn't fit it into my purse."

"Well, could I see your medals, at least?"

"You can have them. My military days are over."

"Is there an eye behind that bandage or will you be wearing one of those black pirate patches now."

"Chet!" Martha said.

Taking advantage of the silence Julia looked around at the

distant hazy foothills of the Rockies along the old U.S. 10 highway and knew she was close to home by the unique rise and fall of the peaks at twilight. Big Sky country. This was the America the beautiful of song, of purple mountains majesty, amber waves of grain, and the fruited plains. She drew a mental comparison of the vista before her to the moonlike topography of Iraq. But after three years there she knew the Iraqi people dearly loved their country as much as she did hers; so different, yet it was from where their roots sprang. Home. Family. Be it ever so humble. Soon the familiar four-rail black fencing of the Abbott ranch came into view. The wheat waving in the wind calmed her. There was something genuine about it, timeless. Along with some grain crops, Norman Abbott had been raising grass-fed beef for nearly twenty years, and while it was never a solid money maker, things were picking up as more and more consumers demanded natural beef.

If people knew the many American farmers were raising cattle and crops for profit and not for nutrition, I'd bet there'd be hell to pay, she could hear him say. Profits could have been much greater if Dad had cut corners, injected this or that drug or hormone into the beef cattle. But the family always took pride in raising healthy cattle with no growth hormones, no pumping them full of antibiotics, and no corn to eat. Cattle grazed on grass and not on corn. The herd grew naturally and ate prairie grasses, and if one died, well it wasn't meant for the table anyway. They could sleep well at night and face themselves in the mirror next morning.

"I don't know what's going to happen with this ranch, kids," Norman said. "When your mother and I pass on, the inheritance taxes are so stiff that you two will never be able to afford to keep this place. Looks like my generation of ranchers are soon gone with the wind. Do you know that the upper 20% of Americans pay 70% of the taxes in this country? Now there's talk of taxing the rich. That will keep the government running for about a week. I don't know if Americans today are too stupid or ambivalent to believe those damn hypocritical politicians. I sure hope someone would attack the U.S. Congress instead of the Middle East. We haven't had a just war since your grandpas fought in WW II."

"What the hell are those?" Julia said, pointing to the near pasture. "Giant sheep?"

"Alpacas," Chet announced. "That's my herd. I'm a livestock breeder also, and I'm going Green, too."

"Well, they do look cute from here."

"They are dear," her mother said. "The babies are adorable, and we've given each of them names."

Julia smiled when she saw her father's less-than-pleased expression reflected in the rearview mirror. A raised eyebrow was a sure sign he was skeptical.

Collapsing in her childhood bed was an absolute delight. It was as if a chapter of her life had come to an end. She could take a break from whatever next was coming her way. Tee shirts and sweat pants, unlimited time for a shower or lingering bath, no testosterone-rabid males in every direction attempting to bed her for "a stress reliever." It was no longer necessary to keep an ear open for the whine of incoming armament, the whoosh of a sniper's round past her ear, the smell of blood mixed with that of urine, sweat and feces, or worse that all, decaying flesh. She was home in Montana, with the Rockies ringing her home, in the land of the free and the home of the brave. *Do any of these people who never experienced what the rest of the world was like know what a gift living here was? Do they take it for granted?*

Chapter 9

Four soft-boiled newly laid hen's eggs in a bowl, crispy bacon, orange juice and hot coffee. Mother knew Julia's breakfast favorite. Dad, usually out of the house with the sun, sat at the head of the table this morning with his scrambled eggs and most of the bacon. Chet stayed with coffee and half a loaf of buttered toast. There was no guilt over too much fat, white flour, cholesterol here. This food "stuck to their ribs," supplying energy for the constant manual labor required to run a farm.

Norman Abbott peered over his newspaper. "So you got a decent education at West Point, graduated from the Army War College, you're a Medal of Honor winner and are in tight with a U.S. senator. How do you leverage all of that? Even looks like the governor has hot pants for you."

"Norman," his wife exclaimed. "Is that any way to talk to your daughter? Julia, your father here has become addicted to some of those nighttime television soap operas. Trash, every one, and their gutter talk has been rubbing off on him."

"Even with one eye I can see what the governor is, Dad."

"Your left eye is bad?"

"Just a little. The scar can be covered with makeup."

"I think it's distinctive."

"The governor couldn't take his eyes off it."

"Don't think you can read Cowel either. You can be safe next to a snake, until you let go of its head. Then you'll see its true nature. They're both lying politicians. To remain in office they must go with the flow; bow to power. While one bad apple can spoil the bunch, I don't think one good apple can revive the rest."

"We're humans, Dad. Not apples. Senator Cowel has always been there for me, got me into West Point, and he ensured I had the best care possible when I was wounded."

"Nearly got you killed if you ask me. I knew his father, a no-good crooked politician and an apple never falls far from the tree. It's pretty well known around here that his father had ties to the Spokane Mob that controlled the poker rackets and the gold and silver interests. Your grandfather knew him well and often would ante up against him at The Silver Bag of Dollars Bar. Someday, look into what he did to our Governor Morales. Dirty tricks. That's politics."

Marta signed. "Norman, we need a day or two just to be thankful that we are together again as a family. Don't spout your political sour grapes right now."

"Grandfather didn't seem like a poker player, Dad," Julia said.

"That's because you only knew him when he was old, sitting around with his quart of beer, watching baseball, right?"

"Yes. Fond memories."

"In his day the miners from Kellogg and Wallace could ante up some high stakes. The lucky ones would leave with bags of shiny silver dollars. All there was on the West side of the pass was Wallace with railroad track and a sewage river running through the center of town, and bars and whore houses on each side of the street. The more respectable miners came to the East side of the pass across old U.S. 10 when it was passable to get into real Montana gambling and drinking without the stench of Wallace. Dad used to say you had to keep both eyes on Cowel and make sure both of his hands were on the table. He could charm a two-headed rattlesnake into making one head bite the other!"

"Norman," Martha said, "I'm sure Julia and Chet would love to hear more about the whore houses."

"Sorry. But Grandpa once quoted Mark Twain when I asked about Cowel senior's funeral. 'I did not attend his funeral, but I sent a nice letter saying I approved of it.'"

"Dad, the senator has secured a free ride at Harvard Business School for me. Room and board included. So I'll be off to

Cambridge soon."

"Humph. Their motto is *'Veritas'* – truth. Should be *'Lucrum'* – profits."

"Most prestigious university in America."

"And coupled with Yale it's where all the billionaire crooks send their brood."

Martha banged a pan on the griddle and stared at her husband.

"What's the game plan with the exotic alpacas, Chet? Aren't they just small llamas from South America?"

"They are related to llamas and to camels. They are mostly from Peru. When the Spanish Empire invaded Peru, they slaughtered natives and animals alike. Many retreated up high in the Andes and brought the alpacas with them for meat and clothing. The people stayed there even after the Conquistadores left. They were up about three miles above sea level and the alpacas grew some of the warmest, finest and strongest fiber in the world. It was prized by Inca royalty for clothing."

"And we have them grazing our pastures...because?"

"Same reason we're raising grass-fed beef. It's natural. If you're wearing nylon, you're wearing petroleum products. If you're wearing cotton, you are wearing herbicides and pesticides that are poured into our ground water to protect the cotton crops. If you are wearing wool, you're wearing lanolin – chemicals that pollute our water also. But if you're wearing alpaca, you're wearing alpaca."

Chet went on between bites of toast. "Natural. Green. With fleece stronger than wool; more durable. Warmer than anything. We gotta get back into making our own textiles and not just buying that cheap crap we got used to importing. Alpaca is a gold mine, particularly here where it's cold nine months out of the year!"

"Chet, I smell 'lucrum'," Julia said, smirking at her father. "When did you submit to the god of marketing? You were an animal-nutrition major."

"Still am. That's how I found alpacas. Eat light, drink light, and poop micro-nutrient-rich fertilizer. You wouldn't believe how the price of fertilizer has skyrocketed since we ship most of ours to China where they pay a premium for it. The American suppliers make a profit and leave us ranchers and farmers with stiff prices here at home. That's 'lucrum' for the few and crap for the rest of us."

"What do they taste like?"

"Low in fat and carbs, high in protein. Haven't been injected with growth hormones and God knows what else to put weight on and improve taste just to turn a buck. I hear tell that those doctored pork roasts sold in the cities these days glow in the dark."

"Julia," her father said, "why don't you and I go for a walk? I'll show you some of the improvements we've made on the ranch and we can visit the alpacas, too."

"Sounds like a good idea," her mother confirmed. "You will love the alpacas. Our local spinning and knitting circle is turning out some of the best yarn, roving and products on the planet. Half the people in the county now wear alpaca socks. The hikers, winter-sports enthusiasts, hunters and everyone who has ever ridden a snowmobile buys them by the dozen."

Dressed in her barn clothes, as she called them, she and her father walked out into the fields of their ancestral ranch. The ultra-soft but thin alpaca jacket her mother let her wear outside was actually surprisingly warm, given its light weight. Even the relentless wind didn't sting her chest or arms either. The wind was near constant on the flat prairies. The sky, blue as Julia's eyes, was true to its Montana moniker of "Big." Julia felt like a speck of insignificance under the limitless heavens as cows looked curiously at her, two farm dogs yapped at her heels and the panorama of grassland and horizon opened before her. There was no smell of auto emissions or factory production offshoots or sterile and dead concrete and steel. Everything around her was alive. She was home.

"Remember when I first took you hunting?"

"Of course."

"You were squeamish at first. Didn't want to shoot a deer, even though we only hunted when the herd was overly large and we knew many would starve in the winter. But you did it. We ate the meat. Saved us money for other food. We lived off the land."

"The bow hunting was difficult. I didn't want to make a deer suffer. The kill shot was almost impossible and the fear of making a mistake made my hands shake at first."

"I started you with the long bow for a reason. Once you mastered it, we moved up to the cross bow."

"That was great. No missed shots, no waiting for a deer to suffer while it bled out."

"No tears either. Then I bought you your own Remington 700 rifle for Christmas."

"We ate like kings that winter."

"I think you became the expert shot you are because you started with a bow, then the crossbow and then the rifle."

"I see your point. I learned the hard way, and I appreciate the lesson."

"I know you feel Senator Cowel has done a lot for you. And he intends on doing more."

"He has helped me enormously."

"He helped you get up to bat, but it has always been your sweat and blood. Not his."

"What are you saying, Dad?"

"Even though you have all those womanly curves, you have the appearance of a young and innocent girl. And in many ways you are. It's always easy to prey on naivety."

"I may have a baby face, but I am not naïve, squeamish or a pushover."

"I've certainly known that for years. I remember when you

tried out for high-school cheerleading. You made the team but found the social politics and pecking order seriously demeaning. But you didn't quit. You became captain of the team and turned the program around from one of flaunting your body to one of supporting the team with enthusiasm and energy."

"It was the only way I could stay on the team. I'm not a quitter."

"Exactly. And you are clever, but not deceptive. The difference is that deceptive types love deceit. Someone like the honorable and esteemed Senator Cowel can see you are talented, hard-working, driven, and yes, I'll admit that when you turn on that feminine charm you are fetching."

"Are you saying you finally see me as a woman?" She weaved her arm through her father's.

"Never," he replied with a fake scowl. "I'm saying if you get too deeply into something you will not back down to deceit. Those who have plans to use you...well, it will backfire badly for them. I don't want to see you hurt. They might come at you with a vengeance."

"Too many of us are standing down, enjoying our comforts, ignoring the threats to our way of life. Someone has to stand up."

"That makes me proud but also scares the daylights out of me. You will stand your ground. You will do the right thing. But if you step in shit, it's hard to shake it off your boot. And it smells. If you do the wrong thing the stink never goes away. It has been said for thousands of years that doing the wrong thing is never right."

"Let's go check on the alpacas. That little one looks like it just swallowed a hot pepper."

"That is youthful exuberance in motion. It's called pronking. That baby is celebrating youth, innocence and freedom. One reason we love them so."

"Do you eat them?"

"We don't. Some do. They are too cute. Each has a name and a distinctive personality. As for a meat source, there's no way the pork, chicken and beef lobbies are going to allow congress to sanction a competitor."

"I thought the people decided what we should and should not eat."

"The dues-rich unions, mostly infiltrated by the Mob and the for-profit corporations whose short-term-profit-crazed stockholders, meaning us, tell Congress what to do. The peoples' apathy confirms it. I guess you would call it a monopoly."

"This jacket is incredibly warm."

"Yep. Don't have to dress up like the Pillsbury Dough boy when I go hunting anymore. Many of us are returning to going green here in Montana. I think most city folk don't even know what that means."

Father and daughter walked arm and arm back to the old ranch house that had acted as external shelter and internal family and close friend shelter for the Abbott family for several generations.

"So what are your plans going forward?" her dad asked, obviously anxious as the family ate lunch.

"After MBA school, Senator Cowel has kindly offered me a job, and I've accepted. With luck, I'll save enough money to support our ranch."

"You never liked budgets or accounting or any financial stuff. Is this MBA stuff right for you?" Norman drilled.

"A free ride at Harvard grad school, Dad? Who could turn that down?"

"What's the catch?"

"I asked the senator the same question. His immediate response was 'none.'"

"What will the job involve after you get this financial degree, dear?" Martha asked.

"I'm going to be a lobbyist or aide for Senator Cowel."

Norman Abbott, in mid-drink, sprayed his coffee all over the table.

"Dad, it's a much-maligned profession. But it is worthwhile. You might even read about me in your newspaper."

"I'm inclined to agree with Mark Twain on that subject. *If you don't read the newspaper you are uninformed, if you do read the newspaper you are misinformed.*"

* * *

After lingering and tearful goodbyes, Julia boarded a plane chartered by the governor and flew off to Helena, the state capital of Montana. Yet another parade, this one in an open-air limo with the governor, waving and smiling all along Last Chance Gulch, Helena's main street. She was blessed by its prelate at the steps of the Cathedral of Saint Helena, one of the beautiful neo-gothic focal points of the city. After a long day of questions and bluster, Julia found herself exhausted. *Saying cheese all day is hard work.*

Dinner with the governor followed where she sat next to him at a raised table in the Capitol Building, his political allies and Montana "people of note," which Julia interpreted to mean campaign contributors, spread out before her.

"Julia," he said softly as the live band played and couples danced. "First, thank you for being a good sport and putting up with all this fanfare. I think everyone in the state of Montana who wanted to see you and shake your hand, did."

"I think it must have been everyone. My right hand is swollen and sore."

"An occupational hazard. Many of these cowboys and ranchers shake your hand with a death grip. By the end of the day it's pure torture."

"Hopefully, my days in the sun are over."

"I hope not. I do not know your parents, but quite a few

people have told me you come from true American stock, and your family is well thought of."

"I'm flattered."

"So please listen to some advice. As governor, I do some good things for our state. I ensure I get our share of federal funding and push for funds if they are held back. I make sure we work hard and in support of our citizens. That said, politics is a game of compromise. Sometimes you have to do things you don't like, you don't want to do, but do it in the name of choosing the lesser evil. That isn't moral. Two wrongs do not make a right. This profession can eat you up. It begins to dim your soul. Just please remember that while politicians can confuse your senses and torture your body, your soul is yours. You are the gatekeeper and only you say what you allow into it. Finally, Julia, the senator and I are of the same party, but that is about where it stops. Parker Cowel has done a lot of good for Montana over the years just like his father did before him. But with power comes corruption. I hope someday you will continue to serve Montana and our nation with integrity."

Julia kissed the governor on his cheek, whispered a thank you and received a solid hand of applause from those in attendance.

Chapter 10

AJ Morales looked over the shoulder of the copilot at the green and red colors of the radar terrain and infrared tracking screens. He was on a rescue mission in the Afghan desert along with twenty or so like men and women with various essential skills needed to retrieve a U.S. and coalition team downed behind enemy lines. Part of a combat search and rescue team, AJ served as a U.S.AF Pararescue member, his assignment was to provide immediate medical assistance to any and all traumatized survivors. Two A-10 Warthog jets trailed the CV-22 Osprey helicopter as it approached its target. The cabin was bathed in a blood-red color. This helped prevent any vision-contrast problems with the moonless desert night. It also served as an indication of imminent deployment.

AJ was on his third tour in Afghanistan; seven years post Rose Bowl, now a decorated master sergeant, and wore the medals and scars to prove it. When he enlisted the same day his best friend had betrayed him and walked away from an NFL draft pick opportunity, most thought he was nuts. *Sports Illustrated* called him the "Nutty Patriot." Perhaps he was. But the grueling challenges he had gone through in PJ training had kept his mind from recalling thoughts of walking in on his fiancé lying under his best friend. He finished first in his class, got his wings, his maroon beret, believed in the Pararescue code of "These things I do that others may live," and rarely looked back.

A subtle change in altitude and direction instructed every team member to check gear, whether feeling for the rifle safety position, ensuring key equipment was properly attached, or to whisper a favorite prayer. AJ put his hand on his 1911 Colt .45. His was a close-encounter weapon. Given his mission, where even emergency surgery was demanded, he had no time for an aggressive firefight. He relied on his teammates for that. His job was to provide immediate medical assistance. And if he had time and the situation was right, he even offered his services to the enemy.

An explosion knocked him forward; his body jammed against his safety harness. His brain swirled inside his head; the Osprey spun as a ground to air launched rocket clipped its tail. The bird spun and went down hard. Automatic-weapon fire. Cursing. Shouting. Blackness. AJ awoke to a foreign tongue spoken too fast for him to understand. Then he understood a few words. It was Dari. There were no native Afghans on the rescue mission. He lay on his back and slowly opened an eye. A black turban. Then, maybe thirty or more. He was surrounded by agitated enemies. He began to pick up words. "Kill him, too. Medic. Enemy. Interrogate." The familiar sound of Warthog machine guns scattered the group. Explosions. Shouts. Cursing. Conscious thought left him. The rhythmic rocking of some sort of vehicle. The Colt was gone. So were his boots.

He awoke slumped and tied to a chair, his head and back throbbing. A cup of warm water was offered, and he slurped at it.

"My name is Shapoor Mamadzai. I do not care about your rank or your serial number. A medic such as you saved my brother; a rare act of kindness from a soldier of the Great Satan. Honor demands I return the favor. I need you to remain calm and act humbled. If you do not, my comrades will separate your head from its shoulders."

"My team?"

"With their god – or in hell. Most died when you crashed. The others were shot. The Warthog jets that followed you limped back to whatever toilet they sprang from. Your CIA Stinger missiles and drones are such effective deterrents. A cowardly way of waging war, but effective."

"Bombs in mosques and in crowded market places are a hero's way of fighting?"

"You do not fear me, do you?"

"You speak English well."

"I learned at your universities. But did not drink beer and plow the female students. I studied."

"You are Al Qaeda?"

"CIA trained. Explosives and small arms."

AJ frowned.

"Trained by the best. Seals, Rangers, Special Ops."

"What a war."

"Yet you Pararescue types save lives. Even ours when there is time."

"I'm not a killer. I'm an American patriot."

"Defined as one who defends your republic and its constitution or as one who fights for the American Empire."

"Empire? We're Freedom Fighters. Since 9/11. Why the hell would we want to invade this country otherwise? There is nothing here."

Mamadzai smirked, shaking his head as if in pain.

"Twenty-three hundred years ago Alexander the Great was said to have remarked that 'Afghanistan is easy to march into but hard to march out of.'"

"These days we fly."

"So did the Soviets. They eventually flew out again in 2003 to watch their empire unravel. This country is known to be a graveyard for empires. Welcome, America."

"We helped you against the Soviets when you were the Mujardeen."

"More correctly, you used us to further your own ends."

"We helped liberate you from the communists. Don't you believe in freedom?"

"When I am on my horse, riding among the mountains of the Hindu Kush, I am free. The Mongols could not find me there; neither could the Mughals, British India, the British Empire, and the Russian Empire. And now the American Empire. Come for precious resources that can be turned into gold. It is an old story that mankind is more inclined to suffer while evils are sufferable, than to right themselves by abolishing the forms to which they are accustomed."

"You are quoting from our own Declaration of Independence to me?"

"You are one of the few Americans who would even know that. Most of you only know the words to your asinine pop-culture songs."

"What exactly is precious in this giant rock heap?"

"Rather ask yourself why have so many come here? Your people no longer know their own brave history much less that of the world."

"I majored in history. We have excellent universities, which is why you were schooled in America. You are the bridge between the Caspian and Arabian seas. Oil and gas and pipelines criss-cross our country. You are entirely landlocked, ringed by Iran, Pakistan, India, China, and Russia stretching above you. You are a country others travel through to get someplace else."

"And you American Freedom Fighters are here to—"

"Prevent terrorism from spreading. Nip it in the bud."

"You are here to profit financially. You are here by the authority of a corrupt empire. You are here because you believe the lies your ideologically compliant media spews day and night. If there is an antichrist, my deaf, dumb and blind friend, it is surely your American media. It promises everything and gives you nothing. In the end, it wins your soul."

"Can I give you my name, rank and serial number now? Do you follow the Geneva Convention protocols or do you and your buddies put on masks, set up a video camera and saw off my head at this point?"

"You are a guest of mine. Honor prevents me from harming you. We hated Bin Laden, too, but he was a guest, also."

"Thanks for your hospitality. Untie me now and I'll just mosey on back to my base."

"Then you would lose your head. You are my guest, not one of those men outside. Each has lost several family members because of what you represent. And keep your voice down or their passions will overwhelm their reason and they will drag you away."

"I'll submit for now," AJ said.

"One day you will submit to Allah."

"One day Jesus will return, remove your blindfolds, open your hearts and set you all straight."

"Your country will soon collapse from within."

"You have crystal balls and fortune tellers here?"

"I have no need of them. One of your own clerics condemned your country in the time of Charlemagne. *Nec audiendi qui solent dicere, Vox populi, vox Dei, quum tumultuositas vulgi semper insaniae proxima sit – The voice of the people is the voice of God.* My father insisted on Latin classes for me through high school. The entire quote is, *And those people should not be listened to who keep saying the voice of the people is the voice of God, since the riotousness of the crowd is always very close to madness.* You are a spoiled and arrogant people who taint the entire world with your movies, songs and decadent culture."

"I agree my people are risking their souls in the name of sloth and our politicians encourage it. And your people tend to look to the letter of the law rather than to the spirit of it. Something Abraham's God reminded us not to do."

Mamadzai studied AJ for some time. "I did not intend to have this type of conversation. I have a duty to my brother who was saved by a PJ. You will be returned safely to your base. I face substantial risk to do this. I must remain with you to help you get back to your base. But if you want to see the truth for yourself, come with me on a reconnaissance mission tomorrow night."

"A U.S. Air Force special ops sergeant on a mission with Al Qaeda? Just chop off my head now."

"I said you are free to go. When it is safe to travel. And you are not curious why you American Freedom Fighters do nothing here but guard our poppy fields? Do you know that opium profits are up 700 percent since you arrived? If you believe life is sacred as I do, you cannot be for the global markets of heroin and cocaine."

AJ thought for a moment. There was much frustrated talk all over the barracks and mess halls about America's role in Afghanistan, the hands-off policy and any discussion of poppy fields and the opium concerns with the numerous foreign contractors and mercenaries from numerous countries. Most everyone was in the dark about much that went on in Afghanistan.

"You're going to let me tag along on poppy-field harvest?"

"We will let you watch one burn; to prevent profiteers from committing sin. After that, I will show you a mining operation managed and controlled by a company known as SMS, run by one of your U.S. senators who is in our country as we speak. His mercenaries have been killing our people, paid by the head, raping our women, stealing our resources and doing so in the guise of building roads and hospitals to improve our country's infrastructure and to bring democracy."

"Why the hell would a private U.S. contractor be running a covert mining operation in Afghanistan?"

"Lithium. Once processed it will be worth many trillions of dollars on the global markets."

"Lithium? The third element on the Periodic Table. A drug to treat bi-polar mental disorders."

"Do you know what the G8 is?"

"Eight of the largest world economies come together now and then to discuss the world food shortage."

"The United States, the United Kingdom, Russia, France, Germany, Italy, Japan and Canada. Not China. Yet. They work together as a cartel. The men and women who control G8 are the same who control the world. Their information clearing house is Interpol."

"I must have died in the crash, and this is Hell."

"The uranium and lithium you plunder from my country flows to the United States. The gold taken from Libya is flown to Germany. Much of the Middle Eastern oil ends up in Italy and France. The UK receives access to the new economic entry points to develop as their own. And when we were occupied by the Soviet Union, they constructed an oil and gas pipeline structure that flows directly to the Indian Ocean. Try to look at a world map and see something besides your own country."

"If this is true, it sure the hell explains a lot. Why isn't this general knowledge?"

"Do the shepherds share their plans with the sheep? My country's veins have been opened, and we bleed our natural resources into your coffers."

"This scares me. If it is true—"

"I offer you a chance to gaze upon some of the truth. Perhaps you fell out of the sky at my feet for a purpose."

"Well, Shapoor, I have personal and painful firsthand experiences with political corruption and what the powerful can do to decent people. And that is not what that Declaration of Independence or the U.S. Constitution is supposed to protect us from. Lately, it has been failing miserably. So I got to see this."

"Address me as Mamadzai. Here, we address one another with our surnames. Let us hope it will be your first lesson of many with your new eyes and ears."

Chapter 11

Disguised as an Afghani, sneaking through the desert at night as part of an insurgent spying operation on illegal mining operations was the creepiest experience of AJ's life so far. The bone-chilling cold and the vast expanse of sheer nothingness coupled with the expectation of imminent attack from American forces unnerved him. The Afghanis also had a sense of the satellites hanging all around the sky; never sleeping eyes in the sky that could pick their company out day or night and follow them from some control room connected to drone technology that could launch a flying robot loaded with explosives silently at its prey. There would be no fear, no apprehension, no logic involved by the operators. Nothing personal. Nothing human.

AJ watched as Mamadzai's men first picked off the guards protecting a poppy field and then torched it. The odor of burning poppies didn't seem dangerous but the smoke did burn his eyes.

"Who are the guards?" AJ asked.

"Usually Al Qaeda, sometimes your men. It is no concern to us whom we kill to achieve our goals. The drugs these lovely flowers can produce kill souls and create untold suffering. We move on now. This fire will be noted from your silent sentinels up there soon."

AJ had more questions, but followed Mamadzai into the darkness. Finally they stopped for a few moments in a sunken part of the desert.

"Today oil is the pumping heart of the world, especially the gluttons. Your country owns about 1% of the world's oil reserves, yet consumes nearly one fourth of that which is produced daily. Those fortunate enough to have vast reserves control and sell them with a smile. How do you say, they have you by the short hairs."

AJ nodded. Mamadzai spoke the truth.

"Much of your military action around the world, in the name of democracy, of course, has to do with protecting that daily oil production. Imagine the American war and consumer-production machines sputtering to a dead stop."

"Right, I get it. Food no longer flows into the cities. People turn into Mobs. Chaos."

"Given that your economy is based on promissory paper and not hard assets like gold or silver and that there is little confidence in America since your banking and Wall Street buffoons caused the financial meltdown catastrophe, things are not well in River City. Oil is dirty. It pollutes the atmosphere. It spews acid rain. Destroys crops, taints water. Your people speak of environmental stability. The Green Movement. How long can you appease them with promises of change when your most powerful tycoons profit from oil?"

"I don't know," AJ shrugged. "We don't talk about these things."

"You should. Shifts in geo-political power are accelerating. A growing base of Chinese and Indian consumers demand their share of wealth and are hungry for power to run their nations, also. Try as your technology wizards will, they have not produced a clean and powerful energy source. Past and current efforts at efficiently storing electricity are rather anemic, until recently. Imagine if something came along that could better power to iPods, MP3 players, laptops, Nooks, Kindles, cell phones. And then there is your archaic and soon-unsustainable power grid. Further imagine lithium powering electric cars, able to efficiently store energy from solar panels, wind turbines, ocean currents. And it can do it cleanly and quietly. Of course, it comes with low carbon footprints, good for the environment and improves Mobile Internet communications."

"You're speaking of lithium?"

"Yes."

"And it is here in Afghanistan?"

"Yes."

"It must exist in other places."

"It does. Bolivia, China and others. But why pay for it there when you can create a small war here, rattle some sabers and under the cover of darkness mine it and ship it home?"

The sound of rotor blades stilled the caravan. Camels were pulled to the ground. Surface-to-air missiles pointed toward the whirring sound in the distance and over a dune. Nobody moved until the sound faded.

"We are close now," Mamadzai said. "The potential profits for your military and industrial entities for lithium are immense. They defend their stockpile of gold with a greedy intensity. The American profiteers, like the SMS Corporation, buy elections for their politicians. The politicians, in turn, rattle sabers, deflect attention from their true goals. Your American media moguls are given ample payoffs to scare the public into believing that terrorists are among them. The American people vote for this corrupt politician. All this thanks to lithium. True, it costs American lives, but when did human life ever matter to profiteers?"

"You are telling me I am here to help turn a buck for wealthy big shots."

"Of course. Bin Laden blew up your twin phallic symbols of economic greed and corruption. Dish washers and corporate lions were both incensed at that. Retribution. Justice. Fuel up the war machine. America is immediately at what it does best – justifying foreign war. And it is a costly fight now, fuel the economy and pay later, when the 'other' political party is in control. Play the blame game. It is the former leader's fault. Everyone is guilty except for the American people. You are hypocrites. The Evil Empire."

"Our politicians—"

"At Cambridge I sat for physics and learned in 1932 lithium atoms were split to transform into helium. The first nuclear reaction. Lithium today serves as a fusion fuel in staged thermonuclear weapons. This made me fear not only the U.S. and the Soviets, but now China, Pakistan, Israel, North Korea, France and now Iran. As they say in your country, 'a fool with a tool is still a fool.'"

Just over the hill, AJ focused binoculars on a well-camouflaged and closely guarded facility that was perhaps four football fields in width and length. A small airfield was defined by makeshift walls that kept the shifting sands at bay.

"Seeing is believing, Sergeant AJ Morales. It is an image that will burn into your memory. American colonialism in action. Are you man enough to report the deeds of the country you serve? And to whom?"

The binoculars trembled in AJ's hands. He had to sit cross-legged in the sand and rest his elbows on his knees for a clear view. Two men walked up the airstairs. One turned. It was the man AJ had seen at the Rose Bowl game years ago. A U.S. senator. A friend of Charlie and his family.

"If memory serves, PJ, your first president was morally challenged in a potential revolt they call the Newburg Conspiracy. It is little known in America. But the father of your country refused the offer of dictator, king or emperor. He reminded the conspirators that a patriot is not someone who defends his government but one who defends its constitution."

AJ's cheeks expanded as he forced air from his lungs while dropping the binoculars. "I have faith in the American people. You do not know them as I do."

Over the next several years that challenge was whispered and echoed through AJ's entire being. After his release from Mamadzai, as promised, AJ returned to his unit and during debriefing played the part of a luckless prisoner of war who escaped from his captors. He was able to explain away his entire absence but never divulged the true nature of his release or the lithium-mining operation. He could trust no one with this information. His new goal was to return home once his enlistment was ended and avenge his father's death by awaking his fellow Americans; to awake the American Eagle.

Over the next several months he completed his duties as required but constantly planned his future. He hit on a plan to run for public office. To the U.S. House of Representatives. If he could get elected he would be daily rubbing shoulders with the man who ruined his father. Whether Cowel knew who he was or not didn't matter. AJ would be a crusader to end at least one facet of the rampant political corruption in the American government.

He spent all his off time reading constitutional law, how political campaigns were forged, waged and won, and decided that the Austin, Texas congressional district was where he had the best shot at election. There was a large Latino contingent there, they were being neglected for lack of a power base and he could offer one to them, if elected. Austin was also the scene of his second greatest heartache – where his best friend and girlfriend betrayed him. Why not launch his payback plan there?

Chapter 12

Freshman congressman AJ Morales looked out the window of his dingy hole-in-the-wall Washington D.C. office, recalling his days in Afghanistan, the lithium mining, the U.S. Senator inspecting his corrupt cash cow; and his own road to election; a first tactic in a payback strategy. He opted out of the freshman lottery and chose the first vacant room. This one was on the fifth floor of the Cannon Congressional Office Building, known to be the worst of the worst of the buildings, where the elevators stop on the 4th floor and staffers and visitors were forced to walk up or down from the 5th floor. The interior lighting was poor, and as for an outside view, one had the option of a sheer wall of crumbly bricks of an ancient and windowless old building to the east or an unending stream of trash dumpsters tending the neighboring complex. AJ felt he had to earn his status just as he had done from the early days of Pop Warner football, through high school and on to becoming a College All American at UT. In his military career he had refused several promotions to stay close to the real action. He had seen firsthand as a child what big egos could do to simple folk. That would not be his style.

He told his tiny staff the stairs were going to help everyone stay in shape and to remember you could walk up, but you could also walk down to anyone's level. It had been a real learning experience to be able to run for public office in the Austin, Texas district. While he met and spoke to the local people who would soon become his constituents, spending every evening and all day on Saturday and Sunday walking door-to-door, he listened intensely to their concerns until he understood the challenges they faced. He did not criticize his opponents, nor did he patronize his neighbors. His goal was to become a statesman and not a politician. His father was his role model. Most of the locals knew of AJ from his UT football days. It was his unassuming, genuine and straightforward manner that helped people remember the young Morales.

Working through a tough primary as the number three candidate early in the process then winning handily over two established party stalwarts, he convinced the Democratic Party of Texas he was the man for the job and could get the votes for a party win. But AJ did not like the BS he had to endure. The cheap-shot attacks from his rivals when they debated in public made the hair on the back of his neck rise. He consciously held himself back from punching the daylights out of those who hammered away at his lack of party experience and youth, thereby avoiding the issues. He remembered his father saying "use your powers of reason, not your emotions," and "get mad at the issues, get mad at injustice but never at your opponent." And when it turned bad for his father, Governor Morales once quoted Abraham Lincoln with, "I am not bound to win, but I am bound to be true. I am not bound to succeed, but I am bound to live up to what light I have."

AJ studied and analyzed issues in every free moment available. He read voraciously from the best of both the liberal and conservative pundits, finding a middle ground, a balance and a synergy as to what was needed to benefit his district and his nation. He found early that his small election team, mostly young volunteers, was the true backbone of the American political system, and a necessity to keeping current, separating truth from fiction and statistics from emotional rationalizations. He was a populist, much in the same way as John Kennedy, Ronald Reagan, Jimmy Carter, Bill Clinton and Barack Obama. They all inspired people to like them and to want to jump on their bandwagons and be part of a magic moment in time.

When the relentless anti-Morales campaign commercials started running in the fall campaign, he felt like screaming. The media quickly researched and dredged up information about AJ's father's disgrace as well as the nagging gossip on his mother's suspect citizenship status. People he never met were quoted with nasty slurs – calling him a half-breed or not a true son of Texas. These unsubstantiated polemics filled both printed and cyber-space media. But he kept a short rein on his emotions. He had learned this skill playing football and in combat. The game was supported by brute force. But rage would surely land you hurt or defeated. The game was won by a balanced combination of intellect and spirit. They were fueled by the emotions, but not controlled by them. He brought these lessons to his political career. There was little leisure, entertainment, social contact or dilly-dally. His career was his life.

If he felt low, or nearly beaten, he would visualize the "honorable" Senator Parker Cowel, sitting on the deck of his mentor, the former U.S. Senator W.E. "Billy" Kiddenly, Gatsbyish 72' Hatteras yacht. Both sat in deck chairs like kings on thrones, smoking Cuban cigars, drinking Kentucky bourbon, all the time planning to sweep AJ's campaign for the Austin district congressional seat into the gutter. Neither power monger wanted to see another Morales rise to power. If AJ could defy them and win the seat, so too could others. A deadly precedent would be set. Much money was thrown the way of AJ's competition. The one-on-one interviews the media scheduled with AJ were usually with beautiful women. All showed more leg or breast than brains, and blatantly flirted with him in pre-interview discussion to tempt him into misspeaking. They pushed at his football hormones and his military muscle asking how he felt about women in combat, or something macho-like which could be used to derail his 70% positive polling with female voters. They complimented his chiseled Latin looks, his war record, then instantly morphed into agenda-driven serpents the second the cameras rolled.

"So, Mr. Morales, while you're known as an all-time illus-trious University of Texas wide receiver and an American war hero, most of our leaders have exemplary legal or business experience. How do you respond to this deficiency?"

"I don't think it's a deficiency, Ms. Brown. Considering the congressional records of the lawyers and corporate types who have served this nation, many have proven to be disingenuous and unproductive in doing the work of the people, but darned good at serving their own personal agendas. For this reason alone I think our voters would love to give me a shot at the job." He would then finish with, "I hope this answer satisfies you." And always add a warm smile.

"While that sounds like a nice sentiment, Mr. Morales," the bushwhacker would continue after clearing her throat, "you've been labeled a long shot candidate who, if elected would then vie with seasoned professionals in both the House and the senate. How can you assure the numerous skeptical voters in your district as to your ability to help pass appropriate legislation and obtain needed funds against such senior opposition?"

"Well, first, I was not aware that there are numerous skeptical voters in my district. Could you share these numbers with me later?"

"Of course. After the interview."

"As for your question, I know of no other candidate in my district that has taken a bullet for his or her country on two separate occasions and still continued to complete both military objectives despite the setback." He let the dead air during his interviewer's silence build and then followed with, "I am more than just another political voice. I am the voice of the people. I have walked my entire district and met thousands of citizens and learned a lot about their concerns, dreams and expectations. The current representatives and candidates are just not acquainted with the constituents. Putting up garish signs with a candidate's name on them and some bumper-sticker philosophy cannot win an election, can it? I am committed to serving my country and have offered my life to that end. It is obvious that the people here are not happy. So what can these seasoned but ineffectual professionals you speak about do better than I can? These political leopards we have in office now will not and cannot change their spots. So put a lion in their seats instead. A lion does not get scared when he hears a herd of impalas are hunting him. I'll get the job done, if elected."

While comebacks like that brought out the Austin freethinking independents, Hispanics, female voters and veterans in droves, it did not endear him to the status-quo media. The china-doll interviewers made a career out of skewering the candidates their media mogul managers did not like, and fawning over those they crowned as media darlings. But the public was growing sick of being manipulated by sugar talk now that their taxes rose yearly, their salaries fell and their job benefits evaporated. In the end, AJ Morales trounced his evil-tongued opponent handily with a coalition of voters who represented 60.2% of the vote.

So here he stood, a U.S. Congressman looking out the window of his congressional office. He was a newbie, for sure, but an elected member of the U.S. House of Representatives for the Austin, Texas 17th congressional district. His job description, to create and pass appropriate federal laws was straightforward on paper; but the map was not the territory. AJ was expected to serve on various committees, to introduce or participate in creating resolutions and legislation in support of his own district. His term was for two years, which he was beginning to think was too brief a time to be productive for his district. In that time he had hoped to build a record to campaign on for a second term to garner the party's nomination once more as an incumbent and win the majority of the voters to return him to do their work for another term.

But he could already sense that to stay in Washington he had to be "one of the boys" and support the party on all things. His district became almost a distant second cause. He wondered how much of his time would be campaigning for the next election iteration and how much time would be spent on actual accomplishment. He realized he would need to create, modify and pass laws. He could not stand in front of his constituents and tell them no new laws were needed. Even if that were true, it was a legislator's job to make laws. He believed the more laws a country had the more unjust its people. This type of thinking went back to the early Greeks. Many of his peers in Congress would indeed make laws. They had another agenda, different from AJ's, whether wealth, power, or prestige, they were there to feather their own pockets as an elected official. Benefits would come for their constituents for sure, but only as a way to reelection so as to point to financial gain for "the people."

AJ's ulterior motive, however, was more than one of revenge for the brutal injustice handed to his father and family. His was a mission to expose and prevent those self-serving ogres from ever sending Americans off to war for a financial agenda or devastating and defacing the earth surface in some faraway land under the cover of the American flag – for defiling the flag as a shield to hide behind, while treasonous acts were being committed right under the nose of a self-serving Congress.

Austin felt a long way from where AJ stood now; Helena, his home, seemed even farther. A beeping phone brought him back to his desk.

"Yes, Crystal?"

"Congressman Hernandez–Gibbons, from the Texas 22 District in Houston, has requested a meeting with you this afternoon at three in her office. Shall I confirm?"

"Let me speak with her."

"This is her admin on the line, sir. Shall I request the congressman on the line?"

"No, Crystal. I will be there at three."

A summons, AJ thought. *Who am I to refuse?* He still didn't know his way around town yet. Like the first day of high school. Steer clear of the bullies. Some quick research showed Congressman Juanita Hernandez-Gibbons to be a twelve-term Democrat, representing a Hispanic district in the Houston area.

She was a former federal judge, married for ten years to Marcus Hernandez, the famed mystery writer, until his death six years ago. She remarried Theodore Gibbons two years ago. He owned three Jaguar dealerships in the D.C. area. The Gibbons part of the hyphenated name fooled him. He knew of her as Juanita Hernandez.

He was ushered into an A-list office that was a contrast to AJ's bare and freshly spackled walls. Pictures of well-known politicians, celebrities from movies and sports and others spoke to a senior political presence. AJ took a seat after announcing himself. A heavy oak door opened, and a smartly dressed handsome woman with graying hair, thick-rimmed glasses hanging from the tip of her nose and an inscrutable smile greeted AJ.

"I'm glad you could make it, Congressman," she said as she showed him entry to her private office, closed the door behind them and offered him a seat across from her desk. "Do you remember me at all, AJ? It's been years."

"Yes, ma'am, I do. I called my mom to get the lowdown on you. Before she told me anything she said to say shame on you for not calling and being 'busy' was no excuse."

"Ouch. Give me her number. I have much penance to do. So what did she say about the lowdown on me?"

"A once good friend, an ally from Mom and Dad's political days and hopefully still a good Catholic."

"I am, but I have to admit it's been a long time since the holy water has met my forehead."

"That's Mom's way of asking if you are still one of the givers and not one of the takers in our country."

"Understood. Anything else?"

"She said you understand what happened to my father and might take pity on me in my new job."

"Which is why you are here. I hear you are nosing around, asking questions about the SMS Corporation. That is career limiting."

"I am not here for a career."

"Then you are your father's son. Buenos *días, hijo de Don Quijote.*"

"Is the Morales family such a joke?"

"I apologize. I did not mean to infer you or your father was a fool. He dreamed that impossible dream. It cost him his life. He never backed down. Then *soy hijo de mi padre.*"

It pleased AJ when this old family friend, this senior congressman beamed a smile when she replied that he was indeed his father's son.

"Oh boy," the congresswoman said. "When your father died it broke many hearts. It is awful to see a good man suffer, much less die. Those who get themselves elected to make themselves wealthy were tremendously pleased when the news of your father's death came out. Your father as Governor of Montana was always bothered by Senior U.S. Senator Kiddenly's blatantly corrupt methods of wielding power, and he expressed it vocally to oversight committees. That made him disliked – not a team player. The senate could easily swat any allegations of corruption down like a fly. When the seat for a Junior U.S. Senator representing Montana became available, and your father decided to run, Buford Ebers and his best pal Senator Parker Cowel did not want a Democrat to share power with him in the senate. So along came the outright lies about your father, strong-arm tactics for shaking people down to get campaign contributions and votes, offering exceptional favors for votes, offering to pay off gambling debts from those illegal Kalispell poker games..."

AJ's stomach soured at the rehash from the congresswoman's perspective.

"...and so on. This became Cowel's campaign strategy to help his own Republican choice for the seat. When it looked like your father could conceivably win, the Cowel dirty tricks team went into action. That is when the fictitious mistress story hit the media. Those of us who are here to serve a just nation and to keep it just put our tails beneath our legs and ran. Our only excuse for the cowardice is that many of us have endured and held back the flood for a time. But these 'get elected at any cost' and 'a slap on the hand' corruption sentences have soiled our constitution until it has become more of a guideline than a moral way to govern."

"I want to change, to divert the flood, Congresswoman."

She smiled. "Your parents and I and others were lions at the democratic presidential conventions once. The dogs you must fight, AJ...these are large dogs that go for the throat. Even retired, former senator Billy Kiddenly would be a nightmare to take on as you found out during the election. I'm sure he even knows about this meeting now as he floats around the Gulf of Mexico on his Hatteras yacht. I crossed him once, and he nearly ran me out of office during my third reelection. I won, but curled my tail again."

"So he is the big gun in SMS?"

"Above him there are guns many times his size, and I do not even know any of those names."

"That's how big it is?"

"Oh, it is even bigger. What are your plans?"

"Simple. The enemy has taken from me. I will put the enemy down."

"The vast majority of your peers in Congress sacrifice principle for ambition. You risk it for revenge."

"What would you have me do?"

"Seek justice."

"They are the same to me."

"No. Two wrongs never make a right. You are in the right when you want to take down a corrupt politician on behalf of your father and America. That is justice. But to kill for your own personal rage makes you like Kiddenly and Cowel."

Her statement burned into AJ's head. He heard it. He knew what it meant. He had achieved so much just to be sitting here today, but he had more to think out. He did not want to be a common murderer. Nor should Cowel and now Kiddenly slip through his fingers.

"I am the ranking Democrat on the Armed Forces Committee and can offer you a seat, and mentor you through the rules, regulations, the infighting politics to expect and the pecking order. From here, you can look into SMS with some semblance of legality. I have good contacts with the FBI and will make those introductions. Learn all about your foe before you even consider a move. Learn about the head of the snake."

"Sound advice. Who is Kiddenly's boss?"

"Organized crime."

"Dear God."

"I'll help as I can, given my permanently curled tail."

"How do you manage to—"

"Live with myself? Take this advice to heart. In time, you will come to know this as truth. All young people want to change the world. The problem with this is that young people neither understand themselves nor the world around them. So you will be viewed by many as a naïve and dangerous loose cannon."

"I've already been called a thumb-sucking gadfly."

"I have done much good over the years from this office. I do believe that a people deserve the government they have. Most do not care about national or local politics as long that they have jobs and discretionary income to purchase things of comfort and enjoyment. We've raised several generations of children and grandchildren in my 71 years of life who know and care more about Luke Skywalker and the personal lives of celebrities than they do about the great history of our nation and the value, even the meaning of freedom. Your enemy is greedy men and women manipulating the entire world. The weakness they exploit is the apathy and softness of the people."

"What can I expect from the Democrats and the Republicans?" he asked.

"Our forefathers had been victims of monarchies, aristocracies, feudalism and chaos, for lack of a better term. All of those who came here in the early migrations from Europe were all victims of the whip, the abuse of power. So they built a new format on what they knew, took the best from what they has seen and infused it with Christian morality. God's law."

"God is not popular these days."

"And is there any wonder America is lost in the dark?"

"I know the history. Monarchy breeds tyranny. The people were treated like dogs. The aristocracies breed feudalism, a politically correct term for slavery. And democracy? On the surface government by the people sounds good but can backfire if the people are all mad hatters."

"It's called Mobacracy, for lack of a better term," she said.

"Our constitution is set up to prevent that kind of thing. It protects the people from the government but can also protect the government from the people."

"If our constitution is strictly followed and enforced."

"Touché."

"From what I've been able to glean from studying, the presidency is like a constitutional monarch, he's elected by the people. He's the figurehead of the country. A king with limited powers. The senate resembles an aristocracy. Powerful and wealthy men and women. Law makers. The House represents the democracy. Only a two-year term. That precipitates change through voting. And they control most government funding. Through this process we've managed to build and maintain a great nation."

"Don't forget the media's hand in things. 16th-century American journalists were a relatively noble lot, reporting on issues and events to flush out the truth. This was a major factor in the preservation of liberty. Crooked politicians were smoked out and exposed to the entire country in the American press. There were few spin doctors, empty talking heads, and the bad guys did not own the newspapers. The evolution of a 'just the facts, ma'am' journalist with integrity to what we have today is a sad story. Today you can pretty much think of the media as public relations for government. They can make you or break you depending on what fat cat or ideology owns their particular tabloid."

"Thank you, Congresswoman, for your honesty."

"Thank you for your sincerity, Representative Morales, and for your willingness to fight a just fight. There are always good men and women waiting for inspiration and a leader to come forward. Perhaps that leader is you. Avoid grappling with our immense and ever-growing government bureaucracy. You'll find it is self-serving, morally bankrupt and politically inept. Bypass the red tape and go for the jugular. Now give me your mother's number. I have many apologies to make. Welcome to Capitol Hill."

Chapter 13

As time passed and his experience grew, AJ's imagined victory and ascension into Congress did not match reality. This was more like high school. Chaos with a pecking order. As a freshman, he knew few members, if any. Getting from meeting to meeting was a chore and he needed a map. He feared being late or imposing on others as he had all of his life. The prominent names intimidated him, holding his eyes, smirking at the small fish in a large sea of sharks. The seniors were the predators; he was the prey, a toy to play with for his one vote. Then there were the lobbyists. They came bearing gifts like the three wise men, but not to pay homage but to get their bills passed, their funding met, even their special agendas tacked on the end of legislation as secret legislative hitchhikes, known as riders.

While on a $178,000 yearly salary, he originally believed substantial, he soon found himself invited and expected to attend or donate to hundred-dollar-a-plate campaign fund raisers. It was disrespectful, and career limiting not to attend. While assigned a congressional budget, covering his staffers – young lawyers, research assistants, and so forth – he soon spent his allotted budget and was forced to kick in his own money, while not touching campaign funds. Although invited to share an apartment with two other freshman congressmen from Oregon, he found the D.C. housing and rental costs sky high. He also had to maintain an office in his Austin district. Expenses mounted. The big fish established multi-term, winning representatives, and senators owned million-dollar houses in Georgetown and other wealthy suburbs. Thank you, Mr. Taxpayer. The lobbyists and others who came with their checkbooks in return for whatever AJ could offer them became suddenly more appealing. Tempting.

So this is how our country works. The golden rule – he who has the gold makes the rules. America isn't for sale. It is already owned. AJ opted to be his own man yet again. He found a first-floor studio apartment with outside parking in Alexandria, VA, close to the rail service to his D.C. Office where he would walk to the Cannon building and then up the stairs to this office, then down again to attend committee meetings, luncheons, briefings or votes and Capitol Hill. He would reverse the process late every night to return home to a light dinner, time to do a quick regimentation of calisthenics and then another two hours of work in front of his computer, personally answering messages from his constituents.

AJ was always conscious of the senate's one hundred in the upper chamber, the president in the White House, and nine Supreme Court Justices. But, less than 600 men and women were left to run the most powerful nation on earth by being the closest ears to the people in the entire federal system. Bureaucracy was supported in numbers few knew or wanted to know. A growing army of law makers and in some case, law breakers, became a growing cancer of those in support of the 600. Perhaps the 666.

AJ smiled as he recalled Parkinson's Law, describing the rate at which bureaucracies expand over time. How could he be Morales for the moral agenda; not the moral majority, but for what was the right and just way to manage the people's business of social maintenance? Was this going to be just another Hail Mary pass that he would have catch to find the voice to convey the message of clearing out the graft, manipulation and outright lies being fed to the American people and the world? Would he even survive exposing the ruthless warlords who manipulated America for their own agendas?

"And I'm here to understand the institution, challenge it when necessary," he affirmed, but also to expose those who would not take a bullet like he had for their country by putting their personal interests first, ahead of what was the right thing to do; the right thing that the people wanted and expected. He recalled some of the lyrics from a Steppenwolf song his father played over and over again: "The Monster."

America, where are you now? Don't you care about your sons and daughters? Don't you know we need you now? We can't fight alone against the Monster.

Yeah, right. Who the hell were those idealistic and wet behind the ears poets praying to? Me? Am I America now? Have I been elected to serve the people of my district at the expense of all the others, or do I first represent the people of the purple mountain majesty, the amber waves of grain, from sea to shining sea? Am I a representative of America or of those few locals who elected me? Where is the balance? Do I keep the big picture in mind or just my own little group?

* * *

They voted him into office. "Have a pleasant day, Congressman Morales. Let's do lunch. Don't forget to write." He'd met quite a few of his party's representatives. They didn't stop by; they summoned him, probably because of the inconvenient walk up in the Cannon Building. They hosted sophisticated meet-and-greet sessions where they drank white wine and ate shrimp and Russian caviar, while all pretending to be cultivated representatives of the world's lone superpower.

These elected representatives of the people raconteured political correctness enough to make AJ puke from the vile righteousness and false patriotism, name-dropping of all the big-gun names in society, and giving him tips on who was who, and whom to avoid. They preached the Bible and evoked the name of God in one sentence while dropping F bombs in the next sentence. They were the anointed righteous who were quick to judge, condemn and execute anyone who stood in the way of their narrow personal agendas. Most were shameless hypocrites, professional profiteers, cunning backstabbers, and eloquent speakers of patriotic rhetoric – rhetoric one must support for fear of being shouted down. Most believed the truth was what they could convince the media and public to believe. They were not the representatives and the voices of the people. They served the highest bidders who worshiped and supported their rigid tribal system, with foolish traditions and faux patriotism.

AJ wondered where the America he believed in was and his father adored? *The people do deserve the government they genuinely want and need; maybe I can be the catalyst. Stay focused!*

He relished his own little "bureaucratic team" and he had some good plays in their playbook with a two-year season to win the championship. At the office the next day, AJ thought again about his team: two professors – one finance, the other global politics; a research assistant and a part time gaggle of pages and interns, half high on power and career dreams, the other half naive kids who wished to serve their country, but instead would serve their government; professional, self-serving politicians and an executive assistant who was the smartest of all of them and knew her way around town and which buttons to press.

"Congressman Morales?" A voice came out of a speaker phone on the large wooded desk.

"Yes, Crystal?"

"FBI agents Sampson and Putney are here for your 9 a.m. meeting."

"Please send them right in."

Agent Sampson fit the bill of a law professor replete with a grey goatee and hounds tooth sport coat. Agent Putney was six-foot-four at least and probably weighed in over three hundred pounds. Neither was what AJ expected as experts on the National Crime Syndicate.

"Thank you for coming, gentlemen. Please take a seat," AJ offered and the two FBI agents sat across from him.

"Welcome to Washington, Congressman."

"Thank you. As I said on my call, I wanted a briefing on organized crime. I hope it was okay to invite you here."

"No problem," Agent Putney replied. "We usually do dog and pony shows for Congress at our own building. We have stock presentations there, but Agent Sampson and I wanted to meet the wide receiver, AJ Morales."

"That final catch still hasn't run its race then."

"I thought the game was lost," Agent Sampson said. "Then that incredible pass, you turn and leap and catch that ball one-handed and then backpedal over the goal line. I nearly pissed my pants."

"Me, too," Agent Putney said.

"And I'll make it unanimous," AJ smiled.

The three men shared a laugh which broke the ice.

"A one-in-a-million catch," AJ said. "Only afterward did I think about how I would have felt if I had dropped it."

"But a legend was born," Putney replied.

"Now the legend needs your help. I'm a rookie here."

"Congresswoman Gibbons vouches for you. We both have years of experience with the Mob," Putney said. "That's what you wanted to discuss, correct?"

"To start with, yes. I think I'm not alone in believing the Mafia once existed, but by is now mostly fodder for movies. Cold-hearted killers coming back to the Godfather and all acting as if they are men of honor."

"The honor part is pure fiction. But whether you call it the Mafia, the Mob, the Cosa Nostra or the Syndicate, it exists," Sampson said. "On TV and in the movies those wise guys are kinda glorified. But the fans don't see the dead bodies, or hear the weeping of a ghetto son who overdoses at ten years old. The Mafia brings those drugs to the kids."

"Or the fourteen-year-old prostitutes who look thirty after being hooked on drugs and forced to peddle their asses in the street," Putney added.

"It breaks my heart, Congressman," Agent Sampson said. "And it infuriates me, that in sixteen years, I've done little to help. I'm a product of the ghetto. I've felt and seen the hopelessness, the trap. I was lucky. It ain't a racial thing to me. It's about greed. I don't blame the white man for the black man's drug problems. I don't call myself an Afro-American. I'm an American, and there is no place here for corruption."

"I'm not a Mexican-American, Agent Sampson. I'm an American like you."

The two men looked into each other's eyes; AJ believed both gaining some insight.

"You intend to go after the Mob, Congressman?" Agent Putney asked.

"Yes. But please don't give me that naive rookie speech about taking on the impossible. I want to know what we are up against."

"First off, we've seen our share of Lone Ranger types getting elected and showing up here to right all wrongs, or with specific personal agendas since their individual rights have been trampled. Some fizzle immediately and others go out like a gigantic firework display. But after that, the sky is dark again."

"I admit I am working my mission alone right now. And I do have a personal agenda. America is blind right now, blind to the U.S. Constitution, which I have sworn to defend from both foreign and domestic enemies. Our greatest enemy is the internal enemy. Ours is a moral problem. I hold the American people responsible for our vulgar and corrupt society. I mean to call it to their attention, transparently, openly and brutally if I have to."

Sampson and Putney looked at each other.

"I don't believe in this *'Too big to fail'* excuse. For us, I think it should be *'Too immoral to endure.'*"

"Well, Congressman Morales, start looking for the perfect stone and get your slingshot ready. Goliath is going to come looking for you. Let's do the organized crime dog and pony show for him, Bobby."

"Give 'em the truth, Steve. They always run."

Agent Putney eased into a lecturing mode. "The old days of bootleggers, protection schemes, loan sharks and Vegas hookers are small potatoes these days. The Internet is a massive business channel. Things like Craigslist money laundering, sex trafficking, the ever-growing texting drug business, sophisticated computer tax schemes, offshore banking, email a hooker – and every high tech gadget is employed. Computers do the work at the speed of light. The Mexican cartel has submarines now. We're being outspent."

"So there's blatant corruption everywhere and you only have the resources to investigate what your boss tells you is the flashing-red-light issue du jour."

Putney grinned. Sampson raised one eyebrow.

"What do you know about me, guys? You must have done some research."

"Mexican-American representing an Austin, Texas District," Putney said as if reciting a shopping list. "Football hero from the University of Texas."

"One of the greatest pass receptions in college football ever," Sampson added.

"Three tours in Afghanistan, Air Rescue Pararescue," Putney continued. "As a former Marine I have nothing but respect for the PJs. Fearless and compassionate. A rare combination."

"Politically?" AJ asked.

"Father was Democratic Governor of Montana years back," Putney continued in his matter-of-fact drone. "He ran for the junior senator opening but lost big time due to some kind of scandal."

"In your experience have scandals ever been manufactured?"

"The more they want someone gone, the bigger the lie," Sampson said. "La Machine knocks politicians out of the game mostly with scandals. They will embellish them, for sure, and manufacture them if needed. Where are we going with this, Congressman?"

"I would like to convince you that I am a straight shooter. I come from a family that has served our country. I have also. I intend on doing more of the same. My father was an innocent man who believed fully in the U.S. Constitution. That scandal was manufactured, and it cost him his life. The shame impacted his health. He died from those lies that went public. Those who orchestrated it have no shame."

"So you have an axe to grind with our American National Crime Syndicate."

"More like a bazooka to point and shoot than an axe. My father's treatment angered me. My experiences in Afghanistan drove me over the edge. I thought crime and political corruption were two different things. They are not. I am here to fight government corruption. I don't intend on leaning into you. You can both stay in the background or tell me to have a nice day and leave now."

Agents Putney and Sampson exchanged glances, mutually nodded and began to bring the history of the Italian Mafia into the light of day for a junior U.S. congressman.

"You can think of the Mob as an organic and well run business," Putney said, "a business that is willing and able to enforce its will illegally, often with the threat of violence and sometimes brutally. It's a worldwide loosely connected conglomerate. Run by individual families. Its goal is the same as any corporation – financial gain. The days of 'Take care of your customer and your business will be successful' are long gone. The idea of making a quality product and the profits will come went with it. In a sense, in today's world any profit-driven corporation is the same as the Mob. They work for money. The advantage the Mob has is that they are not subject to the rules of American law."

Agent Sampson ran his fingers through his hair. "They make

money illegally. Collectively American crime takes about one trillion dollars out of our economy."

"A trillion?"

Agent Putney confirmed with a slow nod. "It is documented that during Prohibition Al Capone was pulling in about one hundred million dollars a year – in cash."

"And without taxes paid. An example of how it used to work: A load of Makers Mark bourbon is loaded on a truck at Loreto, Kentucky and departs for Cincinnati. It's hijacked in Bardstown on Dixie Highway, U.S. 31, and then driven to a warehouse in Oldham County, Kentucky, just off of Interstate 71. The truck is repainted; the serial number changed and it's sold to its sister operation in Mexico. But since they came by the whiskey illegally they have to sell it illegally. Crooked buyers take the load for a well-reduced cost and fence it in Jasper, Indiana or Evansville. The owner of each joint pays whatever the market will bear for the product and accepts the risk for receiving stolen goods. The motto is 'Never look a gift horse in the mouth.' Their customers, who include the police, judges, and top city officials drink Kentucky's finest Bourbon and are as happy as a clam."

Putney leaned forward and grew intense. "Today the Mob has consolidated the whole stream. Illegal cash gets laundered by Mob-run businesses. There are no taxes. The money that is not allocated for operating expenses gets invested as venture capital – off-the-books venture capital. It's big time these days."

"Or a few mill donated to a movie producer under the table, and the movie is a go," Sampson added, arms extended, palms facing up, "just as long at the lead actors puff on the coffin nails. Movies are made for young, naive people. That's why we see so much crap on the screen – huge profits and the Mob is in tight with Tinsel Town. Sex, drugs, big money – a marriage made in Hell."

"These Mob families, they run their business out of different cities?" AJ asked.

"Yes," Putney replied, eyes locked on AJ's. "We have the New York Mob, founded by the Five Families, the Lucchese, Bonanno, Gambino, Luciano/Genovese, and Profaci/Colombo. They started with the protection rackets, and the longshoreman unions, then gambling, union corruption, drugs and prostitution. The Chicago Mob, founder Al Capone, was first bootlegging – moving moonshine up north and bourbon from Canada. His gang made a fortune. Then protection, drugs, firearms and prostitution. The Detroit Mob, founder, the Purple Gang, aka the Kosher Nostra, ran pretty close to the Chicago families. There's the Vegas Mob, founders Frank Costello and Lucky Luciano, Meyer Lansky, and Bugsy Siegal, experts in gambling and prostitution and corrupting politicians from California who came for the whores. They would film the politicians with the girls in hotel-room beds, and they were forever in the back pocket of the Mob. *Godfather II* did a bang-up job of dramatizing that."

"I am having trouble believing this."

"Congressman," Sampson replied, his mouth contorted in a grimace. "I live this every day and still sometimes don't believe it. So how can we expect the American people to? See what you're asking us to take on with you? It's like landing at Normandy on D-Day on your own. Great ambition, wonderful intentions, not many smarts."

"So the War on Drugs is impossible to win."

"The way we are fighting now, yes."

"It's the same business principles these elite East Coast analysts learn at Harvard and Yale," Putney said shaking his head. "Supply and demand. We have illegal product and a demand from many customers. The profits are enormous, and some are earmarked for overhead – paying off corrupt officials, bribes, hiring thugs to threaten and worse. All done under the table, with serious sums of money."

"We've been offered membership many times. The reason we two are together is that nobody upstairs knew what to do with us." Putney readjusted himself in his chair while Sampson looked dejected.

"I've heard the Mafia has always been in tight with unions."

"Sir," Sampson said, "where you have big money you will always find crime. In America, big money always attracts those with few or no ethics. So we are talking organized crime, politicians, Hollywood and American corporations. All of them work together to attract money, launder it and profit from it." Sampson leaned forward, elbows on knees. "Of the ten biggest corporations in America we have three oil companies and two automobile and truck manufacturers. So the fossil-fuel lobby is a massive contributor to our political system. The auto manufacturers have been infiltrated by the Mob for decades. Now, our economy is based on promissory paper – printed money – and not on hard assets anymore like gold or silver. Cash is king. And where you have a lot of cash you will have corruption."

AJ remembered a conversation in Afghanistan with the same story. "So it is everywhere," AJ sighed. "Politicians linked to Mob money linked to oil lobbyists, linked to Hollywood linked to corporate America."

Putney nodded. "They are all hypocrites. Decades ago union leaders were paid off on New York City construction projects by the Mob. If a union leader refused to play the game, he was made to play, or he disappeared. Soon Mafioso puppets became the leaders. That gave them access to the union pension funds. We've been successful of late on cracking down in this area. They flourished during Prohibition. That was the era of Capone, the Untouchables and the Tommy-gun street murders. That's one of Hollywood's favorite eras. Then "Lucky" Luciano came along with his multi-family commission idea to make it a coast to coast operation. The Syndicate is born. So the Mob is not a single group or gang. It's multiple families. Think of the Arab oil cartel – OPEC. These guys probably can't stand each other, but they come together to further personal interests. But given the opportunity they would sell out their fellow ministers and probably their own people for financial profits. Same goes for the Mob."

"Even though the Mafia began in Sicily and spread initially to New York's Lower East Side through the 19th and early 20th century, they're active today along the entire East Coast as well as in Chicago and Detroit," Sampson added, "and Luciano's Commission still consists of the bosses, the dons, of the top families. But today they have competition with the street gangs for drugs and prostitution, the Russian Mafia, Mexican Mafia and on and on. At the top is the Boss, aka Don or Godfather. Then there's the Underboss – the day-to-day chief operations officer. There is always a consigliore, yes, right out of the *Godfather* movies. They mediate disputes. Then comes the captains, the *caporegime*. These guys are the line managers who run the racketeering, extortion, drugs, prostitution and murder. They run teams of soldiers who do the hands-on work. Once they had to be of full Italian ancestry, but today half-Italians qualify if it's on their father's side. And there are associates, basically go-fers. Non-Italians."

AJ's mind whirred. He wasn't so naïve he thought he could fight the Syndicate on his own, but these families had tentacles he hadn't imagined.

Putney waited a few moments before he continued. "You can see that these soldiers and associates get the orders to hit somebody, and they never know where it came from. Runs just like a terrorist cell. Hard to get the guy who sanctioned the hit. The term for it is the same used in our political system to keep the dirt from touching the fat cats, plausible deniability."

"And," Sampson added, "it's difficult to infiltrate the Mob. For a time wire-tapping worked well, but many of our infiltrators ended up in the East River. You're tested by committing crimes and especially murders. I'm sure you've heard of the Donnie Brasco movie. Another Hollywood favorite. Pistone got lots of Mobsters put behind bars."

"What about JFK?" AJ asked. "The Giancana and Marilyn Monroe angle, with RFK as an incorruptible Attorney General."

Putney took over wearing a sardonic smile. "Joe Kennedy had many shady ties, in his bootlegging days. So did Rockefeller. Kennedy senior had Sam Giancana push the Chicago and New York families to help get JFK elected. And Joe Kennedy was a bootlegger. In the 1920s, he was mixed up with the Mob and made a killing in Hollywood. So Joe's son becomes president. Then another son, Bobby is made Attorney General. Joe decides he is not going to favor Giancana or any Mafioso, nor anyone else he owed favors to. The FBI would enforce that."

"I'm having a tough time with this."

Sampson offered a better explanation. "It's the same kind of thing going on today, and you are asking us to take a run at it with you. And remember Marilyn Monroe. She was involved with both Kennedy men – Jack and Bobby. We're fairly sure Sam Giancana was Jack's pimp. But Monroe, a known emotionally unstable woman with loose lips had knowledge she threatened to use to expose the Kennedy affairs. Giancana's men could have killed her, and made it look like suicide to get back at both Kennedy brothers. Sends a stern warning, doesn't it."

"All played out under the very noses of the American people." AJ rubbed his temples.

"And the icing on the cake," Sampson snapped, "we have Frank Sinatra introducing Judith Campbell Exner, a party girl, to both JFK and Sam Giancana. Another link between politics, the Mob and Hollywood. So after Kennedy was assassinated, Giancana is called to testify at a U.S. senate hearing on suspected collusion between the Mob and the CIA to kill the president. He's being guarded by a police detail that is mysteriously recalled to their station. He's shot in the head. Oswald's dead, Jack Ruby, a Mob boy dies and Giancana is hit. No loose ends."

"But why the hit?"

Putney rubbed his thumb and fingers together. "Kennedy

brought us extremely close to a nuclear war. That would have been terrible for global business. And for those who run the country it's all about business, isn't it? Nuff said."

"It is the right place to start, Congressman," Sampson nodded. "November 22, 1963 and the farcical events and investigations that followed is when America lost its virginity. It's been a downward slide ever since."

"So, was it Oswald?"

Sampson smiled. "It was. And it was a shot any average Joe could make. In my opinion that's as far as the assassination went. But ten seconds after it happened every corrupt man and organization on our government began cover-ups to keep from getting caught. So hundreds of documents were disposed of, evidence disappeared, alibis could not be corroborated, and a thousand loose ends were made visible. It was a conspiracy all right – one of numerous individual corrupt officials sloppily covering their tracks."

"I'd like to meet in a couple of days. I have some research to do, and then I want to add more to our agenda."

"It would help if you told us specifics so we can come prepared," Agent Sampson said. "Focus."

"I have extremely damaging information and a resource willing to testify about a private military contracting firm. I've already started forming a congressional subcommittee to analyze the facts. So I'd like to get as much information you have on a company called SMS and its chairman of the board, Nicola Scozzari."

Sampson and Putney both sat back in their chairs and exhaled forcefully.

Chapter 14

Through several levels of unauthorized digital computer security encryption created by the U.S. government and paid for by the American taxpayer a conversation between Capitol Hill high rollers and a cell phone in Kentucky occurred with complete anonymity.

"We have made contact with an ambitious general in the Bolivian army who is also part of a secret left-wing anti-government para-military group we've infiltrated."

"Go on."

"He's hungry, spouts Che Guevara kind of crap, believes in the people, hates capitalism, but wants to feather his own nest."

"Perfect. A typical ideologue hypocrite. What are the obstacles?"

"First, he doesn't believe in us or what we can offer."

"That's normal. Buy him a hacienda or whatever the hell they call it down there. Hand him the deed written in his name and also the account details for one hundred grand in a Cayman account also in his name."

"Second, he's pissed off his general and is frustrated over no promotions or future opportunities."

"Get me the bio, pictures and everything else you can on the general. I'll send Smith."

"Excellent."

Two weeks later an adolescent boy rested his weight on his back leg, the friction with the pavement quickly bringing his skateboard to a halt in front of a U.S. Post Office in a suburb of Newport News, Va. He pulled a key from his jeans, fiddled with one of the boxes, retrieved a translucent baggie, pocketed it, and headed across town on his wheels. A gray metallic object, silent, the shape and size of a medium sized bird hovered above him, perhaps fifty feet above him, just above the power lines and the top of the trees. As the boy's direction became clear, the drone gave him a one-hundred-yard lead then matched the pace of the skateboard. As the boy entered a leafy park, allowing gravity pull him down the slight incline of the winding path, a single pop was heard. Not loud enough to cause much attention, the sound was quickly muffled and lost in the trees. The drone fell to the earth, eventually to be examined by a city worker who cut the grass and dismissed as a broken child's toy. As the boy reached the opposite end of the park a man on a racing-style motorcycle stopped, handed the boy a five-dollar bill, accepted the package and drove off into arterial traffic, zigzagging around vehicles before disappearing into a non-descript alley in an industrial section of town.

James Smith unzipped the baggie, retrieved a thumb drive and pushed it into his laptop computer's USB slot. There were three files. Smith selected the first, clicked his mouse again and the image of a South American general – heavily mustached, twenty or so ribbons and assorted medals covering his chest – filled the screen. He studied it. Memorized it. Estimated the man's height and weight. The second file was the man's bio – the one for publication of the CV or bio of the general's history and accomplishments. The third file was a list of observations, habits, and addresses, everything needed to hunt the man, written by someone who was exceedingly familiar and good at giving information to a hunter. Smith relaxed in his office chair for a moment, mentally going over a newly forming plan before removing the thumb drive, crushing it with a hammer, then watching it turn to dust in his heavy-duty blender. All record of the files was deleted from his computer and the hard drive reformatted.

Though graying, Smith looked to be in his early thirties but was a decade older. Of medium height, he was thicker than lean but not overly muscular. He trained his body for endurance, not for bull strength or show. This afternoon he would visit the woods just north of his home, a nondescript trailer in a shabby trailer park, and go for a run wearing $200 running shoes, paint-stained blue-cotton jogging pants and a wrinkled grey hoodie. He would run along the railroad tracks that cut through the woods and be fairly unremarkable – except that he would be covering six miles in this session and would finish it in less than fifty minutes. While this time for the distance was unremarkable for any trained athlete, Smith would not run in a straight line but veer up the mound of earth covered by fist-sized stones which supported and served at the base of the tracks, down the other side, and back up again at an accelerated pace for the entire run.

He carried an iPod with earphones. His favorite was Beethoven; the symphonies. The often raw and measured immediacy and emotional lift inspired him. Mozart put him to sleep. Sometimes he played Wagner. He was partial to "Die Walküre," the opening passage, especially the James Levine, 1989 recording. Smith, his earphones blasting music into his brain from both sides, imagined himself a force of nature, an avenging juggernaut coming at his victim with an unrelenting passion. The victim changed from run to run. Today it was a Bolivian general, a man he had never met, a man whose crimes he did not know. His employers deemed the man a target and Smith would pull the trigger. An accidental death or the victim of a robbery.

Chapter 15

"Thanks for coming back, gentlemen," AJ said as Agents Putney and Sampson took seats across the desk from Congressman Morales.

"We thought long and hard about it," Agent Putney said. "I increased my life insurance to one mill, and Sampson here purchased a plot in a beautiful Virginia cemetery."

"But here you are."

"My daughter just announced she is pregnant," Putney offered. "She's full of happiness, love, belief in a future. I want to do what I can to ensure my grandchild lives in a better America than we do now."

"We did more homework on you, Congressman," Sampson said. "You have a reputation for keeping your word. We respect that."

"I won't leave you high and dry if that's what you mean."

"Good. Normally we'd tell you to formally contact the CIA on SMS. The FBI handles internal corruption, not global," Sampson said. "But SMS is a domestic and foreign organization. We have some trustworthy contacts in the CIA, and we mentioned a congressman who claimed to have damning information and a source in Afghanistan ready to help us."

"So you vouched for me?"

"Let's call it a strong probability that you're telling us the truth. Our CIA contacts are particularly interested in hearing more."

"Good."

"Now," Sampson said, "We need you listen to us carefully about what you can share with your subcommittee and the media. You'll need to sign papers that threaten long prison terms. And if you talk about any of these things—"

"Plausible deniability will reign."

"He's a quick learner, Steve."

Putney started the rundown. "Okay, Congressman, this is privileged information and something you should know. The FBI has a snitch inside SMS. His name is Diego Salvador. Diego uses his mother's surname. His father, we suspect, is someone high up in the Mob. His mother, Louisa, was an illegal immigrant. She was a mob housekeeper and obviously a mistress for nearly ten years. It seems when she got pregnant in 1983, Nicola Scorazzi had her shipped off to Monterrey, Mexico to live with a Cartel family. Dieg, as the boy was called, was privately schooled, well-educated by the Jesuits. He holds dual citizenship, is fluent in Spanish and three other languages and has no accent when speaking English or dialectic Spanish. He attended the University of Louisville Police School, then joined the U.S. Army as an MP and counter-intelligence specialist, then worked for the Defense Intelligence Agency. He's FBI now and worming his way deeper into the muck that is the Mob."

"Sounds incredibly dangerous."

"Dieg is fearless. He feels abandoned. He only reports to a few of us. There are undoubtedly mob agents above us in the bureau. And he is also digging into the story of his mother and her role in both the U.S. and Mexican drug cartels."

"Right," Sampson took over. "And it is not uncommon for rogue operators to get too close to someone big and then just disappear. We are not a seamless top-to-bottom organization but fragmented, like a piece of Swiss cheese. I've been in briefings that sounded like the famous Abbott and Costello 'Who's on First' routine. Same goes for the CIA and every other A in Washington."

"I am beginning to understand Washington, gentlemen. It's like any corporate job. The peons have no idea what the executives are doing. The majority of us work for wages only."

"Ours is not to reason why..." Agent Sampson said.

"Back to Diego, er Dieg."

Putney took another breath. "So upon leaving the DIA after twelve years of service, highest grade attained, major, he was recently recruited by the Domestic Intelligence division of the FBI. He's become a vital player in unraveling who's who."

"Why did you pick him up?"

"He has very specialized contacts in the Mexican cartel and hates their immorality. Seems the Jesuit training took root in this boy. We wanted him welded to our mission. Some research revealed that his mother died suddenly just after Dieg finished college. This seemed curious. We had the body exhumed and told Dieg it wasn't food poisoning that killed his mother but cyanide, Dieg promised to cut the head and balls off every mob leader."

"If his mother was a Mob mistress, any idea who Dieg's father might be?"

"You learn fast, Congressman."

"She kept house at Nicola Scozzari's Kentucky estate."

A low whistle came from AJ. "Does Dieg know that detail?"

"Yes. We told him primarily because if Dieg is indeed Nicola's illegitimate son, he could be a target if any one of Nicola's hundreds of enemies found this out. We did not know of the DNA match until recently, or he would not have been assigned to the case, so now we are scrambling to substitute another agent."

AJ shook his head. "And they'd love to knock off his son. Deliver a head in the bag or some such thing."

"Bingo. And watch Nicola possibly fall out of favor for having an illegitimate son with a Mexican housekeeper. You are a natural for this work, Congressman," Sampson said.

"I'll take that as a compliment," AJ said before smirking.

Putney didn't miss a beat. "We put him to work with a new unit created to track Mob activities in scamming the U.S. government. He is no dummy and understands that if Nicola falls, he stands to inherit a vast fortune if he can prove it, so he works for us to take down Nicola, and any other bigwig Mafioso. He's the type of man who would use that vast fortune to go after the entire organization."

"I think I'm starting to like this guy."

Both agents smiled.

"There is an ulterior motive here, sir," Agent Putney said with a bit of apology in his voice.

"Let me anticipate. Antonia Scozzari, my former fiancée, might be Dieg's half-sister."

"Yes, sir." Putney exhaled. "But neither Dieg, nor Antonia knows of each other. Add Nicola's wife, the former Benedetta Cortese, who is wired to her father, the New York don, to the mix and this thing becomes volatile."

"So Nicola and his wife, Benedetta are not officially divorced?"

"Can't happen in a Mob family," Sampson stated with zero emotion. "The dons would not allow it. Nicola and Benedetta just tell the world they are legally divorced. Theirs was an arranged marriage to unite the Boston and New York family in an effort to thwart the Chicago, Detroit and Nevada Mobs. Laundered monies were used to acquire legitimate businesses – a tobacco company, a distillery in Kentucky, recently a synthetic growth hormone lab which supplies the livestock and food processing concerns in North America – located in southern Ohio and of course, legal gambling along the Ohio River. A divorce would make the contractual relationship messy. The 'family' wants to maintain a low and legitimate profile for their 'laundry business.'"

"But legally," AJ pressed, "Antonia and potentially Dieg are solid heirs to a heap of Mob money if anything suddenly happened to Nicola and Benedetta?"

"Correct. I love *Game of Thrones*," Sampson said. "It unfolds just like my day job. But I know the fictional series will end with all loose ends tied."

"We assume that SMS start-up funds came from crime-world sources and the business was quickly aggregated to other interested parties who would politically gain and increase their control and then profit heavily, but we have not found the 'deep throat', as they said in the Watergate days, to come forward."

Sampson echoed his partner. "Every story is hooked into a global web, and nobody knows all the links. The way to wield power in the game is to know things about everyone, know what makes them tick, what moves them, what they will sell their soul for, and how to buy them. It's the game that sucks us all in, Congressman. A multi-level chess game. And for your first time on the playing field you are going to face off with the undefeated Super Bowl champions."

"What are you asking me?"

"Congressman," Agent Sampson, asked with some emotion in his voice, "are you prepared to help us take down the head of the Senate Foreign Relations Committee and the key player in the Appropriations Committee?"

"Yes."

"Many of us are sick of our vulgar American culture, of our politicians, and most of all with our inability to set things straight. We're a David going after a Goliath. And I don't think we have God on our side."

"Really? Have you asked him?"

Both agents chuckled.

"Is there anything you aren't telling us before we share our information and formulate a plan of attack?" Agent Sampson asked.

"I know SMS is taking C-130 cargo plane loads of lithium out of Afghanistan; and at the expense of the American taxpayer. The war torn country may actually have the purest and largest lode on the planet. Easier to mine than the Bolivian lode. Much of the technology that's coming, meaning battery-driven cars and the like, will depend on lithium. We do not want China taking it. The former Soviet Union tried and failed. Now we've been in the longest war in our history while telling the people it's a war on terrorism, and that we are freedom fighters. Much of that is a lie. I have some proof and can get Afghani help to fill in the blanks."

"Excellent."

"Hold on. Back to my ex-girlfriend, Antonia Scozzari. I have no doubt Scozzari knows what I am doing right now. He knows I have a personal issue to settle with one of his bought-and-paid-for U.S. senators. They will both go down."

Putney wiped the sweat from his forehead with the palm of his hand. Sampson shook his head in disbelief.

"Congressman, you do play your cards close to your chest," Sampson said. "This will become personal for Scozzari. Steve and I are sitting here spilling our guts on Kentucky's answer to Darth Vader and you are mixing the Kool-Aid."

"I never met Antonia's father. She spoke rarely of him, only told me he was way up there in the Mob and that she was the daughter of two Mob families. I did not understand the significance until lately. She is the living proof of a business merger of two devils."

"Is she as...as—"

"She's a poorly raised girl. She's spoiled, has low self-esteem, been in rehab numerous times but I felt for her and thought I could bring her around, release the real woman from behind those walls of rage inside her. I failed. Nuff said there."

"She married—"

"Charles Prendergast III. Given you are both football fans you have surely seen the picture of the three of us. I will not autograph a copy for either of you. I do remember her saying that her father was the chairman of SMS. When I was in Afghanistan, I heard several names, including his. Does this jive with your knowledge?"

Putney offered more background. "Scozzari, is the son of the Don of the Boston Mob, graduated from Boston College Phi Beta Kappa, and has a Wharton Masters degree in Finance. For some time, he ran the Boston Mob's laundry business. Known to be cunning, vindictive, and preferring to stay in the shadows, he lets his bought politicians take the limelight. He's dug himself deep into Kentucky and Tennessee politics, as well. Lives in a European-style hunting lodge on large acreage guarded better than Fort Knox. Once he married Benedetta Cortese, and connected the two city Mobs through marriage, both dons let him run their western flank of the U.S.. Making investments as the CEO of a tobacco company, distillery, food processing, feed lots, insurance interests, and a river-boat gambling business as well as making him chairman of the board of SMS, made him fabulously rich. Keeps a low profile and lets his pawns take the limelight, particularly the high-profile politicians."

"His estranged wife, on the other hand," Sampson added, "is the daughter of a New York don. The families merged and produced Antonia as insurance because neither side of the family would harm a 'love child' made from both families."

"In addition to his role at SMS, your almost father-in-law is an underboss for both families along with his former wife, Benedetta. Nicola is charged with investing a hefty sum of the Mob's profits most recently in growth hormones, and also genetic crop engineering. Our research suggests that the stuff he is supplying has addictive features to give the consumer an affinity for other products with the same ingredients. We have CDC and Mao Clinic trying to determine if there are other side effects linked to this crap. So far he has only operated in North America except once, when 100 metric tons of beef loaded with the concoction was sold to feed the Russian Army the winter before last. He is the New York Mob's front man to slow down the expansion of the Chicago, Detroit and Nevada Mobs into other businesses – especially the growing military's use of mercenaries and in the war zone construction business."

AJ leaned back in his chair. "This explains why tobacco just won't go away."

"The tobacco companies have known the dangers of tobacco

for decades. They buried the findings again and again. Yet they are untouched, other than some fines, and we see our teenagers smoking like chimneys due to the behavior of their idols in Hollywood movies. Want to get rid of gun violence and tobacco usage? Get rid of Hollywood. But they are deeply in bed with the mob and Washington – the unholy triumvirate."

"Smoking kills about half a million Americans a year," Agent Sampson added. "But it's big business. My son smokes. Thinks it is fashionable. I can't stop him. Steve's kid was arrested last year with pills."

Putney frowned. "The Boston and New York Mobs are spreading westward. They set up shop in the Covington and Newport, Kentucky area, across from Cincinnati years ago, but failed because they got too cocky. That was the Chicago and Detroit families at work then, so the race for re-domination has been underway ever since to see who'll run the lower Midwest. Nicola and his supporters took brilliant steps to squeeze out the Chicago and Detroit family. This union of the dons' children helps prevents turf wars. There is lots of competition these days with illegal activities. The mob is now buried in our political system. It's just like the unions getting infiltrated with Mob leaders."

"And SMS?" AJ asked.

"It's an industrial military operation," Putney explained. "It builds and supports infrastructure in countries we invade. It makes or buys the weapons, the munitions, and all the goodies that go along with war – food, uniforms – hell, the whole damn country benefits as product and service go into supporting a war and money and jobs grow here."

"To pay for it, they raise taxes on the people later, after the current administration is long gone," Agent Sampson added. "And it's all buried in politico-babble that pits the rich against the poor, black against white, liberal against conservative, men against women – anything that can keep the American people from the heart of the matter."

"So Afghanistan and Iraq are not moral wars?"

"The wars are economic wars – fought for profiteering. Imperialism, the American Empire. We're Rome, the new British Empire," Sampson said.

"And as long as the American people have their comfort, safety, and entertainment, they don't give two shits," Putney added. "We're pissing all over the U.S. Constitution daily, and all we hear is some mumbling. Everybody looks at each other and asks why someone else isn't doing something about this."

"Then they go back to their *burrito grandes* and supersize their fries," Sampson said. "They demand their pensions be paid, no matter what. Now we have the country split between tax payers and tax eaters. The mainstream media peppers us 24x7 with – we're all too fat, asteroids are going to slam into earth and kill us all, End of Days, Armageddon, the Apocalypse, and endless awful zombie movies."

"Easy big fella'," Putney said with a chuckle. "Whether learned at Harvard, Yale, Wharton or all three, the mob has found innumerable ways to launder their cash and cook their books with the backing of the U.S. senate and a huge list of sub-contractors with a vested interest in profits."

"You mentioned that Scozzari owns politicians."

"Anybody on the SMS board is either totally corrupt or incredibly naive and used as needed," Sampson said. "And I forgot to mention that string of adolescent sluts who can't really sing those crappy teenage love songs or dance well and must throw a handful of fleas down their pants to gyrate that way on the stage."

Putney raised his eyebrows and turned to his partner. "Not everyone can appreciate Nat King Cole or Sinatra the way you do, pal."

"Now that's adult music."

It was AJ's turn to chuckle. "Or Julio Iglesias."

"Well said," Sampson replied.

"Tell me about a man whose name was whispered in hatred to me in Afghanistan. Buford Ebers."

"Senate Majority Leader (R IN)," Putney moved to the edge of his chair. "He's been in for five terms, elected in 1988 as part of the Reagan landslide in Indiana. Replaced retiring four-term Senator Herschel 'Smitty' Smith who had inoperable lung cancer – real heavy smoker of Dragon Brand Cigars. Prior to that, he was the chairman of the GOP in Indiana and made or ruined many a political career. He's made a fortune on insider trading tips. JD degree from Indiana University. Divorced twice, no children. He is an expert on historical political coups and makes it his business to know something about anyone who got or gets in his way."

"So we can never let go of the head of the snake," AJ said.

"Next up," Sampson took his turn, "is U.S. Senator Parker Cowel, a Montana Republican."

AJ's jaw tightened noticeably.

"He heads the U.S. Foreign Relations Committee and also holds sway over the Appropriations Committee. He's called the 'Teflon Senator.' He was appointed to complete his father's term in 1977 and has been reelected repeatedly. He is from Butte, and his family was heavy in the mining and silver business. Runs a lobby in both houses for SMS. Not voting his way can be career limiting."

"I'm all too familiar with Cowel," AJ seethed.

"Finally," Sampson continued, "we come to retired Senator W.E. 'Billy' Kiddenly (R, TX), a six-term retired patriarch of the Republican Party from West Texas and tied to oil money, lots of it! He is the party figurehead, respected and consulted by all and most importantly – feared by all along the Gulf coast, as well as other areas of the GOP. He was the U.S. Senate Majority Leader, and on retirement turned the job over to Ebers. He is the man who can sound the alarm to get a caucus fired up or get an immediate response from a political action group. To intimidate or oppose him is to take on the entire GOP and its funders."

"So what now, Congressman?" Agent Putney asked. "You're about to kick a sleeping dragon square in the nuts and are asking for our help. We see freshmen congressmen come in every other January, and there are always a few who start out gung ho about just what you are. Most are turned by the system and cash in. A few stay on. The rest drop out. Naïve kids."

AJ massaged his face with his open palms. "Someone once told me all young people want to change the world, but they neither understand themselves or the world."

"Smart person. We see it all the time here in Washington. The world is an ugly place, and it takes ugly men to stand up to it."

"It's so huge and interdependent." AJ's stomach turned. "What about going to the media?"

"First, look at who owns the world banks and related financial institutions. Then look who owns the television, radio and movie businesses. Then look at their backgrounds, friends, investments and contributions," Putney replied. "Hollywood is wired to D.C. It is Capitol Hill's single biggest political super PAC and campaign contributor. Illegal drug profits need to be laundered. So the mob gives cash to a Hollywood producer who will put on the screen what he is told to put on the screen. I can give you the ins and outs in-depth."

"Not now, thanks. My father was a state governor. He was able to look past the corruption to strive for the good he could accomplish. But when he ran for the senate, he never even got a punch in. Ebers murdered his good name and did it in his stride. I want to bloody and embarrass them. Overseas I've seen what exploiting young girls as slave-prostitutes does to their lives. I've seen young boys given to male perverts for their pleasures. And it's happening here, and it's a growing business. You both have children. You've seen what this rotten system has done to them, and you're powerless to stop it."

Both agents frowned, looked at the floor.

"I want a family someday. How do you protect yours from dying of drug overdoses, from adolescent sex, from AIDs, from pornography, from losing all respect for the value of human life, from losing respect of their parents, teachers, for learning personal responsibility, our faith in God and the American values? How do we protect them from school shootings, angry ghetto music? From losing their very souls?"

"We try," Agent Putney said. Agent Sampson merely shrugged.

"Right now, these gangsters, political and media ghouls are bending and warping our culture. For the last fifty years they have been manipulating us, telling us all the crap that happens is because we are essentially animals and the vulgarity and violent horrors we endure daily are unavoidable unless the government runs everything. And our government reeks of corruption."

"Amen," Agent Sampson said.

"You're talkin' the talk," Agent Putney added. "How do we walk the walk?"

"We start now."

"Just a heads up," Putney offered. "The FBI, CIA and all the other departments are bureaucracies. That means most everyone's first thought when dealing with a situation like ours is for their own careers. The directors are going to wet themselves when they hear of your congressional subcommittee's goals."

"Understood. Bureaucracy has killed more than one dominant nation."

"Yes," Agent Sampson said. "I'd like to get a few more agents involved so when we light the dragon's asshole on fire we have some loyal American firepower on our side."

"We start now. So help me God. My mother often told me that life was not so much about accomplishment as it was about faith," AJ said, eyes off into memories. "So, gentlemen, I believe what we are doing what is right – right for us and for our country. Let's get to work."

"Sir, would you mind if I gave your number to a friend who can talk turkey about a strategy here."

"Absolutely. Bring him here or I'll go to him."

"It's not that easy. This guy is a shadow. A hunter and hunted shadow. He'll give you the code word – Popinjay."

Chapter 16

Julia leaned back in her desk chair, stretching her arms, massaging her neck. Two colorful boxes of half-eaten Chinese takeout lay pushed to the corner of the desk, a few fortune-cookie crumbs still on her notebook cover. The fortune read, "A love interest is in your near future." *Sorry, but there is no time for that right now. Prince Charming will have to wait a long time.* While her time at West Point and the relentless graduate work at Harvard had always been challenging, what she was up against now was truly monumental, baffling, and impossible to keep all in her head. Senator Cowel had painted a pretty picture of lobbying, but somehow neglected to touch on the complexities of what she now faced.

"Julia," she could hear the senator say, "you were there, on the front lines, and you fought for your country, bled for your country. You can leverage your experiences like few others can. I am asking you to once more stand up for your country, to become the spokesperson for your fellow patriots." He certainly convinced her of the value of SMS. Somehow, in her two tours in Iraq she had taken the supporting infrastructure for granted. SMS teams had been working alongside her, before she even got there, and after she had left, all in support of the freedom fighters of the American military. She remembered driving on paved roads, built by SMS, living in new bunkers, built by SMS, driving in heavily armored trucks, much heavier armored trucks than the military had available while brandishing the newest and deadliest of modern weaponry, furnished by SMS.

Then there were the new hospitals and the schools, requiring physicians, nurses, and the new infrastructure designed and built by engineers, bringing clean water and disposing of disease causing waste – something Iraq desperately needed. All built and staffed by SMS. These private-sector consultants, engineers, laborers faced the same daily threats she did, and worked hand-in-hand with the combat and support teams. But they rarely got their due. Their deaths were not reported as military deaths, their wounds never covered with Purple Hearts, or their country's thanks. They got their compensation from SMS and that was that.

There was a lot of talk about high-paid mercenaries. A story made the rounds of private security contractors making six figures per year. Sometimes a grand a day, plus expenses. Sometimes they were off for six months at a time, sometimes worked six months straight, seven days a week. They received supposed medical benefits and 401K. Worked for an upstanding company. Had an inflation-proof job. Some called them trained assassins. They were called mercenaries or soldiers of fortune. Like in the movies. Fly in, get settled, take out the bad guy, disappear. Wasn't the military's mission to engage in violence? Wasn't it their duty to fill the jobs nobody else wanted? Those deemed too dangerous.

Now she was hand-picked by Senator Parker Cowel to communicate the importance of SMS to the war effort, and to ensure the voice of SMS echoed through the halls of Congress. And that job description was "lobbyist," – the word her father almost choked on four years ago before she left for Harvard. Her father defined a lobbyist as someone who attempted to influence legislation of the House, senate and the Department of Defense on behalf of special-interest groups. The logic that followed was that wealthy organizations bought votes with campaign donations. For the congressman to stay in office, he or she needed a campaign war chest to fund TV commercials, host dinners, speak all over their district and on and on. Special-interest groups gave the congressman the funding required. He or she with the biggest war chest usually won the election. The financially poor, therefore, had no say in attempting to influence decisions made by government officials or regulatory agencies. The tyranny of the wealthy – a class-war chant. A twisted Golden

Rule – he who has the gold makes the rules.

Julia tasted sour grapes, not fortune cookie.

She looked at a poster hanging on her wall – a John F. Kennedy quote: *"Lobbyists are in many cases expert technicians capable of examining complex and difficult subjects in clear, understandable fashion. They engage in personal discussion with members of Congress in which they explain in detail the reasons for the positions they advocate... Because our congressional representation is based upon geographical boundaries, the lobbyists who speak for the various economic, commercial and other functional interests of the country serve a useful purpose and have assumed a pivotal role in the legislative process."*

How indeed was a senator or representative to keep up on all the proposed laws which needed to be voted on? How could they manage the work of all the committees and sub-committees; the constant change? This was the world of the professional lobbyists. They researched pertinent information on specific issues, they analyzed it, interviewed the key players, and then they presented this information to the appropriate individuals or groups. They arranged testimonies of key individuals for hearings, and prepared information. They ensured that whoever their client was got the information they needed. And it had to be a thorough analysis and evaluation, for just like a legal case where two lawyers went at each other with effective strategies, tactics, and most of all facts; a lobbyist had to present all the facts: the pros and cons of the law, the risks, obstacles and opportunities spelled out in mind-numbing detail. The goal – simply a positive impact on decision makers. SMS was a private-sector war-support operation. Who better to explain the thousands of moving parts than Julia Abbott: West Point graduate; two tours of duty in Iraq; a living Congressional Medal of Honor recipient; a Harvard MBA and protégé of Senator Parker Cowel.

As she sat at her desk, the first signs of light brightened the horizon. She had again worked through the night. Her current load included keeping a close eye on all legislation moving through the House and the senate and its potential consequences to SMS. A daily summary was due on the senator's desk at 6 pm every afternoon and was always marked "Top Secret" even though it was not actually top secret. Earlier in the evening she had completed a review of current congressional budget and funding status that could have an impact on SMS. Pulling funding from her initiatives could prove detrimental for support of the all-American troops fighting on foreign soil. This required daily contact with legislators and key staffers in House and senate to both garner information and disseminate it. She had just finished a review on the funding SMS had circulated to the appropriate political action committees (PACs), the groups who campaign on the senator's behalf and that of his legislation. In the end, if people wanted to know what was actually going on in Washington, they needed to enter the realm of the lobbyist. And it went without saying that the reputation of a lobbyist was central to his or her value. If you were an SMS lobbyist, you were the go-to person for information, status on bills, on operations. Your contact list would easily reach into the thousands, your cell phone ringing day and night. *Stay away please, Mr. Prince Charming.*

A quick glance at her Samsung Droid tablet showed a fully booked schedule from 8am through dinner at 7pm, including her appointment at 4pm to testify on SMS's behalf at yet another congressional hearing. A two-hour catnap and then Show Time, yet again.

The results of lack of sleep crept up on Julia in an afternoon meeting with the senator. But she knew how to wing it after years as a female in a male university and male-dominated war zone.

"Julia," Senator Cowel said from across his congressional desk after reviewing his reports. "What you've done here is excellent work. I know it is a heavy task, sometimes like trying to pick fly shit out of pepper, but I dearly need these analyses."

"It is an enormous learning curve, Senator. I want to deliver top-notch service, accurate and timely. And I want to represent SMS to the fullest."

"I have two experienced staff members who are expected to complete projects soon and will be instructed to assist you. They can do the research and reporting while you continue with the face-to-face work."

"That is excellent news, sir. Sometimes I think a law degree would have benefited me more than an MBA."

"Both staff members are lawyers. I need you to understand SMS. I've been holding back on the minutia so as not to bury you."

Julia paused, then finally stated her misgiving. "I love the job, the multi-faceted aspects of it, but the term lobbyist has a dirty connotation to it."

"You, as a lobbyist, and those like you help make our country live up to her ideals. I am the first to admit that a lack of personal integrity and blatant profiteering go on here daily, but we must hold true to our course."

"Hypocrites abound here, and it is tempting to play evil against evil for a good outcome." Julia sighed, wishing for a good eight hours of uninterrupted sleep.

"Keep honest, Julia. Remember, that at any time, you may be called in to testify in defense of SMS. You don't want any indiscretions that could harm our mission goals."

"I sometimes feel like a hen in the henhouse with the fox asking to come in just for a friendly visit."

"That's the Beggar's Banquet, girl. This is a world of compromise. Everybody wants something and has something to barter. Cold cash is the best, but there are other things to sell. Think of it as a Mexican standoff where you each have your revolver aimed at the other's heart. You talk it out. Like it or not this is how we help our constituents and thereby, the country."

"And get reelected."

"I may not sit for another term, Julia. And I may be grooming my successor, of which there are several candidates. I have even though about resigning early so long as our GOP Montana Governor appoints my choice. Governor Bowie thinks highly of you, as do the people of Montana. I will make my decision soon."

Julia let that comment pass with a polite smile. It was amazing to her how the chubby old red-faced senator with a constant sourpuss could deliver good news or a stern warning with the same expression.

Don't ever play cards with this man.

While she realized the senator was implying something truly compelling, he did not say anything directly, only that he thought highly of her. This was a trained politician; a man who said nothing no matter what you heard. Besides, she thought she was not qualified to become a senator. Cowel not only knew Washington backwards and forwards, he was one of the elite that called the tune. She did not have the political-speak necessary just to survive. She knew everyone in power looked at each other searching for a weakness to exploit. This job was a calling for fast-talking illusionists with thick skin and situational ethics.

Not me.

"We endure here in D.C. by votes through promises. But we thrive through compromise by lobbying."

"I understand."

"You just need to develop a thicker skin. Everyone here knows who you are, your record, and your potential. They will play ball with you, but you need to know how to catch as well as throw."

"Thanks for your help."

"I see your eye is healed and the scar is quite alluring. Somehow sexy."

"I see just fine in both eyes again. One inch to the right and I'd be dead and buried."

"That was a lucky day for all of us. I have a budding lobbyist with an exciting career ahead and you the Congressional Medal of Honor. Did you know it was only awarded to five living soldiers?"

"Yes, and I do not feel qualified or deserving. I did my job."

"So they all say."

"You didn't jury rig the award, sir? You certainly have the power and the knowhow."

"I'll never tell. You are the girl to talk to the Armed Forces and Foreign Relations committees. You hold a medal most only dream of. In a sense you are the real Miss America. We do not want to pull out of Afghanistan. You know how democracy is finally dawning on the Afghan people."

"Yes, sir."

"You've fought and suffered for both our peoples. The Senate Intelligence Committee was impressed with your last review on the Afghan war and is behind us one hundred percent. On another topic," Senator Cowel said as he adjusted his considerable bulk in his chair, "have you looked at the financial information I gave you on SMS? These are close friends of mine and will be extremely vital to you and our cause in the future."

"Yes. If the prospectus matches their internal books, they run a clean ship and have become quite profitable since 2002."

"I can vouch for them one hundred percent. I sit on the board of directors. They are an American company, and we rely on their security and service capabilities to support our war needs. The CEO, Nicola Scozzari is a dear and long-time friend."

"That's a new name for me. His name appears nowhere in my material."

"Nicola is a behind-the-scenes kind of guy. He's a genuine Kentucky gentleman. A weekend at his estate in the Frankfort horse country is in our future, Julia. For now, I want you to get in touch with one of the SMS senior VPs: Charlie Prendergast. Charlie knows the charitable parts of SMS backwards and forwards, and I can tell you he is proud of our efforts on that front. He's a Harvard grad like you, former star quarterback for the University of Texas and son of Admiral Prendergast, as well as a personal friend of mine and former Senator Kiddenly's."

"Prendergast as in the Joint Chiefs of Staff?"

"The very same. So, with that it is time to get you more exposure into SMS. While the letters stand for Security Measures Services, it does not indicate a whole hell of a lot about what we do. For that matter, what does IBM stand for? International Business Machines. Does it have much meaning today other than by its initials? HSBC Bank once was the Hong Kong Shanghai Banking Corporation. Meaningless. We must now understand each other clearly and in the spirit of our Founding Fathers. Top secret from here on out. Understood?"

"Of course."

"There are times when in the name of freedom those of us entrusted with the power to rule must act in ways which are not to be shared, or traceable by normal diplomatic channels. We must protect our troops against self-interest – foreign or domestic – political squabbles and ideologies. Companies like SMS work on behalf of our government when the government's direct involvement isn't the most effective solution or not in our best interest to be visibly or actively involved." Senator Cowel's lowered voice conveyed the seriousness of the conversation.

"So the State Department plays a big part in SMS strategy."

"To the point of having select members on the SMS Board of Directors."

"So many of the spooks I ran across in Iraq were probably CIA?"

"They could have been SMS employees. We do provide our own security and support forces. We do work with both the CIA and DIA and some like-minded allies, to...to...ah provide the additional protection for our troops and civilians. We go in as road pavers, building and water construction and the like. There are times that we have to do what we have to do and the CIA, DIA and sometimes the Joint Chiefs of Staff pay us handsomely to ah, haul out their trash and ensure that confidentiality is maintained and then disavow some of our operatives if necessary. SMS folks you might say can be visible when required and invisible and not traceable when required. Hence, spooks."

"We always heard rumors that some of the thugs were hired mercenaries. Covert operations."

"The term mercenary has a sinister connotation. We have employees who provide a private extension of peacekeepers supporting the Stars and Stripes. If certain funding or programs get cut, innocent people might lose their lives, the infrastructure would collapse, and everything you and other patriots fought for would be lost, and in vain. That's why we need you on Capitol Hill lobbying for appropriate covert aid in the event of the media, some liberal lobbyist or some greenhorn senator or congressman raising a threat to our initiatives. This is an exceptionally crucial link in the safety of our country and our overseas initiatives. Our country is counting on you, Julia!"

"You may count on me, sir."

"I was groomed for my job years ago when my father – the late senator – died suddenly. It fell to me to take up the cross and maintain our dedicated service of what our forefathers began. I was a greenhorn: naive, trusting, poor in spirit. But I learned. I saw the importance of politics – a cultural struggle if you will, and I totally believed in the America of my father and my ancestors. I learned, I excelled and I triumphed. I believe I have made a difference. And I've fought my share of dragons. I am beginning to see myself on a flowered and leafy porch, sitting in a comfy rocker, an elder statesman holding court with old cronies, perhaps an autobiography. My late wife, Sadie, and I never could have children, so I have no blood relatives to pass the torch on to. So do you get my drift, Ms. Abbott?"

"Are you saying that—"

"I have about 200 acres in a remote part of western Maryland, near Fredericksburg on the lower slopes of the Smokies. I have plans to build a beautiful estate there. The main house will be in a clearing, about a half mile in diameter, with a cluster of pines, oaks and maple trees circling it. You should see it in the fall. It's where I want to be laid to rest. If things work out well, you could inherit it. The fishing is fantastic!"

"I don't know how to respond, sir."

"I have been slowly grooming you into someone with the right stuff to join a very elite group of American patriots. While the people vote, and tell us who they want in office, some of us must act as shepherds and see that they hear the truth and make the responsible choices."

"So it pays to know the right people here in Washington, correct?" Julia held the senator's gaze for a moment.

He cleared his throat, before pushing a thumb drive toward her. "Go over this, Julia. It's all the financials on SMS. Study it, learn it, dissect it. I want you up to speed when I set up a dinner with you and Charlie Prendergast."

That evening Julia went through the packet of information created especially for her to "get up to speed" on SMS. The bold red letters of "Top Secret – SMS Confidential" and the fact she had to sign a Non-Disclosure Agreement for the document before a U.S. senator as a witness raised her adrenalin to that of going in combat. Each stern warning in the smaller print made her heart race. It seemed as if she was now a part of the leadership of the United States of America, and with America.

Her first surprise was a picture of the senior SMS VP the senator had asked her to meet at an upcoming dinner. Charlie Prendergast. It seemed so long ago, but there he was, the towering handsome quarterback with the looks of the late Christopher Reeve, a Superman-like hero of the Rose Bowl victory from the University of Texas. She turned the pages enthusiastically.

Over the last several years the privately held entity spent $55.5m and made $18.2 billion in U.S. dollars for road and infrastructure construction in Afghanistan, made another $800 million for building schools and hospitals in Iraq, and yet another $3.5 billion for the development of GPM and laser-guidance systems under the operating company, Indiana Ordnance and Research, located south of Rising Sun, Indiana, along the Ohio River, not far from the river boat gambling casinos. Incredible, but there it was – $300m to develop new armor and equipment for covert operations, and $13 billion for special counselors, security guards and trainers in Afghanistan. SMS was a privately held company with Nicola Scozzari and his estranged wife Bianca controlling 89% of it and another 11% split among five to seven others.

She knew that to win this type of business, and without the formal bid process, the notice of the government compliance eagles, other lobbyist or the media, that the CIA, DIA and JCS had to have blessed the deals. She wrote this off to Senator Cowel's involvement; the best interests of her country were being protected. Julia kept reading, seeing an entry for Perimeter Security Services Corp, a subsidiary that had several thousand private contractors working for it, based in Cookeville, Tennessee, not far from Tennessee Tech. It provided the services of retired or no-longer-active soldiers from countries around the world, both friends and foes. Kind of strange to bring in exclusive services types for former foes and friends alike. The names were only numbers and the duration of contract per resources ranged from a few weeks to a few months. Who were they? Snipers and assassins or special protective forces for diplomats or even guarding sensitive items? Curious, specifically because the expenses were in the billions, yet the income and compensation sources were nowhere to be found. There were also no assets, how could this be? *Too secret to divulge in this report?*

Next, Julia noted donations: hundreds of them, totaling in excess of $975 million dollars, primarily to various veteran aid organizations, but also including contributions to candidates of both major parties and political-action committees. The grand total approached two billion dollars over the last eight years. The senator had shown his trust in her by allowing her access to the SMS books. Chairman of the Board: Nicola Scozzari. Chief Executive Officer: Tyrell Landecker. CFO: Aren Steinman, PhD Wharton College, General Consul: Nicholas Cantino, PhD/JD Harvard Law School. Chief Security Officer: Retried Marine Commandant Finley Q Frederickson. Officially, SMS was headquartered in a small, bland building in the southern suburbs of Cincinnati, in Covington, Kentucky, just around the corner from former Mob town of Newport. Easy access to the I-71 and quick access to the private airports, military bases an hour and a half or so from Frankfort and Louisville.

The other board members consisted of Senator Parker Cowel and Senator WC "Billy" Kiddenly (Texas) – Ret and Tyrone Wood – MBA from UCLA, CEO of the International News Networks (INN), which has outlets in every country internationally with operatives worldwide; he was a regular on the Sunday morning new show syndicates. He was both loved and hated, depending where you stood ideologically. Monique-Rose Wallace, PhD – CEO of the Center for International Integrity and a former Assistant Secretary of State in the previous administration and a renowned expert on the covert laundering and transfer of funds internationally. She had over 20 books published and was highly respected in both parties as a "tough broad" for backing down many heads of state publically, but with fairness.

Rumors had run the gamut for years of her preference in "girls"; she had never been married and was a Dominican nun for fifteen years and taught at prominent Nostros Dominos Center for Advanced International Studies – a think tank for academic research. The CIA depended on it during the Cold War to predict the Soviet's next moves and because they had operatives on the inside of major enemies of the U.S.A. She spoke five languages fluently and was thought to have one of the highest IQs on the face of the planet. Her parents were French Canadian Academy and worked in the Consulate for Canada in New Orleans, where she was born as a U.S. Citizen with dual citizenship.

Everybody here is wired. And loaded. Plus it's a far cry from my life growing up in Bozeman, Montana.

The board met quarterly on a private island in the French West Indies, not far from St Martin. SMS owned four aircraft: a Gulf Stream; two 737 long-range jets loaded with unique equipment, one in rural Odom County (Kentucky), and one located outside of Covington, KY at the Northern Kentucky International Airport; and a high speed state-of-the art helicopter at Chairman Nicola Scozzari's estate, just outside Lexington, Kentucky.

She scanned through a few of the senior VP bios and stopped at Charles Prendergast's. She read through the football-hero stuff, his certain NFL draft pick ruined because of the injury, which also forced him to decline his family's long patriotic history, the military service at the highest rank.

"Wow," she whispered, "this Charlie has it all – great looks, wealth; prestigious family history, political and military connections and a senior VP at an ultra-wired security services company with billions to invest and donate to charity and support veterans."

Julia willed herself away from Prince Charming's face and studied the remainder of the immense file: various SMS training centers, documentation purposely vague on their locations in remote and secluded places around the globe. She refilled her coffee cup and wondered where she should store this bundle of confidential information. What if she lost it? The press could have a field day with it. That alone could negatively affect the war in Afghanistan.

I must be careful with this new knowledge.

Chapter 17

On his way to an interview with a former SMS employee who claimed to be a mercenary, AJ knew the man wanted immunity for past crimes in return for incriminating information concerning SMS. While driving through the southwestern quadrant of D.C, his cell phone rang, and he took it through the Bluetooth connection in his car.

"Hello?"

"Congressman Morales?"

"Yes."

"Are you alone?"

"Yes, I am in my car."

"I highly recommend you do not complete your visit tonight."

"Why is that?"

"Because you will run right into a police team investigating a suicide."

"Who is this?"

"Popinjay."

"Er, was I in danger or something."

"Yes."

"Did you kill the guy?"

"No. He was already dead. I killed the two men waiting for you."

"So my SMS contact—"

"Is a dead end. A mutual friend asked me to help you with your go-forward strategy."

"Let me pull over."

"I suggest you keep driving. You may be followed."

"Sure. First let me thank you for—"

"I never met a PJ I didn't like. Sometimes what goes around comes around."

"I understand."

"Ever hear the name, Hajduk Kabotinsky?"

"No."

"He was an old Al Capone crony. Big on process. Self-absorbed intellectual. Typical type with no experience other than reading books and gassing with like-types in coffee houses. His shtick was that the masses are disillusioned. He was big on how to grab power – the Lenin, Marx, Stalin disease of the ego. His forte was stirring up trouble, citing class struggle."

"Which we are seeing now, in spades, in the media."

"Your enemies believe you have some power. So they will move on you. While you do not have the money or staff they do, you do have some excellent assets. Greed and pride will eventually always lose to spirit. After the failure of tonight's plan they will come at you with slander. They will ridicule you in the press. Don't get angry. Live through it. Keep the pressure on them. When they screw it up another level, screw it back at them two levels higher. You understand flanking maneuvers better than most. Ignore threats. Think of them as being in the school yard years ago and one kid says to another, 'I know you are, but what am I?'"

"Thanks for that. I can see that kid's face."

"Watch your loved ones, but don't warn them. They will go nuts with fear and anticipation. Have them watched. The pressure you apply will unnerve them. They will crack before you will. The soldiers they employ have combat experience like you. But the brains of the operation are always armchair pencil necks. Use that to your advantage."

"Good advice."

"Finally, focus on people, not the organization. Project a smiling face that you are just itching to bloody. That's how Humpty cracks."

"I can see that smug face now. Did you build this strategy yourself?"

"No. Kabotinsky did. And these are the exact strategies that the enemy is rolling out right now, and with you in mind."

"Thank you, Popinjay. I could sure use you on my team."

"What makes you think I'm not on your team?"

The connection went dead.

Chapter 18

Julie guided her white 2012 AUDI convertible into the private driveway of the fashionable 1789 Georgetown restaurant housed in a two-story federal townhouse. The valet opened her door, greeted her and she was waved into the restaurant. She was enveloped in a refined atmosphere, cozy and eclectic, fireplaces and antique gas-lit rooms. The tables were set with Limoges and silver. Jackets for men were required, a place for the D.C. movers and shakers. The Maître d' asked for her reservation, and was duly impressed that Senator Cowel's office had arranged it. She was formally ushered to the second-floor Garden Room with floor-to-ceiling windows covered with lattice, lace curtains and floral prints. Seated in a private alcove, close enough to the main dining room not to feel alone, Julia felt far enough away to relish the privacy. Her waiter explained the 1789's renowned 11,000 bottle wine inventory with 250 varieties stored in the basement cellar and that 1789 was the year that the United States of America really became united.

Damn! Julia had sipped the first bit of wine when her phone vibrated. The text message from the senator offered apologies. *Can't make it tonight. Have fun with Charlie.* Before her phone was back in her purse, a gorgeous hunk of All American man filled the doorway of the dining room where she sat alone, his eyes scanning the room. There was something both distinctly masculine and devilishly boyish about him. *Maybe he really is Superman.* His eyes settled on her. A flash of white teeth.

She smiled a warm recognition, sensitive to how she looked – polite, feminine but not immature or on the hunt.

"Ms. Abbott?" He approached her table, head bowed.

"Was it the lobbyist horns or clove hooves that gave me away?" she asked, taking his outstretched hand without rising.

"I confess that once I saw you I decided to have dinner with you no matter who you were."

"That seems a bit impulsive."

"Impulsive is my middle name. But truth is, Senator Cowel texted 'petite beauty, regal, elegant, ex-Army highly decorated colonel, Harvard MBA.' I couldn't miss."

The scent of his cologne affected her.

"I'll answer to the MBA part."

"As usual, Senator Cowel was accurate. You are beautiful."

She accepted the compliment with a nod and a smile.

"A far cry from the 'Hawk Eye Abbott' moniker."

"They actually use that name for me?"

"Last week, in an SMS board meeting, the senator said, 'we're doing quite well on Capitol Hill with our current initiatives and 'Hawk Eye Abbott' is as usual on-point, not missing a trick."

Julia blushed and shook her head. "Excellent imitation of the senator. But in the description, why do I visualize a girl in oversized fatigues with an M16?"

"I visualized a Schwarzenegger in a green Dago tee with a tramp stamp on each arm."

The couple shared a laugh.

"Well I knew you immediately," Julia said.

"How? Ah, the SMS prospectus."

"Not quite. Years ago, after the University of Texas cardiac win at the Rose Bowl."

"The silly TV interviews?"

"The picture in every newspaper on the planet, with you, that raven-haired beauty and one of your teammates."

Charlie's pursed lips made Julia wonder what the negative implication of mention of that picture implied.

"Guilty. Well, the raven-haired beauty is my wife and the teammate, was my best friend, but someone I've lost track of over the years. So goes life."

Julia was careful not to reveal her disappointment over Charlie's admission of marriage. A quick glance revealed no evidence of a wedding ring or a tell-tale white line on a tanned ring finger.

"Have you ordered yet?" he turned, probably looking for a waiter.

"No, just arrived a few seconds before you. I sat down and received the senator's text."

"Me, too. How is the wine?"

"Perfect," she said, flashing a warm smile, despite the fact that what she had envisioned as a business meeting with the senator and a VP from SMS was now some kind of date gone wrong. Here was this luscious man; a luscious married man, alone with her at dinner. But a 2006 vintage of a *Montalcino Brunello* Italian red with warm bread dipped in olive oil and garlic eased inhibitions and kept the conversation well away from SMS business. She was attracted to him and wanted him to know it. It was flirting, the first she felt worth experimenting with since way too long. Harmless.

"So you took your football and beauty queen, turned your back on pro sports, conquered Harvard, forged a career, a family and are living happily ever after."

She noticed Charlie's mind must have wandered a thousand miles away. His eyes watched the dark red liquid roil as he gently swirled his glass.

"I was seriously hurt that day. My knee was shattered; my last gridiron performance ever. The NFL was informed, and I was dropped from the draft. The story went out that love kept me from accepting the first-round draft pick. Friends in high places can do that. But I did marry the girl."

Julia saw a frown rather than a soft smile.

Can I say anything right?

"Helping to drive a force of nature like SMS must be exciting," she said, changing her tack.

"Yes. CEO Landecker is a good man. He's a soft-spoken leader with a truly committed management team. We all get along well, and the board of directors. And our coffers are full."

"What leadership style makes that happen? Most companies today are driven by sheer greed and executive golden parachutes, short-term goals, and bonuses."

"That does seem like the real world, doesn't it?"

"They didn't teach that when I was at Harvard."

"I didn't get that either. Maybe someday Harvard will begin to believe in their motto of 'Veritas'." He touched her hand with an affectionate pat as they both shared a moment of similar experience. "We're both alums, and here we sit, heavily dug into the American capitalist bureaucracy. So what is your style of management, fellow barney?"

"C. S. Lewis. Picture a fleet of ships, an armada, ready to sail out of the harbor to do some extraordinary deed. What does it take to do it well when so many initiatives with so many moving parts fail or produce less-than-stellar results? Lewis maintained it took three things. First, the ships needed to cooperate with each other to avoid smashing into each other, squabbling with each other, wasting energy and resource. Second, keep each ship in good working order. Third, the entire fleet must know its ultimate purpose. And now you know my secret sauce of management."

Charlie offered her a nod and a smile. "Your number one is a social ethic – how we live together in harmony. Number two addresses personal ethics. An organization cannot be superior if the individual parts are inferior. One faulty link and the chain collapses. Number three is individual character, integrity, self-control. It implies a goal with a shared vision."

"You figured that analogy out from the top of you just now."

"Yes, but an undergrad in philosophy made me very familiar with the great C. S. Lewis."

They shared a laugh again. This was a warm laugh, a comfortable one. Each took an involuntary deep breath that went unnoticed by the other.

Julia tried her best prominent Boston Harvard accent. "Should we order some chodaw?"

"Yeaah. This chowdawhead loves that stuff. Then let's take in a game at the Gahden."

"Then to a who banga to top off the night. Okay?"

Laughter and back to small talk saw another bottle of ruby-red *Brunello* arrived with some *crostini al Pomodoro*. The background music was neither the frustrated anger of the ghetto, nor the sugared naivety of 50s/60s love songs, but a soft blend of jazz, Italian Neapolitan classic songs, seasoned with Sinatra and the French Sinatra – Charles Aznavour. Soft, beguiling, romantic, immediate. Several couples were dancing, lost in each other, wrapped in each other.

"So you're a Montana girl, right?"

"Hawk Eye here grew up in Bozeman," Julia said after the wine cleansed the garlic taste from her palate. "Home of the University of Montana, my alma mater, and also Bozeman High School, where I graduated valedictorian. I still have nightmares about my words-of-wisdom graduation speech surfacing somewhere on YouTube."

"I know that feeling. I was so naive."

"So Bozeman is best known for growing and canning peas and the town most tourists pass through on their way to Yellowstone."

"So it must be a great place for hiking and such."

"Along with white-water kayaking and mountain climbing."

"Prom queen?"

"You're psychic, Mr. Captain of the football team, right?"

"Guilty. Go on."

"Student council, editor of the school paper, a few other things. I have one brother. Mom is a homemaker and never forgets to beg for grandchildren. Dad still runs a family cattle ranch on the outskirts of town. Natural beef, no corn, they graze all day. It's a modest operation. So when Senator Cowel wrote me about an interview and a possible appointment to West Point—"

"Your life changed."

"I was naturally thinking University of Minnesota and maybe a geology degree. No one in our family expected me, at my size, to end up in Afghanistan in the middle of a firefight. Nobody."

"Yet, the Purple Heart, the Congressional Medal of Honor—"

"All achieved from Senator Cowel's West Point recommendation."

"I read the background on your CMO. Got me thinking that maybe I'm lucky I got my knee crushed back then. I come from a military family. So I know your parents must have been proud of you."

"Getting the CMO was my dad's proudest moment for me. And the senator stayed true, landed me into Harvard graduate school, and he's still grooming me for heaven knows what. It has been a wild ride."

"My story was somewhat different. Having an Admiral as a father piled on enormous pressure. Everyone expected me to fight the good fight and come home a hero. You could say I was bred for war, politics and exceptional achievements. Duty always came first. So of course my flaws and upcoming responsibilities were discussed over dinner. I was to be a blooming symbol more than a man."

"Sounds like a Kennedy family story."

"While my father helps keep the free world free, my mother is always in the garden helping to make our family appreciate the beauty of life and nature. I majored in philosophy so I could understand her better. As for war, all I know of it is from fireside stories, the parades, and the movies. It sounds too good to be true somehow and also too gruesome to be true."

"I thought of the glory when I enlisted. I ended up killing two young boys in a raid."

"They were the enemy in a just war."

"But I killed them. I am responsible, too. Once home, most of us forget, or rather hide the distressing memories. So the stories are always funny or about bravery and sacrifice. We were talking about you being Kennedy-ish."

"But the Republican version. Senator Cowel attended more than a few of those dinners. Imagine being tutored by the ranking member of the Senate Armed Forces Committee and the Chair of the Senate Intelligence Committee and the Senate Majority Leader, former Senator Kiddenly. I call him Uncle Billy. He used to take Pop and me on his hunkin' yacht. Pop used to tell him that his fleet of aircraft carriers would dwarf his yacht, the *West Texan*. They would both laugh and order another bourbon."

"And I see he sits on the board of SMS."

"Father of the Grand Old party. But Senator Cowel set the pace. He's the career builder, groomer and planner. Senator from Kentucky even showed up now and then. But that was 'adult' talk, and nobody wanted me around. Senator Cowel always looked like a big bag of bones and when he looked at me I thought he wanted to bite me. Maybe he did, you will meet him soon."

"So we both have Senator Cowel to thank for who we are now and where we are."

"The jury is still out on me. My parents are none too pleased with my career to date."

"I can commiserate. My mom told me she and my dad hardly know me anymore, what with the media attention, the Ivy League schools, the complex lifestyle."

"I'll trade you parents. I'm all for the simple life."

"A life of public service doesn't suit you?"

"At first there were some benefits. My talent for football brought the cheerleaders' attention. Living behind the iron of a gated estate in North Houston helped me feel exceptional, better connected than most felt good, but that soon wore off. We also had a stately town house not far from here as Pop had to be in town often for his military and political duties. When I shattered my knee, my football career was over, and I quickly lost the attention of the ladies when all the publicity left me."

"So here you and I sit with our prestigious resumes talking SMS. And our mutual mentor seems to hold the reins and is a no show tonight."

"That pleases me," Charlie said, raising his glass. "This is the best night I've had in some time. Tonight *Je vois la vie en rose.* That's French for—"

"*When he takes me in his arms and speaks softly to me, I see life in rosy hues. He tells me words of love, words of every day, and in them I become something.*"

"*Mon Dieu*! You speak French!"

"High school and university and I spent a year in Rennes as a foreign-exchange student. You?"

"My mother *is* French. I heard the language first in her womb. Damn, I should have ordered a Bordeaux!"

"No way. The *Brunello* is superb. It's a new friend for sure."

"The wine must be getting to me, quoting French and all. Kind of pretentious of me. French seems out of fashion lately to Americans."

"Americans seem out of fashion lately to Americans. *Quel domage!*"

"My mother still has an accent and sure 'nuff she gets flack for it sometimes."

"One can only imagine a French accent mixed with a Texas drawl. Must beggar description."

"Shoot. Mom has no Texas talk in her and Dad had to learn a Middle West accent for his political speeches. I was the only family member blessed with this American accent."

"Yet your French is spoken precisely, without that—"

"That slow drawl doesn't mean I'm slow upstairs. It means I'm proud to let everyone know where I come from."

"Well, here's to Texas," Julia toasted. "You know France went bankrupt funding our revolution. And here's to the Marquis de

La Fayette, French aristocrat, and American Major General," Julia said, raising her glass.

"Brandwine, Albany, Yorktown," Charlie added.

"To Lafayette, a man who put one belief over all others, that of human liberty."

"Why isn't there a major movie about Lafayette's life and contributions to America?" Charlie asked.

"Same reason there was a movie made that glorified Che Guevara. We've somehow become a self-hating nation and think we're a nasty people, that freedom is free, and all of us have rights but no obligations."

"Here's to your beauty, your brains and your patriotism," Charlie said.

"Here's to your beautiful drawl, your cockroach stompers and your mother," Julia echoed.

"Mom would like you," a suddenly down Charlie said. "Dance with me, Julia."

"What?"

"Please."

"I believe that they are playing what is called a tarantella right now. Not a good song for high heels."

"If I get the waiter to play something appropriate, something French, please?"

"Well—"

"Just one dance. Help me make another memory of a wonderful night."

Julia complied with a nod. Charlie signaled to the waiter and whispered in his ear. The waiter nodded and left. At the end of the Italian song, Charlie rose and extended his right hand, which Julia took. They walked to the small wooden dance floor and joined several other couples who waited for the next number to begin. A single strum of a guitar, then the familiar voice of Texan, Roy Orbison, filled the room with his 1963 rock and roll ballad, "In Dreams." Julia found herself dancing a cha-cha with a man a foot taller than her, with shoulders that filled doorways, yet he moved with a soft elegance as he guided her across the floor. Without awareness of when and how it happened, she found her head resting against his chest, moving as one to the soaring music, which took her from a dream of a woman and then the realization where it was "too bad that all these things could only happen in dreams."

Julia, softly held in the massive and protective arms of a lonely man who gently turned her in small circles until the master songster whispered the final "in beautiful dreams," struggled to compose herself. She knew it was somehow an intimate moment for both of them. Returning to the table Julia could not meet Charlie's eyes at first. She finished the dregs of her wine, sampled some spiced and oiled bread. Eventually, the silence became too deafening.

"So, who do you work for at SMS, Charlie?"

"The CEO, Tyrell Landecker. And he in turn reports to the SMS board of directors, and ultimately the rarely seen chairman, Nicola Scozzari."

"Do you know Scozzari?"

"Yes. But I doubt if I could get you an interview. He and I are not on the best of terms."

"Why is that?"

"He's my estranged wife's father."

"I wish your wife could have joined us," Julia said. "I would have liked to meet her."

Charlie sighed. "No, you wouldn't."

Julia's wine glass froze in mid-air and returned to the table without a sip.

"Antonia and I are no longer together. I married the big boss's daughter, got a cushy job at Daddy's firm and even with money and connections things went south. Sounds like something out of a soap opera, doesn't it?"

"I'm so sorry."

"Not your fault, Julia. I wanted the wife and kids, house in the suburbs, eternal romance. Antonia likes to swing. See why my job is my life?"

Silence. Eyes averted.

"Whoa. That is too much wine and too much information. I apologize," Charlie confessed.

"Too much for me, also, and my fault. I've been asking personal questions, and you've been gracious enough to answer them. This is supposed to be a business meeting. Can we reschedule when the senator is able to join us?"

Charlie raised his finger and mouthed "Check please" to the waiter.

Julia reached for her purse.

Charlie put his hand softly on her arm. "This is on SMS, Julia. I had forgotten what delightful company was like. I'll ask the senator about a good time to meet and let's get you out to SMS soon."

Charlie was suddenly all business. They parted formally.

Julia did not sleep well that night. Charlie did not sleep at all.

Chapter 19

"Just keep it away from the media," Nicola Scozzari, growled into the phone. "If one word gets out I'll cut you off financially."

The cell phone exploded against the unyielding wood of the Australian bull oak, which lined his opulent office. The bull oak was the hardest wood in the world and fitting for a man like him. It comforted him that his powerful reach could extend to any point on the earth, and his grasp could indeed reel in anything. But tonight, Antonia was up to her old tricks again. Off the wagon. Nicola looked into his beveled brass-framed mirror, and his reddened face disturbed him even more. His fortune was estimated at over 2.7 billion dollars. As heir to a major tobacco empire based in Louisville and a distilling business in Bardstown, Nicola was the real power of SMS. He was used to getting his way and vindictive toward anyone who challenged him. His hot southern Italian blood spilled out at times like this – fire, rage, vendetta. He owned a stable of senators and through them had fought and defeated the anti-tobacco lobby for decades. Hated by most Democrats and Republicans, he had never been touched by any investigative body in his entire life. Few would even whisper his name.

Divorced from his wife, Nicola had his hands full with his daughter, Antonia, an only child, blessed with a face and a body that few men could resist. Unfortunately her favorite part of sex was neither intimacy nor orgasm but turning her victims into begging boys. Nicola had heard of their pleading and ridiculous demeaning stunts they would perform for her in the heat of anticipation and how they pleaded when she'd tired of teasing them. Nicola's staff would tell him stories of the men. Those who hit her or went too far in pursuit of her were bloodied.

"Please, Antonia, let me come over tomorrow night. I will give you anything." Oftentimes she would force her aroused lover to put on outlandish costumes and snap a few pictures. If they refused, she turned to leave the room. In all the years since puberty, she had never even had to grasp the doorknob. Despite her father's strict grooming attempts and the thousands spent on private tutors, fashion experts, and the like, Antonia was born to develop and employ her greatest asset – the curvy body she had inherited from her mother. From her father, she got her lust for control, domination and cruelty.

Nicola was more than up to the task of covering up his daughter's indiscretions. And many of her "caught in the act" snapshots ended more than a few wrongdoing complaints or threats of law suits for compensation for this or that. No police force in Texas, state or local, would move against the likes of Nicola Scozzari. The only thing he did fear was that somehow one of his enemies, and they were legion, could use his daughter's antics against him. Troublesome people were eliminated. He would only tolerate his daughter's antics for so long. The kitten was running out of lives, and Father was keeping score. While her storybook wedding to Capitol Hill, in the form of Charles Prendergast III fell apart quickly, as expected, she still carried his name and behind that was yet another string for the puppeteer to pull at will.

A crystal bourbon glass shattered against the impervious wood paneling of Nicola's office. "Damn her!" he shouted, loud enough to trigger a bark from one of the numerous guard dogs set loose at night to prowl the Scozzari estate and protect its ten-foot-high iron fencing. The house phone rang, the twenty-four-seven video surveillance team checking on him. "No problem," he responded calmly, pleased with the response of his SMS mercenaries who were not engaged overseas or with domestic issues.

Benedetta, the estranged wife, had to be handled differently. An Italian Mafia don's only daughter was to be treated as a princess. One did not go straight at one of the Mob's ruling family members, but from the side – delivering a glancing blow. You were either chastised, or bowed to your betters, or were never heard from again. But Nicola had leeway with the family. It was Benedetta's grandfather, Sergio Cortese, who had set up Nicola's father in the tobacco business. At one time, tobacco was king. But cotton replaced it in the South for a century. That dynasty ended when Lincoln freed the slaves and Sherman burned the South. The boll-weevil migration from Mexico that infected the cotton crop just about killed it. Production moved to China and India. With the creation of the cigarette, tobacco became king once more. Then the do-gooders prodded Congress to vilify tobacco. And this was Nicola Scorazzi's raison d'être, to keep the tobacco industry alive in the South. He would fight the people, the government and whatever else came at him. While his once billionaire status had dwindled, his SMS dealings funded his goals and paid plenty to the New York Mob, which gave him a long leash. But Benedetta and Antonia were wild cards in a well-greased machine. It was time to send his daughter a message. Her husband carried a prominent name and Nicola needed that to keep SMS running smoothly. Tyrell Landecker, the current CEO was getting a bit too nosey and demanding.

Nicola's informers had been watching Landecker's activities and had tapped his phones. There were numerous encoded calls received at odd hours. Landecker's computer indicated he had been taking confidential information each night, which he diverted to a series of thumb drives. The tracking device on his private car showed meetings taking place in the middle of the night and he had stopped using an SMS driver and bodyguard. His wife and kids left 8 days earlier to stay with her parents, yet there were no known rifts in their relationship. Why did she depart the residence in the middle of the school year?

Chapter 20

It was not just another day of talking the talk in D.C. for Julia, this was her coming-out party, so to speak, where she could apply what she had learned in her many detailed briefings by Senator Cowel as well as with Charlie Prendergast. She had studied the folder and memorized what she needed to speak on about SMS, its value to America. She was a subject-matter expert and could tell the story with authority.

Julia told herself it was easy to sell something you believed in and now was the time to show it!

She walked through the vast historic corridors of Capitol Hill, easily recognizable with her long blonde hair, shapely petite figure and toned legs. She returned nods and smiles of those people who nodded to her, most she had never met. By now Julia had come to accept her celebrity status with the grace and poise that had become as well-known as her military history. It seemed everyone recognized Hawk Eye Abbott. Sometimes she wondered if it was her ever-growing Washington contacts list that were making her the celebrity her well-wishers admired. But she committed to play the role to the hilt, convey the message, and do the job for which she had agreed to do. A quintessential soldier on a mission, she was bound and determined to success-fully complete her job because the senator, Charlie and the country needed her.

She had become an A-list player on Capitol Hill and had access to whomever she needed with even the shortest notice. It was what it was, in her opinion, and she would use all of the above and wrap it in the right clothes and shoes to do her job – to keep the wars in Afghanistan and Iraq going, for they were just, as just as the words coming from Senator Cowel's mouth of freedom for all!

Her meeting today was with first-time congressman, AJ

Morales, a Democrat representing the Austin Texas Congressional 5ht District. She had studied his bio with a curious anticipation and was well-prepared. She knew Morales to be a combat hero – Air Force Pararescue man, three tours in Iraq, captured for several months, escaped, and used his record of service along with the fact that his father had been the Governor of Montana to get elected to the U.S. House of Representatives. Her plan was to welcome Mr. Morales to Washington, commiserate on their experiences in the Middle East then subtly launch into the importance of backing SMS. After all, Hawk Eye Abbott was someone to treat as a friend in the rarified air of incestuous Washington D.C. They had much in common, yet were at the same time somehow so different.

* * *

"Please have a seat, Ms. Abbott," AJ said. "I apologize for the accommodations. Newbie congressmen always get the shabby offices."

"Please call me Julia."

"AJ."

Julia sat, crossed her legs, adjusted the hem of her skirt and opened her briefcase, hoping the ruggedly handsome Latin-lover type approved of her appearance.

"We have military experience in common, AJ."

"My Purple Hearts are trumped by your Congressional Medal of Honor; and, of course, your heroic actions while ambushed and wounded."

"And we both hail from Montana."

"Yes, I was born and raised in Helena. And you grew up in Bozeman. I remember seeing you on TV in a high-school cheer-leading segment."

"Ouch. You've been stalking me on the Internet?"

"No. We all have bios on each other in Washington. Don't we? Here's the public record on you," he said, reading from a computer screen. "Single, former class president, cheerleader captain, prom queen, National Honor Society, class valedictorian, member of the Daughters of the American Revolution. Graduated top of her class at West Point, recommended by Senator Parker Cowel (Rep Mon). Upon graduation deployed to Iraq, winner of CMH and Purple Heart. Wounded in stomach. Recovered. On return to the states attended Harvard MBA school. One of Senator Cowel's hand-picked protégées, lobbying for the SMS Corporation."

"Congressman AJ Morales," Julia said from memory. "University of Texas football legend, mediocre grades, up for lucrative NFL draft, enlisted in UASF Pararescue instead. A difficult program."

"It was. At first I was proud of my accomplishments and new skills. But later, when I could employ them, I was proud to help others as best I could."

"So a man of action rather than words."

"I could say the same of you. Only my actions were in the service of others."

Julia ignored the implication that she was here to feather her own nest.

"To continue with your bio: two tours in Afghanistan, two purple hearts. Represents Austin, Texas. Father was a former Governor of Montana, ran against the junior senator for a U.S. senate seat. He was defeated and passed away shortly thereafter."

"It's a shame how little these bios actually tell about us. That junior senator was a close pal of your employer, Senator Cowel."

"It that a sin of some sort?"

"Cowel and his dirty tricks team smeared my father so badly that the slander triggered his fatal heart attack."

"I'm sorry." Julia was not prepared for this. Time to change subjects – back to the shared military experience. "You were Pararescue. We were always happy to see you guys around in

Iraq. 'That others may live' is your motto if memory serves."

"And it still is my personal motto. I represent Austin, Texas now. AJ is short for Alejandro Jaime. My parents are of Spanish ancestry, and I have many Mexican relatives here and across the border. I ran in Austin as a Latino voice. They need representation in Washington – honest representation."

Julia did not like that last phrase. It somehow called her motives into question.

"Good. Then you and I should get along well and open discussions on bipartisan motives."

"So let's cut to the chase, Ms. Abbott. You're one of Senator Cowel's hand-picked protégées, a lobbyist. Cowel sits in the middle of a self-made shit heap called SMS and he is the errand boy for his Costa Nostra godfather, Nicola Scozzari. Your job is to sugarcoat the industrial-military collusion and corruption that costs our taxpayers untold millions a year and kills our sons and daughters in the name of patriotism."

"I beg your pardon, Congressman. Those are unfounded allegations and I am at least as patriotic as you are."

"A patriot is an American who defends the U.S. Constitution and thereby guarantees the freedom of our people. Your idea of a patriot is someone who makes war on anyone who stands up to our politics or personal profits."

"As a rank newbie on Capitol Hill I suggest you study the facts before accusing a U.S. Senator with libelous statements you cannot possibly back up. Good day, Congressman, hopefully our paths will not cross again anytime soon."

"I don't have to study them on immaculate white paper that's been filtered through an army of bureaucrats. I've seen them firsthand. SMS is a terrorist organization built and operated for economic gain of a few powerful criminals."

Julia stopped walking to the door and turned to the new red-faced Morales. "How can you say something like that?"

"If you remember my bio, I was MIA for two months."

"You escaped unharmed."

"I escaped with my eyes wide open. I saw the illegal SMS mining operations, directed by our own politicians, watched the SMS mercenaries protect their business interests to keep product flowing."

"What product?"

"Lithium."

"Ah, I am somehow in the *Twilight Zone*. I don't even know what lithium is used for. It's not gold, not silver or—"

"It is probably the most valuable rare earth mineral on the planet. Your company digs it out of the Afghan mountains every day and flies it to distribution and manufacturing plants all over the world. We don't want their damn oil. We have enough oil for a century or two. SMS makes serious money using the military to provide the industrial complex with the raw materials they steal from the Afghans. Big money. Untraceable money. Money used to finance revolutions. Money used to create large profits for your pimp, Cowel, and his sugar daddy Scozzari."

"I came here today—"

"I know why you came. I expected you to show up in fishnet stockings, stiletto heels and a plunging neckline. Are you part of my bribery package?"

* * *

Julia's stomach stopped burning and she stopped shaking about ten minutes after walking aimlessly. Who was this monster, Morales, and how could he have been elected to congress? While she had heard most of the urban legends and conspiracy theories from those who had heard it from a friend whose third cousin knew someone who had the truth, this nut Morales actually said he was there. There in Afghanistan, which he was, captured by the insurgents, which he was. Was it possible he wasn't lying?

The SMS books were as clean as the wind-driven snow. Was

she looking deeply enough? Was she blinded by her own ambition? Was this the reason her mere mention of SMS turned senators, aides, and congressmen pale? Why did they cheerily agree to anything she demanded? Something was wrong. She reasoned she could not confront Senator Cowel with this. No proof. Career limiting. If SMS was a front for something nefarious, and the senator was involved, he wouldn't tell the truth anyway. But the conversation with the governor and then her father still lingered in her mind. She had been warned not to trust Parker Cowel. Was she guilty of rationalizing everything just to keep her position in Washington?

But Charlie...she and Charlie had met twice since their disastrous dinner. He knew SMS backwards and forwards. He was proud of the SMS accomplishments. *Perhaps I should invite the nutcase Morales to dinner with Charlie and get the truth out on the table. It may be volatile, but something is wrong somewhere. Charlie could go head to head with this conspiracy theory Democratic liberal. Better to go right at it and nip it in the bud.*

Chapter 21

"Is this guy a nutcase, Julia?" Charlie Prendergast asked over the phone.

"I don't know, Charlie. He seemed at first a very polite, almost humble man. Rare for D.C. Then he seemed to explode; lose control. I admit a few things about SMS have been bothering me, and this man spent three tours in Afghanistan, boots on the ground, a prisoner, probably saw SMS up close and personal. He seemed to be telling the truth at least as he knows it."

"SMS is a global entity, with many hands involved in many initiatives. As you know, I am on the charity and political contribution to PAC side of things and have little to do with the manufacturing or military contracts side of things."

"Then maybe a conference call with the three of us would work better."

"No. Let's stick with dinner. Your instincts always seem to pan out, Hawk Eye. Besides, it couldn't be worse than our first dinner, now could it?"

"I promise no personal questions. So eight tomorrow night where we met last month, the 1789?"

"Looking forward to it."

When Julia arrived at her office her secretary smiled a special smile and Julia caught site of the roses – white roses; two dozen. Assuming a gift from Charlie he did not mention on the recent call to him she ripped open the tiny attached card thinking they should have been red. Why white?

My sincere apologies for yesterday's disastrous meeting. I was out of place and rude. Is there a way I can make this up to you? AJ Morales.

"Well the opportunity couldn't be better to extend a dinner invitation. But in a way I hope this guy is a nutcase."

Julia grabbed the most valuable tool in a Capitol Hill employee's chest – her iPhone.

"Yes, this is Julia Abbott calling for Congressman Morales."

Enough time passed that Julia checked her phone to verify the connection was still working.

"Ms. Abbott. This is AJ Morales. I'd assumed I was on your never-call list. I do apologize for the name calling, but not for the accusations against SMS."

"Apology accepted. Thank you for the beautiful white roses. I'd like to invite you to dinner."

"Will you have a sharp shooter lurking somewhere outside the restaurant?"

"That's called paranoia."

"Self-preservation."

"I'll be giving you an opportunity to spout and back up your so-called facts. A friend and senior VP at SMS will be there, and I thought we could rationally discuss your allegations. I'm all for uncovering the truth."

"Impressive, Ms. Abbott. I accept."

Julia sat facing the door as her vantage point in the 1789 restaurant. Tonight's meeting would be in a private dining room. Charlie appeared at eight p.m. sharp, as was his style. She smiled when she recalled he was one of those Texans with more hat than cattle. He bypassed her outstretched hand, politely brushed her cheek with his, sat across from her, and they engaged in chit-chat. AJ Morales entered, head not moving, eyes scanning the tables. Her raised hand immediately caught his eyes. He smiled, nodded and entered the private room.

As Charlie turned to greet the congressman Julia watched a smile of greeting and an extended hand turn to shock and a trembling hand. The congressman stopped in his tracks, about three feet from Charlie and glared at him.

"First you corrupt Antonia and now she's dragged you into SMS?" Julia heard Morales say. "How low can you sink?"

That comment cowered the big Texan. Charlie's shoulders sagged as he sank into his chair. The congressman's eyes were squinted, holding back tears.

Julia broke the silence. "You two know — "

"That Rose Bowl picture, Julia," Charlie said, not looking up from the floor. "The wide receiver was this AJ Morales."

"I knew you were employed by SMS, Charlie, but not that you'd be Ms. Abbott's resource to defend your corrupt activities."

Charlie recovered and offered AJ a seat. Charlie offered his hand, Morales refused.

"How do I know where that hand has been?"

"Not where you think. Ms. Abbott obviously didn't know we go way back together. Julia, years ago I betrayed this man. He was my best friend. That Rose Bowl picture showed three friends on top of the world. In reality time has faded that relationship to loathing for all of us."

"Do we all run from past actions now or does someone start explaining?" Julia asked, attempting to sound like a first-grade teacher. "I vote for going over your SMS knowledge and initiative, Congressman."

"I erased this SMS stooge from my memory and hoped he was dead, Ms. Abbott."

"I should have tracked you down and apologized, face-to-face," Charlie said. "When I heard you declined the NFL draft pick and joined the Air Force I couldn't believe it. At first I wanted to forget you and what I did, but it wouldn't go away. For years, I expected to hear of your death and blame myself. I know you. You never shied away from a fight, and were never tempted to cheat."

"Tempted to my core once. I was offered a hundred K cash to drop any game-changing passes at the Rose Bowl."

"You never told me that."

"I was already spending the money in my mind as time was running out on the clock. Then I looked back, saw a thousand pounds of linebacker rush you and a perfect spiraling football come up from the collapsing pile and out toward me. I figured that if you could throw that ball under that pressure I could catch the damn thing and to hell with the money."

"Why wasn't I bribed?"

"Because your family is rich. The bad guys always know what buttons to push."

"Damn. I never even suspected that stuff went on."

"Life is a gilded cage for you, Charlie. How could you have expected to know the crap that goes on?"

"You've changed, AJ. You were always calm. Now I see a fury in you."

"That's war. I've seen good men die, strong men crack and cry, wicked men thrive. I've seen my country commit sins in the name of might makes right. Speaking of which, how's your family friend, Senator Cowel? The Charlie Prendergast I knew would never work for a shithole like SMS if you knew their true agenda."

"What true agenda?" Julia asked.

"It's been eleven or twelve years since Mr. Prendergast and I have seen each other. Now I know he and his family have sold out and are secretly in bed with evil."

Julia blinked and tensed as she watched Charlie deliver a right fist to Morale's face, knocking the congressman clean out of his chair and onto the floor. He rose with lightning speed, ducked a second punch from the approaching Charlie and knocked him to the floor with a heel to the back of the knee on Charlie's bad leg. Before Morales could do more Julia was up, slamming her right knee into Morales's ribs. Both men were on the floor of the restaurant now with Julia looking down at them.

"This is no place for adolescent reactions," she said, threatening further action.

"He insulted my family," Charlie said as both men rose, looking like hungry male lions standing over a meal and waiting for the other to make its move.

"Where did you learn that move, Ms Abbott," Morales asked

as he rubbed his ribcage.

"A woman in a war zone has potential enemies even in her own camp. Congressman, if you want to delve into proving your very suspect allegations against SMS you need to get hold of your emotions. Charlie, same goes for you."

The threesome took a few silent moments to regain personal control. The waiter entered, Julia sensed something was amiss, but discretion kept him silent as he took orders and made recommendations.

"Ms. Abbott," AJ Morales said, "while I was flying around in helicopters in Afghanistan then getting myself elected to the U.S. Congress, Charlie here has managed to seduce and marry my former girlfriend. He is undoubtedly in line to inherit a goodly share of his father-in-law's evil empire and then join the most corrupt global conglomerate in the world. Even Hitler's resume reads better than yours, Charlie."

"I made a grave mistake in the heat of the moment, AJ. It's not like I seduced a nun. She showed me her tits for God's sake that day. Remember."

"Granted Antonia was hot and carefree. But she thought using her body was the only way to make friends."

"She got me drunk, made me watch porn and then somehow I ended up at the altar with her. I even had to become a Catholic," he whispered.

"Then you may have swam the Tiber but ended up on the wrong bank."

Charlie squinted with confusion. "My go-to man deserted me. Or rather, I betrayed him and he left. So I suppose I have what I deserve."

That admission cooled both tempers as AJ pursed his lips and offered Charlie his hand. They shook looking square into each other's eyes.

"Nicola Scozzari is Charlie's father-in-law?" Julia asked AJ.

"Yes, Mommy," Charlie admitted.

"Your mother-in-law has ties to the Mob?"

"I am separated from my wife and have not seen my father-in-law for some time and my mother-in-law only once."

"I find this all very fateful, Charlie," AJ said. "We were split apart by a woman, and now we've been brought together by a woman. Looks like it's time to spin that roulette wheel again."

"Call it providence," Charlie said.

"Two things are for certain." Julia interceded. "One, you've just proved my assertion that men are truly just overgrown boys, and two, I am certainly not a woman like the one you two shared."

"So here we are, gentlemen. One of you is a congressman investigating SMS and implying there are highly placed traitors in our government, the other a senior VP of SMS, married to the mob. What the hell is going on here?"

The waiter entered and Charlie quickly said, "a large carafe of Makers Mark 46. One ice cube each in three glasses. And keep the door closed."

The waiter responded with world-class speed. AJ and Charlie each took a healthy belt of the bourbon. Julia had no illusions about either of them. Both were the types that had drank the most beer on campus, bedded the most coeds, ran the fraternities and were masters of all they surveyed on campus. Charlie was the anointed one, thick dark hair, rock jaw, confident and smug. He wore a perennial mischievous face. AJ was a hair shorter than Charlie but built thicker, his skin a sun-kissed bronze color, his hair combed straight back. He was more reflective than Charlie, more humble, reminding her of a priest.

"So fill me in on your experience with SMS, AJ," Charlie said after both men inhaled the first glass of whiskey and Charlie poured the refill. "I've got nothing to hide. I'm just a dried-up leaf floating in a rippling stream."

"After you unknowingly saved me from Antonia I lost my faith in pretty much everything. There was a war on, the recruiters actively clubbing for freedom fighters, I joined up, served my time in support of my country and like to think I did some good. Three tours. Hard to think a lot about painful memories and betrayals when you are dodging bullets. One night we responded to a downed-chopper alert. It was a trap. All killed but me. Seems their leader's brother was saved by a Pararescue guy like me. He let me live."

"You were saved by Al Qaeda?" Julia asked.

"An Afghan patriot to be more specific. We argued about U.S. and Middle East conflicts and the like. He started showing me things."

"Severed heads. Homemade bombs. AK47s?" Julia asked.

"A tour in country, but from the other guy's point of view."

"Don't tell me you went on missions with the enemy, Congressman," Julia said.

AJ took a stiff drink. "Number one, I'm telling my new old buddy my experiences. You are eavesdropping. Number two, I told you a patriot is someone who defends the U.S. Constitution against internal and external threats. I'm an American. Are you, Ms. Abbott? Do you harbor any doubts about curious things happening when you were in country?"

On the surface, it was a straightforward question. But Julia's mind took her back to Iraq and the two boys she killed simply by pulling back a trigger. Facing imminent death, the masks of war abandoned the insurgents to reveal innocent and naive boyish expressions – before she turned those faces into bloody masses.

"Please continue."

"I think she's okay, AJ."

"It's you I'm worried about, Charlie."

"I am an American too, AJ. I do not know of any dirt on SMS. That doesn't make me a spy, just stupid."

"So at least your taste in women has improved."

"I am not his woman."

Charlie refilled the glasses. Julia stayed with the red wine.

The waiter knocked, was given permission to enter, and told nothing was needed at this moment. The door shut silently.

"Yes," AJ said, "I saw what it looked like from the citizen's point of view. The Afghani were invaded. They were again pitting their lives against an empire, like they did the British Empire, the greatest army in the world. They threw the Russians out too."

"Good for them. We sent the British packing here in America. You have to win freedom not just expect it."

"We fought against a tyrant in our revolution. In Afghanistan, I saw a politically manipulated war to plunder natural resources. That is the same thing the British had in mind for us. I went on a mission where I saw the Afghanis torch a poppy field which is no different that our Boston Tea Party motivation and action."

"Why would Al Qaeda or the Taliban or whatever exotic named group do that?" Charlie asked.

"The Afghanis hate what the Taliban is doing to their country. Unfortunately, our forces patrol the poppy fields. And the opium and heroin profits are up 700 percent. And the funds are channeled to the Mob and away from Al Qaeda. But his drug profit still funds terrorism. Illegal drug profits make a few men wealthy and also fund military operations. The trickledown effect keeps quite a few unscrupulous people in the black also. I also went on a Recon mission to see one of the lithium mining sites. Lithium will be a vital resource needed to retool our country for weaning us off of oil. Electric cars, high-tech long-lasting batteries. There is a fortune to be made here. And Afghanistan has it in spades. Up close and personal I saw evidence of foreign mercenaries protecting the mining operations against any and all threats. They wore nondescript emblems on their fatigues, but these boys were former French Foreign Legion, Russian Spetsnaz, and ex-U.S. Special Forces."

"How could our military operate such a large operation and we not know of it?" Julia challenged.

AJ looked around the room to ensure nobody was listening. "It is not our military. It's private for-profit operations sanctioned through the U.S. senate and funded by the U.S. House. They will use our military personnel, equipment and intelligence if necessary."

"How could that be?" Charlie asked, his brow furled. "SMS is an engineering, construction and private military contracting company that helps our troops, our freedom fighters, do their jobs. We privatize some war functions to complement the military. SMS employ specialists to augment the infrastructure construction to fight the war. And America is not going to allow extremists to terrorize our country at any cost. We're bringing democracy to Asia. And we do massive charity work in support of our troops."

AJ shook his head. "And you finance Super PAC groups to get the 'right' candidates elected, so they turn a blind eye to the corruption and collusion within our government."

"Why would people at the top subvert our government?" Julia asked. "I would think skimming would be their greatest scam, but outright traitorous activity? Why?"

"Simple. What's the most addictive drug on the planet?" AJ asked.

Julia and Charlie both whispered 'money' at the same time.

Charlie's face contorted.

"You are saying SMS—"

"Yes, Charlie. I have pictures. Digital data. Reports. My contact can give you whatever you require as proof. And your beloved father-in-law, Nicola Scozzari, and Senator Parker Cowel, your favorite sugar daddy, have their mugs on video also. Their DNA all over this."

Julia's heart sunk in her chest. There it was – the name she did not want to hear. Parker Cowel. She pushed her white wine aside, refilled the men's glasses and switched to the whiskey herself.

"I've heard rumors that we're under investigation," Charlie said.

"What?" Julia asked.

"The FBI is working closely with a U.S. House congressional committee," AJ said. "Why do you think I ran for Congress? Many remember my father as Governor of Montana. I remember the dirty politics, the smears against him. My district is progressive and brown, white and black. I'm here to clean up Dodge."

"And you began with me, in your office," Julia said. "Thank you for that."

"I told the truth. But you thought I was a madman."

"I still do."

"The investigation may explain why the board has been so preoccupied," Charlie sighed.

"Yep," AJ said, sitting back in his chair. "Charlie, it's essential to answer this truthfully. Do you have knowledge of any illegal SMS operations?"

"No, AJ. I do not. I'm on the donation and grant side of things. I fill pockets, not empty them."

"So both you and 'Hawk Eye' here are SMS patsies."

"Charlie," Julia, "a nice fist in the chops might cool the congressman down."

"Would you two like to help me and the Feds get the goods on these crooks or let the crap continue to grow?"

"Do you have a feel for the size of this thing, AJ," Charlie asked.

"Unfortunately, yes. This is huge, and it is dangerous for all of us. And just like with the banking meltdown, no major player will ever go to jail and the Mob will continue."

"The Mob is in this?" Julia asked.

"Charlie's estranged wife, Antonia Scozzari is a grand-daughter of two Mafia dons. Nicola married into the Cortese family, hence his chairman-of-the-board position at SMS. He also runs a tobacco and whiskey empire and is moving into riverboat gambling and has growth hormone labs in Ohio. God only knows what profits he sees in growth hormones."

"So the Mob is not just the stuff of Hollywood melodramas," Julia said.

"Junk movies are actually about laundering Mob money, no need for quality. Sell cigarettes to young people. Hell, their brains aren't even fully developed, and they fall for the propaganda hook, line and sinker. Make movies with enlightened teenagers and corrupt hypocritical airhead parents. Wish fulfillment. Works every time."

"This is somehow beyond belief," Julia said.

"Most people just shake their heads and leave it at that. 'What can I do?' they say. 'So much power in the hands of a corrupt few.' And when asked to stand up and fight, they usually wet their pants. Julia, Charlie, you could drive this investigation to a real head. Open the oyster. Are you in or out?"

"We meet again after a decade you remind me that I'm married to Antonia, you propose to prove to me I'm a numb-nuts VP for a corrupt company with government, military, industrial and Mob collusion. Then you ask me to help you take them down."

"I've seen you under pressure, Charlie. It brings out the best out in you. So, yes, I am asking for your help."

"All these names you've dropped as corrupt traitors I've known for much of my life. I cannot make that decision here, at this minute, after a quart of whiskey."

"Julia?" AJ asked.

"I echo Charlie's reasoning."

"Julia, my gut tells me you are being used by Senator Cowel. If you are astute as the local gossip says, you have qualms also."

"But I want to be certain of what you are implying."

"Perhaps you don't want it to be true and will ignore the evidence. That's what the majority of the American people do today."

"I want to be sure about your view of SMS before I become a traitor to my country. But I don't like being thought of as you put it, 'a soul-sucking lobbyist whore,' and I do not, nor have I ever owned any fishnet stockings."

"Whoa. A few rounds of Maker's and 'Hawk Eye' starts talking trash," Charlie said. "Sure wish I could have been at yawl's meeting. Must have been juicy stuff."

"Charlie, I did not come across your name in any of the documentation on the crooked side of SMS."

"I want to know more, AJ. These are serious allegations. For me it is life-changing stuff."

"If evidence emerges tying either of you in SMS's ongoing effort to defraud the U.S. government, it's my job to ensure you are prosecuted to the fullest extent of the law. We are talking treason. One last question. Are you two a couple?"

"He's married," Julia fired off.

AJ chuckled, shaking his head.

"What's funny?" Charlie asked.

"Julia is naive enough to think marriage would be an obstacle to a relationship these days. A Bozeman girl."

Charlie leaned forward. "AJ, is this a personal vendetta to get revenge on Cowel for belittling your father?"

"At first, yes, but then I began to see the negative effects on our entire nation. These highly placed dogs are slowly destroying what's best about our country so they can benefit financially while controlling a dumbed-down and rootless people. There are powerful, highly placed men and women who are making a mockery of the U.S. Constitution and orchestrating foreign wars to turn a buck."

"A conspiracy theory comes out once a week," Julia said. "And the proof is always 'he said, she said.' But you are telling us you have proof."

AJ finished his drink. Charlie refilled.

"This is not just about a few corrupt fat cats. There is an inclination to abuse power at all levels of our government. Many of our elected representatives have no idea of what is good and what is evil. That 'everything is relative' crap is bringing down our nation. There is no truth, no freedom, no integrity anymore."

"Who cures this problem if the people in power are the problem?"

"The laws of our country. We wake the people up. This cancer is pervasive throughout our entire political system. This is the historical empire killer in action. The entire American government needs a collective enema."

Charlie whistled through his teeth. "Talk about WMDs."

"I'm serious."

"Where would we start cleaning house? Pun intended." Julia asked.

"With treason."

"We commit treason?" Charlie asked.

AJ frowned. "We go to the top. We grab the snake by its head. We find one treasonous act by a high-level official and we make an example of him or her. We start with SMS, Charlie, and follow the money."

"I'm bought and paid for," AJ said. "I do what I am told, do the best I can for others and myself, within the parameters I'm given."

"That sounds uncomfortably like my story also," Julia said. "How do we snare the prey?"

"With the U.S. Constitution."

"Why and how?" Julia asked

"Because it is based on natural law and the reason we've become the greatest nation in history."

Julia recited from memory. "The rational vision of how we can flourish as a society using the morals which are written on every man's heart."

Charlie and AJ looked duly impressed.

"Your girl here is not just another pretty face," AJ said.

"I'm not his girl and I can knock you flat on your ass yet again, Congressman."

"So, in summary," Charlie asked, hands open to AJ.

"In summary," Julia said, "Americans are fat and spoiled. You don't see this in the city, but on a farm when the pig or turkey is fattened up, it never bodes well for the pig or turkey."

"We are becoming a defenseless and rootless people by conspiracy, Charlie."

"So," AJ asked again, "are we going to 'hang separately or together,' as Ben Franklin asked of his fellow conspirators against English rule?"

Julia studied her whiskey. "As a country we are becoming an empty vessel. We are spoiled hypocrites. Is our nation worth saving?"

"When did you become so persuasive, AJ?"

"When my eyes were opened to the truth, buddy. American universities no longer train us to search for the truth. They're just high schools with ashtrays now. We're being socialized – trained to get in line and listen. The ideology is enforced by Hollywood and the media. The fat cats want a complacent people. Both of you need to look into SMS with your American souls and not with your career goals in mind," AJ cautioned. "Time is running out. The SMS big boys know about the investigation so I would assume both of you may be on SMS's radar. Remember, they are large enough and strong enough to take on whole countries. The three of us are just piss ants."

At that, the meeting ended. The participants parted cordially. The young woman who walked into the restaurant a few hours ago, proud of her career and service to her nation came away with severe doubts; events she did not fully understand were becoming clearer. The Wild West fisticuffs had been child's play next to the political and moral allegations raised. And then there was her career. Who or what ethic was she serving working for SMS? She now felt as if she had been chained to something,

something she could not run from; something that needed to be exposed to the light of day. She reminded herself of what it meant to be effective and efficient. Effective meant doing the right thing. Efficient meant doing it well. If what she heard tonight was fact, corrupt U.S. officials were efficiently sucking the wealth out of the pockets of the American and putting it into those of a few ultra-wealthy criminals and traitors. These men were parasites, living off an unknowing host. Like a cancer, it would devour all until it ultimately devoured itself. If true, Julia was helping them. This did not only affect her and her career and sense of duty to her nation, it affected everyone in the most powerful and just nation in the world.

Chapter 22

With the lingering twilight still illuminating the town of Puno, Bolivia, a single U.S. military Recon helicopter without a registered flight plan flew through the snow-capped Andes Mountains and entered the Altiplano, set high in the range at nearly 13,000 feet. Flying just above the water of the huge Lake Titicaca to avoid detection by radar, the copter slowed at the shore then hovered for a mere few seconds as a single shadowy figure lowered by a cable from the belly of the chopper detached the instant boots hit ground. The silent war-bird turned and lifted, disappearing into the twilight sky as its passenger ran off to his predetermined destination.

Puno was a thriving black market town. The outskirts were nearly barren, populated by subsistent herders and shepherds who lived off the llamas and alpacas for food and fur. The terrain reminded James Smith of Iraq. He carried enough Bolivian currency to bribe half the town if needed. His target was a Bolivian army general who was an obstacle to his organization's plans. Smith had over thirty scenarios in his head ranging from a surprise attack by the Bolivian army to a bystander noticing his kill. He would elude the army after a fire fight, circle them, and then continue on his mission. In the case of a bystander, Smith would make him or her appear to be the general's murderer. Once in Madrid he bribed a bystander with cash to leave and pretend to have seen nothing. Then, in perfect dialectic Spanish, Smith phoned the local police, reported the murder and gave a description of the witness. Who would believe a man with pockets stuffed with cash, fingered by a witness, albeit unidentified, with an assassination tale?

Although Smith was in his element and lived for this thrill-jockey work, he had no idea why the general was to be eliminated without suspicion of a hit. This would not be a murder for statement to elicit fear but a subtle execution to extinguish a fly in the ointment. He could not have been prouder if he had known this was the first action on Bolivian soil to ensure an invasion, soon to be unfolded slowly and sold to the American people as a just war to put down tyrants and prevent WMDs in South America. The process would begin with propaganda specialists, experts in South American politics, feeding the American media with rumors of an antagonistic Bolivian government and growing concern of military action against the poor and the disenfranchised Bolivian people.

Within a few years American soldiers would have boots on the ground on Bolivian soil. SMS would plan and build the roads for the empire to the north's troops to move troops and supplies and for barracks to be built, ammunition to be sold and stored. The support structure for war was incredibly complex and incredibly costly for the U.S. taxpayer. And incredibly lucrative for SMS. And ultimately, the Mob.

Chapter 23

A week after Julia's wild meeting at the 1789 with Charlie and Congressman AJ Morales, she pecked hard at her cell phone.

"Charlie, it's Julia. Are you on a speaker phone?"

"No. Why?"

"Because your god-damned friend, Morales, just subpoenaed me to a congressional hearing. And I have not had enough time to—"

"Julia, listen to me. Our CEO at SMS, Tyrell Landecker, died last night. I'm told it was a heart attack. The guy was forty-two and ran marathons."

"What are you saying, Charlie?"

"Remember I told you that lately he had been preoccupied and seemed to be under a lot of stress?"

"Yes, I do."

"Well, it was the congressional investigation, for certain."

"How do you know that?"

"Because the SMS board of directors has just invited me to an emergency meeting."

"How can that be? They are all over the damn world. It can't work that fast."

"I've been asked to meet them tonight and discuss a congressional indictment as well as my possible new role at SMS."

"Too much for coincidence."

"There's more. I had a friend here, an expert in accounting, dig into the SMS charity foundation I head. The funds do not go to our wounded warriors for rehab but to some as-yet-unknown corporation that looks like a dummy setup."

"The real funds are being funneled somewhere else?"

"Yes, and I think we would both guess where they go."

"Are you in danger?"

"Nothing big yet. I called my father about the investigation and my own digging and though he played his cards close to his chest he assured me not to worry."

"That's good. If anything ever happened to you..."

"Right now I'm married to the Mob because of my estranged wife. I will not bring children into the world with a Mafia princess. I know U.S. senators who are lifelong family friends. I am assuming they would help me by telling to keep my mouth shut or else. I think I am in for an oral exam tonight."

"This is coming to a head very quickly."

"Which is probably why AJ moved on you so quickly with the subpoena. He's telling the thugs 'hands off.'"

"We're culpable. And even not knowing all the dirt we'll look like fools."

"Let me dig into this, Julia."

"Charlie, will this make you a corporate spy?"

"I am not sure. We need to get off our cell phones and get some of those Wal-Mart contract phones. If these people are who AJ says they are, they will have state-of-the-art surveillance equipment and the people who know how to use it. Bye!"

Julia refilled her wine glass while looking out of her bedroom window toward Reagan International Airport and the Washington Monument. This was becoming more than hearsay, gossip, or cheap shots. She reviewed how she felt when she first received a letter from Parker Cowel, U.S. Senator for Montana, complimenting her efforts as a citizen, and her volunteer efforts. With her senior year begun, she was already looking for colleges, thinking of majors, wondering what path to take for a career. Family income limited her choices, even though her grades and SAT scores were top notch. She did not hail from a competitive school district, and was not a stand-out when compared to the best and the brightest. But here was a letter telling her she did stand out. *And if you are considering a career in serving your country...* it read. Julia remembered considering for the first time a career of service to her nation. She loved helping others, the feeling of being part of the next generation to serve the noble causes of America. The caveat here was *a meeting to discuss further opportunities* with a United States senator.

In no time at all it seemed she found herself an incoming freshman at the United States Military Academy at West Point, New York, overlooking the Hudson River. The students and alumni, known as the Long Gray Line, included Ulysses S. Grant, Dwight D. Eisenhower, Jefferson Davis; Generals Pershing, MacArthur, Patton, Abrams, Westmorland, Schwarzkopf. More than seventy Medal of Honor winners attended class here. And here stood Julia Abbott. A free ride, compliments of Senator Parker Cowel. She landed in Iraq as a 2nd lieutenant where she learned to lead by example, taking responsibility for those who served under her. The difficulty of balancing the goal of a mission against the protection of the lives of her men weighed heavily on her shoulders. Then her final action in Iraq came to her. While the confusion was extreme and her memory lacking in parts, the faces of those two boys came to her yet again; those innocent ghosts that haunted her. She had been right to choose her men and herself over the lives of the two images.

But how could she have avoided that confrontation? It was still going on there and in other places. The horror of war was the guilt it instilled in so many. She remembered waking up in the hospital with Senator Cowel there, comforting her, playing down the death of the boys to happenstance and their own faults and "that's war, Julia." She saw herself today, a high-powered lobbyist for the senator, and her fingers in the inner working of the country she loved.

What if I am a patsy?

Maybe she was a naive little girl, a gofer for a powerful man who orchestrated the murder of children for the profit of a few. What if so many innocent boys and girls were dying and getting maimed for immoral reasons, the scheming of men who lusted for money? *What if the American Dream is dead and we are no longer blessed, no longer a people of faith, hope and love?*

"That just better not be the case, Senator Cowel," she said aloud, fists balled, knuckles white.

Chapter 24

Charles Prendergast deplaned from the SMS corporate jet and entered the limo sent to summon him to his meeting with the SMS board of directors. It had been a rocky flight from D.C. to Lexington as gusting winds from a major storm front battered the light plane left and right and air pockets sent the jet into temporary freefall – along with his stomach. This did not bode well for his meeting. An omen. This would be his moment to stand and deliver. He thought of the Great and Powerful Oz and how the Scarecrow reacted with bandy legs. He tried to relate it to throwing a football in a clutch situation without knowing how the defensive plan would evolve. But for sure – both the linemen and SMS were all about testing Charlie under pressure. Football and politics were in a sense mirror images of one another – stealth, compromise, being fast on your feet, never showing your opponent your true goal, the game always changing. A nagging quote from his college days rose up from who knows where. "Just because you do not take an interest in politics doesn't mean politics won't take an interest in you!"

The hearse-like limo pulled into a secluded winding driveway, and although the sun had set, the sodium lighting from above revealed a security fence, replete with vigilant guards who asked for Charlie's driver's license and confirmed the picture and details. When nodded on the driver continued to the front entrance and opened Charlie's door. Charlie looked for a sign hanging above the entryway that said, "Abandon all hope ye who enter here," but there were just heavy limestone blocks, making the door seem like the entrance to a vault. His arrival was orchestrated to a tee; slick as a whistle. A non-imposing balding man extended his arm, the classic butler with an open palm inviting Charlie through the matching and formidable oaken doors and into a foyer that was built to impress. Cherry wood, plush red carpeting, steel and brass armor from various periods on the walls, oil paintings of famous battles, the conquering heroes all looking as if ordained by God for conquest.

Despite his efforts to keep his briefcase, the butler smiled good-naturedly and mouthed "Not allowed" and Charlie entered a candlelit room.

Nobody expects the Spanish Inquisition.

"Right on time as always," Charlie heard a familiar voice announce. "And I guran-damn-teed it."

Senator Parker Cowel (R, MT), leaned back comfortably in a high-back red leather chair, hands folded over his belly. While he had not seen the senator for some time, the familiar inviting smile was there but Charlie now had qualms about what lay behind that mask. Whoever he would be facing tonight, would not be men to respect for their accomplishments but rather a slithering pack of pit vipers to steer clear of. But tonight Charlie had no choice.

What you believe shapes you.

"Good evening, Senator, it has been some time. It's lovely to see you."

The senator's expression changed just enough to show Charlie he got the wry humor and while pointing to a seat near the head of a large wooden table.

"Charlie, to my left is Senator W.C. 'Billy' Kiddenly, retired, from the great state of Texas."

"Uncle Billy, it's been a long time since we've talked, also." Charlie nodded. The senator simply peered through his short glasslike spectacles and forced the edges of his lips upward a few millimeters, his oversized head somehow too weighty for his body.

"To Billy's left is Senator Buford Ebers, Senate Majority Leader, from the great state of Indiana."

Again Charlie nodded, this time to the famous sourpuss from New Albany, who looked like he habitually sucked on lemons, with no visible reply. This intense and demanding senator was always in the news, criticizing someone, making dire predictions if his recommendations were not followed, or browbeating his opponents or one of their bills. Without his "show-time makeup" the flickering candlelight made his eyes look sunk into his head, his cheeks hollow, giving Charlie the impression of an animated corpse.

I just hope I'm not the dead man walking.

"Consider tonight your chance to graduate to the big league or sink back into the rat race," the corpse said, with his characteristic threatening rasp. From out of the shadows to Charlie's right, the head of Nicola Scozzari moved into the light. His thinning long hair was combed straight back, dyed an unnatural shade of red; his face was long, his lips somehow uneven and curled, his skin yellowed from age and bile. His expression was that of a man who terminally smelled a foul odor in the room. His neck was deeply furrowed, with flesh like folds in heavy drapes disappearing into a $500 silk shirt. He wore a bright red tie and a vest to match his $3,000 tailored suit.

Charlie swallowed instinctually as the full force of his estranged father-in-law's black serpent-like eyes rested on him. While they had spoken several times in the last few months over the phone, less a conversation than an interrogation, he had not seen his father-in-law in person for nearly two years. All of the conversations had been about Antonia – Charlie's estranged wife and Nicola's daughter.

Memories of his wedding came to Charlie. The no-expense-spared event where money was evident in every detail. Charlie's mother called it a complete lack of taste where elegance had taken the night off. Nicola and his wife and Admiral Prendergast met formally and emotionless. The three reminded Charlie of magnets that repelled – the closer you brought them together the harder it became to do so. There was little celebration that captured the spirit of the event; a polite tolerance reigned. He remembered his mother's hurt and puzzled look and read her mind.

What the hell are you thinking, Charlie, marrying this girl?

Antonia was not a picture of the innocent virgin bride wrapped in white and veiled until the marriage vows were completed. But she was stunningly beautiful, glowing. Her plunging neckline, figure-hugging bodice and the nearly waist-high slit in her wedding dress showed off her physical assets. A former Miss Texas, the show rigged ala Nicola, was getting married. They made a stunning couple. Superman, god from another planet; Venus, goddess of love. The U.S. Navy meets the Mafia.

On the groom's side of the DMZ sat a significant portion of the power elite of Washington. In a sense, they brought the U.S.S. Enterprise to the table. The American war machine. On the bride's side were the loan sharks, drug dealers, the distribution channels, the enforcers, booze, gambling and prostitution. The American wedding of the future. Charlie imagined everyone on Antonia's side was packing a handgun. He figured if he had thrown a firecracker onto the dance floor, the room would have erupted into a replay of Normandy beach in 1944.

His father, the admiral, was in full formal dress whites. His mother in an elegant cobalt-blue gown that only a French girl could find and wear. Benedetta, Antonia's mother, looked as if the bloom had gone off the rose and then the rose caught fire. Too tanned, too much leathery skin, too much bling. Too little taste.

Charlie realized that day he was caught in a bear trap he willingly put his foot into. Antonia's beauty would quickly fade. She was not fit to raise children. So there would be none. She would shop the best stores and drink white wine. He would golf or sail. This was somehow a mini-replay of that night.

Sitting in the room with these four chilled Charlie's blood. Senator Cowel headed the U.S. Foreign Relations Committee and held sway over the Appropriations Committee. This was the secret of SMS. Cowel could spark a war and encourage Congress into paying for it. Senator Kiddenly ran the influential political-action committee collecting numerous IOUs via veiled but polite threats from his yacht usually anchored in Houston. Senator Ebers was the current U.S. Senate Majority Leader. And finally, Charlie's father-in-law, Nicola Scozzari, the puppet master of SMS.

I'm like a quail hiding in the brush. If I attempt to fly, four shotguns will lock onto me. Better to wallow in the scrub than sleep with the fishes. I deserve this crap.

"Bourbon?" Senator Cowel asked.

"Sounds good," Charlie replied.

"It's in Nicola's hideaway liquor cabinet. There – just push that button on the left side, and the whole unit will slide out."

Charlie complied, and every gesture was magnified a hundred times with complete silence in the room and all eyes on him. Summoned from the salt mines to retrieve his own drink was probably akin to bowing before his betters. These men knew where every skeleton in every D.C. closet was buried and probably had pictures. They were well-versed at getting their way. Charlie knew he could not dance his way out of this meeting, which was no meeting at all and promised to be an interrogation.

Back at his seat, he had enough time for one sip before round one began.

"My daughter and you haven't hit it off, Charlie," Nicola said. "She was raised to be a princess, and you can't control her."

"Can you?" Charlie replied, hoping his defiant attitude was the right strategy. No reply. "If it is any consolation to you, sir, I tried. I honestly tried."

"Try harder."

"Is this the time and place to discuss our personal family matters?"

"Why do you think you're here?"

They will see through a lie immediately.

"There's a congressional task force set up to investigate SMS."

"What else?" Nicola demanded.

"Tyrell Landecker is dead. I assume he had both knowledge of and contact with said task force."

"Go on," Nicola said.

Charlie felt like a rat in a trap. Nicola and his cohorts were no idiots. He had to reveal what he suspected. This was the reigning Super Bowl champion team of liars.

"It seems a stretch to me that Tyrell has a heart attack just after news of the task force came out. First, a congressional task force doesn't go after a for-profit corporation unless they have both suspicions and substantial evidence of wrongdoing."

"What do you suspect we are being investigated for?"

"Defrauding the U.S. government of billions of dollars through warmongering and money laundering."

"And?"

"Second, it's reasonable to assume that, as CEO, Tyrell knew much more than the average SMS employee. Third, if he was approached by them, they would have threatened him to testify, or else. Over the last month, he must have lost fifteen pounds and looked pale as a sheet. Something was eating at him. If he made the wrong decision as to which path to take, he needed to be—"

"Disposed of," Nicola said.

There it was. His suspicions confirmed. Tyrell had been murdered. He had decided to work with the Feds. And that means that SMS was indeed dirty. Charlie took a drink to relieve dry mouth. It didn't work. He took a deep breath to help keep his voice from trembling as he spoke. "Which means Tyrell has to be immediately replaced with some patsy; someone who knows nothing of the inner workings of SMS and cannot do any damage in testimony before a formal congressional investigation. Someone who is loyal to the SMS team. Yet someone who could pass a lie-detector test convincingly."

"Someone with plausible deniability," Ebers whispered.

"Do I get a bullet proof vest or will you boys throw me to the wolves unarmed."

Senator Cowel's faux laughter broke the tension. "Well said, Charlie. We'll be with you all the way. Most of us think this is just a fishing trip for the FBI and a Texas congressman with an ax to grind. Your father-in-law is not so sure."

"What do they have? At least give me that."

"You've lost contact with your former football roommate, AJ Morales, correct?" Senator Ebers demanded.

Charlie gained time by taking another sip of bourbon. This question made his heart pound and his hands chilled.

"We did lose touch."

"If memory serves, he declined to participate in the NFL draft and joined the Air Force some years ago."

"That's how I heard it."

"What could cause a man to—"

"He and I got into a fight over Antonia."

"So it's bad blood over sex?" Nicola hissed.

"Over a woman. We did run into each other last week. Apparently, he got into politics."

"This is an odd coincidence," Nicola said. "AJ Morales is now Congressman Morales representing an Austin district in Texas. He also heads the subcommittee investigating SMS. Some of my longtime opponents have taken him under their wing. Now you run into him after four years of bad blood between you."

"What can I say? Maybe he saw my name on the SMS executive list and decided to look me up. Maybe he wanted to know about Antonia."

"Did you mention SMS to him?"

"I think I mentioned to him in passing that I work on the charity side of the business or perhaps he asked me what my role was."

"And your response?"

"I did tell him I fund accounts that are supposed to be in support of rehabilitation of our wounded warriors. I did not tell him they are dummy corporations, which funnel the money right back into SMS. Where exactly, I can only speculate."

"You are as sharp as a tack, Mr. Prendergast, yet unsure about which of you mentioned SMS first." This was the first time Senator Kiddenly entered the conversation. Staring down his thick glasses it felt to Charlie as if he were under a microscope and could hide nothing under the magnification.

"I had dinner with one of Senator Cowel's lobbyists. The senator even set up the meeting but could not attend at the last minute. The lobbyist was supposed to be prepped by me to explain SMS in detail and show we're squeaky clean. The lobbyist asked for a second meeting to defend SMS against some loose-cannon congressman and AJ Morales showed up."

"I'll confirm I set up the meeting," Senator Cowel said. "Julia Abbott. Just high-level PR stuff. But how is it that Morales shows up right then?"

There was no way Charlie was going to implicate Julia in this, even though she had invited AJ not knowing that there was a history between the two men.

"We met at the 1789, one of the most popular restaurants in D.C. It's frequented by politicians. Morales *is* a politician. When he saw me, he insulted my family. I punched him in the face. We made a sizeable scene. Check it out."

"Something smells," Nicola said. "I got a nose for shit, particularly Texas bullshit, right Senator Billy?"

"I'll run Charlie's story by my new lobbyist," Senator Cowel offered.

"I've no patience with he said/she said crap. Let's get to the heart of the matter," Senator Ebers said.

Charlie noted that Senator Kiddenly was nodding off – having trouble keeping his head up. Charlie remembered him seeming old when Charlie was a boy.

What kept this guy going? Watching rats like me, caught in a trap, squirm?

"Nicola," Charlie said, using his father-in-law's first name for the first time. "I am married to your daughter; I've known senators Cowel and Kiddenly all my life. They are friends of my father. I need to know what I am up against. You've seen me on the football field and know how I handle pressure. I am not a quitter. Who are you people really?"

"Do you know what a Guinea is, son-in-law?"

Charlie shook his head, exasperated.

Chapter 25

"Wop, Dago, Gumba?"

"Slang word for Italians," Charlie replied.

"In my father's day the Limeys, Micks and Krauts ran all the large cities. Heroes to the people 'cuz they promised a chicken in every pot. That image meant wealth. If you could eat chicken, it meant you had plenty others to produce eggs. So we were given two choices – the Democrat or Republican. Both assured the Italians they were friends. We got the table scraps while the politicians got the beef steak. And when it came to money, the Micks forgave their English politician brothers for starving a million of their ancestors in Ireland. Blood is thicker than water, but gold is thicker than blood. The Italians here in America, the lowest of the low, were cheated, then forgotten. So we imported a society from our homeland. *La Cosa Nostra. Our thing.* You know the story?"

"The Mafia," Charlie replied. "A criminal syndicate, mostly preying on their own people – extortion, gambling, prostitution, and such."

"My grandfather was a common laborer when he came here. My grandmother washed his one shirt and a pair of pants every night. He went to work clean every morning. When his hands got deep cracks in them from constant shoveling, my grandmother poured candle wax into the crevices. He had to work. No choice. No healthcare. No time off. My father saw all this. My father was a business man. He hooked up with neighborhood Italians who protected each other. They took care of each other, made money, and invested it back into the community. One day a Mick kid, just out of some expensive dental school, came to my father and asked for a loan to buy the equipment he needed to yank teeth, so he could open his own business. He said he'd offer free care on Saturday for everyone in our neighborhood. My father gave him the money. The deal had a competitive interest rate. Free care to the locals was a win-win deal. They shook on it."

"After the first then the second payment didn't come through, my father visited the dentist in his lovely new office that had three rooms, and a secretary and a nurse. The dentist said he wasn't going to pay. Told my father there was no paperwork so my father could not prove the loan was made. That night somebody mugged the dentist on his way home, extracted two of his teeth with pliers. Back payments were made next day and regular payments after that. The dentist also gave a generous donation to the local church for a new boiler."

"I hope the Church made Nicola senior a saint," Charlie said.

"This isn't a time to be smug, Charlie," Senator Cowel said. "Your wife could end up a widow tonight."

I'm in a meeting with the Dark Lord and Darth Vader.

"None of the politicians nor the lawyers, judges or police would help the Italians. We learned the lesson that we had to help ourselves. America was like everywhere else – the strong survive and prevail. The American Dream was supposed to be a road to riches and prosperity. We had to get our share with or without the law on our side."

"So you threw equality for everyone under the law out the window."

"Law is the ugly shadow of justice," Nicola said.

Senator Ebers leaned his elbows on the table. "These days everybody in America is special, has unlimited rights, cheats on their taxes. It's taxes that keeps us afloat. They are a must. We run American like a business. And as they say here in Kentucky, y'all with us or agin us?"

"Senator Ebers, are you telling me the men in this room are attempting to control our country politically?"

"Politically?" Nicola said in a raised voice. "I am neither a Democrat nor a Republican, a liberal or conservative. Politics is simply a tool. I am incredibly wealthy. So it's not about politics. It is about economics."

"The people want our money, Charlie," Senator Kiddenly said, suddenly animated as if this theme was his utmost concern. "They bitch about me cruising around the Gulf. Know why? Jealousy. Envy. They want what I have. They want what they were never smart enough or strong enough to accumulate. Wealth. Power. So they deserve nothing."

"Charlie," Senator Cowel added, "having millions is one thing. Keeping it is another. I am not going to let a wealth distribution regime or administration hand out my money to the riffraff. And accordingly I am not going to allow congress to make decisions in world politics which would negatively affect my holdings here or in Europe and Asia. And there are billionaires all over the world who are like-minded in this goal. Our business comes first. We have vested interests."

Nicola grunted. "The people are sheep. We are the shepherds. As the saying goes, 'Do the shepherds share their plans with the sheep?'"

Next up, Senator Ebers. "We're telling you things have changed since the U.S. Constitution was ratified and that damn petrified pile of naive intentions keeps us from protecting our own interests. The people are stupid, self-serving, hypocrites. They have enough. More than their share. They will never be happy and do not even deserve 'the pursuit of happiness.' The American people have become spoiled and are now unpredictable and a liability to our business interests."

"So it's the rise of the Second Estate," Charlie offered.

"Meaning?" Cowel asked.

"The nobility. Aristocrats. Obscenely privileged families where sons follow fathers to rule. Where merit is not rewarded, only bloodlines." Charlie was no longer in the mood to make light of something with a one liner or childish sarcasm. This conversation was more than stupid without his foolery.

These dumb shits believe this crap.

It was Kiddenly's shot at the one-two punch as he wiped clean his heavy eyeglasses with a handkerchief. "Once the people in a democracy catch on that they can get handouts from their government, the government is finished. We babysit a nation of deluded fools that can vote for whatever ninny they want in office and with just a simple majority. It is a recipe for disaster. We had to step in long ago."

Cowel took over from Kiddenly who seemed to be running out of breath. "Men like these in this room have come together to help avoid the bloody riots, and the harsh authority needed to stop the riots dead in their tracks. We keep the people in the blissful ignorance they deserve. You're a Harvard boy, Charlie. That's our school, and so is Yale. It's for ours alone. It was difficult to get through, wasn't it? You were not allowed to just drink beer, party and spawn day and night like they do at all the other schools."

"I studied plenty at UT."

"You were bred to be responsible. But most of the others drank and screwed their way through four years of fluff courses while listening to ghetto music. Artificial noise. They didn't learn much. Got out into the real world and found they couldn't compete. Couldn't get jobs. Didn't learn shit in college. Now the whiny buggers want their college loans excused. They want their fellow taxpayer to foot the bill for their sloth and decadence."

"Are people that bad?" Charlie asked his uncle.

"Most are greedy fools with two thoughts; one from their belly, the other from their crotches. The country is in a terrible mess. The 'baby boomers' lead the charge. Their arteries and hearts are clogged with fat. They take pills to mask all the symptoms. They have operations to change out old parts for new ones – new hearts, new lungs, new everything. The doctors prey on them like flies on shit. The medical costs are astronomical. And they want the government to pay for their health care. Lazy cocksuckers. Time to die. And they demand their social-security payments and pensions. All that money is long gone. So we do it through wealth transfer from the young to the elderly to avoid riots. We need more taxpayers. We need younger people to work. We need more consumers, so they buy shit. The damn people have aborted 50 mill babies since it was made legal. That's 50 mill fewer taxpayers. So we limit then gradually reduce what the Medicare boomers can get. We limit the costly heart and cancer operations. It saves the nation money and gets the boomers off the planet quicker. We put the wetbacks into those vacated jobs, keep them in ghettos, and they help fund social medicine. We lose some of our young to war. They have to be replaced. That's responsible economics."

"What about personal dignity and equality under the law? I believe in God."

"So does Satan," Nicola shot back with an expression implying he knew the devil himself.

"God holds each of us accountable for our actions."

"Which is why we must break free of him. Religion is an idea long past its time. We let the people know that it is okay to sin. There ain't no God, so there ain't no hell. It's all about nature. We'll surpass her. Man is in control. And those with power reign over our herd. Money, prestige, entertainment and sex. And we distribute the new order through the global media. Everything from cartoons for the rug rats to TV commercials and the news through today's music and Hollywood films."

Charlie shivered as Nicola's eyes almost glowed, his hands painting an illusion in the thin air; as he whispered a vision.

"You sit in pitch-black halls, the bright light of the silver screen appears up front, like God, and we speak from heaven, teach you what to think and how to behave."

"And with a few titties here and there to hold your attention," Kiddenly added.

"And if the natives get restless, give them bread and circuses. One of my Italian ancestors thought that up. Nero burned Rome in the name of urban renewal and blamed then burned the Christians for it. The public sucked it up."

"So we are just clever apes."

"Want to know a secret about wealth that only the wealthy know? Money doesn't make you happy. Too much sex becomes boring. Too much booze and drugs become addictive and kills you. The people don't get this, or rather, don't want to get it. So we protect them. Just enough. We turn the spigot off or on as needed."

"So why play your game even if huge war profits can't make you happy?"

"War *is* life and life *is* war. We are constantly at war with ourselves – reason and emotion, locked in a lifelong struggle."

Nicola rose quickly and leaned over toward Charlie. Charlie hid most of his shock, but it was noticed.

"As for what makes me happy, and it is delicious, is getting my way. I tell. Others listen. I want. Others give. I orchestrate. Everybody plays to my tempo. That is power. Power buys control. And all of us in this room exert control. We are asking you to join us and rule the world; the world made up of billions of pathetic losers who deserve their fate. Might makes right."

Cowel sighed, and Charlie wondered if the senator was tiring of teaching an ape. "By sacrificing a few we prevent the death of millions. It's simple math."

"And SMS? How—"

"Think of SMS as a foreign war logistics and infrastructure cash cow," Ebers offered. "We use the profits to guide and sometimes prod powerful groups and people along the right path. We know what is best for them."

"We help the people make up their minds by giving them what they need and not what they think they want," Senator Kiddenly added.

"You repeat something in the media often enough and it is believed, it becomes the truth," Nicola said. "Every kid on the planet has a smart phone plugged into his head. The crap they play turns their brains to mush. The movies do the same thing. We guide the people just like a teacher does it in the school room. We decide what is beneficial, we endorse proper behavior."

"What about individual freedoms, the right to choose, personal responsibility and integrity?" Charlie asked.

"Look around you tomorrow. Do the people you see in the streets genuinely deserve the freedom they have? They've turned it into a search for immediate gratification. We supply the drugs, the prostitutes, the technical toys, the Hollywood movies, telling them it is fashionable to be irresponsible. We encourage the merry-go-round whirling lifestyle where there is no time to think between the hunt for the next thrilling immediate gratification. We break up the nuclear family and that puts 300 million bodies drifting in space. We do not want groups confronting us. We want black against white, gay against straight, liberal against conservative, male against female. Each alone. No God, no sin. Everything is permitted."

"Enough of this!" Nicola demanded. "Here it is in a nutshell, junior. America has not been a democracy for some time. It is no longer a constitutional republic. Look around this room. We own the Senate, the House, the judged. We control education, the news media, and entertainment. We run the corporations, control the military, industry and the unions. All production of goods and services and distribution flow through us. You work for us, Charlie boy. You have no rights; you will soon have no guns, no input. Rioting mobs with guns are an obscenity and costly to suppress. We want tax payers, not tax eaters. No Boomers! No Internet! No Guns! No Freedom! Just shut up and we'll take care of you, or else. You are already slaves to debt. Wait until you taste hunger. You'll come around quickly. A government is not moral. It simply serves the interest of those in power. And we are in power. Do you have any questions for us?"

This guy reminds me of Colonel Kurtz from 'Apocalypse Now.' I'm starting to hear Jim Morrison singing 'The End' in the background. I'm in the god damn Twilight Zone.

"Decide which team you want to play on, Charlie."

"My mother has often reminded me that what we believe shapes us. So be sure you know what you believe and why."

"Your point?"

"You said most Americans believe in tolerance for Satan himself. Have you ever stopped to think that you might be Satan?"

Chapter 26

While Julia waited anxiously for a call from Charlie, a thousand scenarios ran through her head. In one, Charlie was found floating in a river. In another, he accepted the SMS CEO position and went over to the Dark Side.

A text message from her cell phone brought her back to reality. It was from AJ, telling her to call one Marjorie Golden and a phone number with a Texas area code followed.

The name brought back memories. Not the best of memories. Cheerleading practice back in high school. Julia and Marjorie were diametrically opposed on the goal of cheerleading. To Julia it was school spirit; for Marjorie, it boarded on exotic dance. Why would AJ have this girl's phone number? She sat back on her sofa and continued to nurse a red Zin and some garlicky crackers – her version of dinner. Curiosity got the best of her, and she dialed the number, not knowing what to expect. Why an Austin, Texas number when Marjorie was from her hometown of Bozeman?

"Marjorie?"

"Who's calling, please?"

"Julia. Julia Abbott?"

"Now there's a name from the past. How did you ever get this number?"

"From Congressman AJ Morales, a good friend."

"Ah," Marjorie said. "I was hoping to rattle a few cages with regards to benefits. Lord only knows how the request came to you, and I'm sure I am the last person you want to speak with."

"Not at all. It's good to hear your voice. When I saw your name on my phone, I immediately recalled petty cat fights filled with tender emotions. While I was sure I had the moral high ground back then, today I realize I was a naïve girl trying to get my way at your expense."

Marjorie let out a gasp. "I see a prim and proper Julia making slutty Marjorie furious because of your popularity, your grades, and your even-headedness."

"Well, aren't we a pair," Julia laughed.

"I had a great body back then, pert boobs and great legs."

"You did. I bet you still have great legs."

"No. I left them in the desert in Afghanistan."

"What?"

"I joined the Army two months after you. I was in country for only three months and stepped on a mine and woke up legless."

"Oh, Marjorie. That is horrible."

"You passed by me on Main Street in your parade. I had a little flag. I was proud of you."

"Why didn't you—"

"I did nothing. You were a hero. The parade was richly deserved."

"We need to get together soon, Marjorie. I'll tell you just how pathetic a hero I was. I killed two teenage boys. I won the Congressional Medal of Honor because of political shenanigans. I'm ashamed over the whole thing."

"I live in Austin now with my mother. It was she who actually called Congressman Morales."

"What about. Can I help?"

"I would feel embarrassed asking you anything after the way I treated you back in high school."

"We both got our wounds in, didn't we? Shoot."

"I want to keep my baby."

"Why on earth couldn't you. Your spouse—"

"I didn't marry. He was my boyfriend. We planned to marry when he came home. Army too. He came home on leave, we planned the wedding, went back to serve, somehow I got pregnant and he came home in a box two months ago."

"What can I do? I don't understand about the baby."

"I'm not getting fair treatment. There's shrapnel in my lower abdomen. It's supposed to be removed, but I can't even get an appointment at the VA for another three months."

"The baby?"

"I'm in the last trimester. The drugs they give me to mask the pain, they, they can affect the baby inside me. It hurts so bad to stay off of them, but I want to keep my baby. I will not risk its life."

"I will help you. How are your new legs?"

"Never got them. I'm in a wheelchair. It's motorized. The VA paid for everything."

"Marjorie, why are you not getting the care you deserve? You fought for our country. Your man died for it. This is a travesty."

"Julia, I don't know a senator like you do. My mom thought that Morales—"

"Between he and I we will get to the bottom—"

"The VA is great. Great doctors, nurses, staff, support. It's just that they are overwhelmed. The wounded are two deep in the halls. I'm told no money is coming from Washington. They are doing the best they can. Not their fault."

Julia did not attempt to hold back her tears. "Oh God, Marjorie. I will take care of this with AJ. I will be at your child's first birthday party. We can talk war wounds. Please trust me."

Both women were crying now. They said goodbye as best they could. Julia finished off her glass and the rest of the bottle before calling AJ.

"Thank you for that text, AJ."

"Then I did the right thing?"

"My turn to send you roses."

"Don't. People will talk. When I saw Ms. Golden's background info I thought you might know her and a call from a friend might help."

"AJ, Charlie has discovered that the charity end of SMS is just a sham for more profits to get laundered and land back at their own front door."

"I can believe that."

"It has affected me personally. While I got the finest treatment possible due to Senator Cowel's pull, a school friend lost her both legs in Afghanistan as well as losing her boyfriend, and is only asking for help to ensure her unborn child survives."

AJ could only gasp.

"Can you please get the best doctor you know in Austin over to Marjorie's house now to help her? I will pay for everything. Then I want to work with you on taking down SMS and every corrupt politician in Washington."

"Welcome to the team, Hawk Eye. Now if we can only get Charlie to see the light."

Chapter 27

Charles Prendergast III was quiet and oblivious to the scenery during the limo ride back to Lexington Airport, his flight back to Reagan International's private aircraft terminal ninety-five minutes later, and the ride in another SMS limo to his D.C. condo. His entire life had changed as he listened to Alexander and Pharaoh and Caesar and Napoleon and Hitler, and Stalin and Mao directly from the horse's mouths.

The arrogance of a few self-anointed kings, full-blown megalomaniacs, confident they know better than an entire nation. That people are inherently sheep in the fields, wanting to be led, looking for security, guarantees, predictability. Dear God! What a bunch of self-delusional dogs. They are sucking the life blood from America's very soul; crushing our spirit; convincing us we are unworthy, rotten to the core.

Multinational corporations, essentially the banking, mortgage and insurance companies who keep us all in debt up to our ying yangs have taken over America. They do it by dumbing down the people and leading us by the noses to be dependent on our government. I thought The Body Snatchers *was damn scary. But 'The Soul Snatchers' is a horrible thing. Democracy is a threat to these shysters. A republic, giving a written constitution, a measure of individual human dignity is Kryptonite to them. So the constitution must go. Soon I will not have the freedom to choose right from wrong. Big Brother will make that decision for me. It will not be about right or wrong but about economic and political expediency based on the profits of a powerful few.*

A powerful group in the CIA has our troops in Afghanistan protecting the poppy fields. AJ asserts this. They harvested poppies, produced opium, then refined it into cocaine and heroin there, and the CIA has carte blanche to bring it to our shores. The Mafia goons have an extensive nationwide distribution network, probably in with the Mexican and Russian and a few other drug cartels and their gofers sell the drugs to our kids. Hook them. God damn the pusher. Dependency increases, theft for drug money increases, more crime, and girls prostitute themselves for their daily hits.

The rich get rich, and the poor get poorer. This is a whopping nontaxable income moving along the distribution system. The money ends up with the Wall Street types who launder it through financial organizations where everybody gets his cut. SMS builds the war machine by building infrastructure and selling munitions in one war after the other. All the cash flows into the hands of the mighty few at the expense of the American taxpayer. Shit, if I ever have grandkids, they are already saddled with a lifetime of war debt mixed with the stock-market fraud bailout and the housing-bubble collapse. What a legacy I'm leaving. I'm selling out family I don't even have yet into economic slavery.

My choice now is to side with the 300 million deeply-in-debt people, working harder and harder to pay an ever-increasing debt and never really getting out of the hole – or join the greedy bastards, the parasites that live off of our labor. A master or a slave, Charlie Prendergast? Are most of us simply cattle in a field, chewing our cud? A republic is a government of laws, not men. So bye bye republic. It's coming. Unless something is done and done quickly.

We continue to grant these bastards authority in our political and economic lives. Even in our educational system. They don't educate us anymore, they socialize us. This political-correctness crap, this equality mania is a strategy of control. Equality must be enforced. This destroys our freedom. It's a tool of control. Americans are asking for more security and that means more government control. And who actually owns the government? The people? No. The multinational oligarchy. A global-archy. It's the House of Hapsburg back from the dead.

Our entire political and economic system needs an enormous enema. Our constitution, our very culture, has been hijacked! The entire soul of a nation. Life, liberty and the pursuit of happiness has been replaced with "It's business," as a motto, all in support of short-term profits for the few. American is not for sale. It has been sold. War for profit must be incredibly lucrative. Use the American peoples' army, its patriotic *young citizens to fight and the U.S. taxpayer foots the bill. Importing drugs must come in second; unlimited customer demand. No record of transactions, no taxes, no receipts, no returns.*

When did truth become the enemy? It was when the greedy began perverting our people with deception and trickery. It was when we stopped being a nation of laws and became a nation of lawyers. It was when Affirmative Action gave advantage to some and discriminated against others. We institutionalized racism. Men in power now manipulate laws for personal power; favored grants and not objective rights.

The hollow fat-cat capitalist with no moral center buys congressmen, probably runs his own stable of fast-talking pretty boys for office, perhaps even one against the other in a critical race. They have the resources to corrupt almost anybody; bank board of directors, CIA and FBI appointees and generals. If cash won't do it, they can blackmail, extort, threaten and even kill with their army of enforcers; Mafia goons and war-blooded mercenaries, trained compliments of the American taxpayer in wars they created and orchestrated.

And I've been invited to sit at their table with Chesterton's merciless and metallic detachment of the Omnipotent Oligarchy. It is not actually about the individual. It is about certain individuals, and the rest are measured on utility and economic value. I can help rape the American people; the indifferent American people. Shit, maybe they deserve it. Everybody has sold out in the name of keeping up with the Joneses, comfort, distraction, apathy toward politics, pervasive childish entertainment, sex-based produce commercials, Ponzi schemes, entitlements, inflated pensions.

There are more takers than givers out there. They all have rights but no obligations. Who would "Occupy Personal Integrity?" Fat chance of that political bloc forming. It wouldn't even get play in the national media. Only political correctness plays, or any self-hating American cultural dig. Tyranny by minority... What's the rationale for this?

Death by capitalism, Hell; death by taxes. Self-delusion reigns. We aren't free anymore but slaves to untenable debt. We've got our children and our grandchildren into debt. We are slaves to debt. The

God-man Pharaoh at least offered something mystical, some hope of an afterlife. How much longer can we go on before we collapse like every empire before us?

"Caesar. We who are about to die salute you."

Our entire nation has freely self-applied golden chains. We've sold our personal moral integrity for shiny things. Our politicians are our sin eaters. It's their fault. Right. I'm actively helping my soul whither for cold cash and prestige. An Italian red sports car in my driveway can reach 200 mph, but it's illegal to drive over 80. Vanity. I lived in a twelve-bedroom estate with Antonia, my trophy wife. Once the sex wore off there was no other language we could communicate in.

For generations, my family served America. Not its politicians but its constitutional republic. Individual dignity. A nation of laws, not men. I've been trained to follow in that tradition and have just bummed about sampling the fruits of the land – a damn parasite living off of the hard work and sacrifice of generations past. We are no longer a nation of quality but one of quantity. Gold plated. But all that glitters is not gold. We've abandoned God, family and truth. For what?

The greatest generation is almost gone. They suffered through a great depression in their youth. They fought and triumphed in a great world war. They saved the entire world from pure evil. Then they came home, never bellyached, went to work, lived frugally, saved their money and built the greatest sustained prosperity ever seen on this planet. They handed it all over to the boomers. They sucked every bit of sugar out of that affluence. Dropped out, drugged out, and sold out. The hospitals are overrun with their obesity-related diseases. Then came my generation, the so-called Generation X. Tests show that most of us cannot accurately answer the question 'In what century was our Civil War fought?' But we do know most of the words to most Michael Jackson songs. That's entertainment.

So I hate this vulgar and corrupt cesspool of a culture. I feel a responsibility to my forefathers. I have a responsibility to my republic, to those who gave all for individual dignity, freedom and truth. I am not going to let it all fall apart without at least attempting to turn things around. But how do I take down a force that can initiate war and destruction to most any country on earth with the support of other nations and the world media?

Knowing that a thumbs down to Nicola on the CEO position at SMS could be a death sentence, even a healthy dose of bourbon couldn't get him to sleep.

What do I do? Join them? Let the Devil have his due, live like a lord with all the wine and women I want? Screw the people, the U.S. Constitution and feather my own pockets?

He suddenly remembered back to a time when he snuck out of his bedroom late at night, curious about the singing he heard drifting from Dad's study. There was Pop, sitting in his high-backed black leather chair, a remote in one hand and a glass of brown liquid in the other playing one part of a song over and over, his face was expressionless. The lyric, *"Guess every form of refuge has its price"* was from *"Lying Eyes,"* sung by the Eagles. So what price was he paying and for what? Did he sell out to Cowel and Ebers and Nicola for a fat-cat job? Prestige? Respect? Membership in the most elite gang in the world?

Lord in Heaven please do not let my father be in with these ghouls. If he is, stop my heart now.

At about three am, weary of constantly searching for a comfortable position, his pillow beat to shit, he immediately arose, put on his jeans, t-shirt then a hoodie, slipped into his luxury alpaca running socks, tied his high-tech hot-red running shoes firmly to his feet and walked to an all-night diner.

After three hours of hot coffee and a Danish or donut now and then, reflecting, watching the nation's capital wake up and fill its streets and sidewalks with the Hoi Polloi – Latin for 'the majority' – he thought as he paid attention to the ever-growing crowd as he never had before the "meeting."

Nicola truly is the Pied Piper, his music mesmerizes us, and we follow him like rats to be drowned.

If the people knew the truth, what would they do? Would they rip this rotten political corruption from the heart of our government or would they simply shrug and expect someone else to do the dirty work so they could go back to their rights to do as they desire and only give lip service to the ever-growing plague of corruption?

Charlie sighed. *Somebody has to do something. AJ and Julia are risking their lives right now for their country – this time off the battle-field which will surely prove more detrimental to life and limb.*

A shaggy scarecrow of a man in a Notre Dame football sweatshirt caught his eye.

This whole damn struggle for our country is like a damn football game played on the gridlines of the entire country from sea to shining sea. It's the Super Bowl. Our politicians against the American people. Their cheerleaders are the national media, whores all; ambulance chasers looking for the next juicy train wreck to confirm that whites are racists and blacks are victims. Up there in lights we have the feminists with their "poor me" stories trading domestic life of the loving nest for the prestige of a day-job profession. These media cheerleaders rally the self-hating white culture into shelling out for black free rides. Tyranny by minority pushing into the people's face. The pols offensive line immediately divides black and white, rich and poor, gay and straight, husband versus wife, old versus young so the President of Quarterbacks can connect with a favorite receiver who can keep them ahead on the scoreboard, keep them the lead dog in the scientific polls. Figures don't lie but liars figure.

The defensive line are the politically correct heavy weights, the secular 'everything is relative' center, the Pro Choice holier than thou victims, the long suffering Gay Movement. The referees are the Seven Deadly Sins; the Supreme Court justices. Those noted for Dred Scott. Those who proclaimed blacks as property and non-human and therefore unable to sue the U.S.A. Those celebrated for Rowe vs. Wade who arrogantly bypassed the human dignity heart of the Constitution and allowed the stopping of fetal hearts; a war on the defenseless, the innocent, the very symbol of the reaffirmation of life. And PETA no longer talks of animal welfare but animal rights. Is it no wonder we are all at each others' throats?

This is a game I want to play, one I was born to play. No prisoners.
No bribes accepted. No holds barred. Winner takes all. It's a compe-
tition for the very soul of a nation. Size matters here and mine is bigger,
much bigger than yours – even if it means cleaning and oiling my
Peacemaker 44s and Remington shotgun.

Bring it on!

* * *

AJ had picked up a tail right after Tyrell Landecker, recently deceased CEO of SMS, suffered his mysterious and convenient heart attack. He constantly ran various scenarios through his head as to how his attempted murder would go down. The typical Hollywood scene with three or four machine guns spewing bullets and casings while never hitting their target was a joke. If someone was going to hit a U.S. Congressman, it would come subtly. But he still carried his favorite handgun in his shoulder holster – the Colt M1911. The expected approach was slander, ruining his career with the media confession of a torrid affair from a woman he had never met. He would be branded a drug freak, a woman beater, a campaign-funds thief or all three. Many righteous men had succumbed to this tactic, and their political careers ended in well-orchestrated outrage from carefully rehearsed witnesses who came forward then disappeared, often forever.

* * *

Julia had it tougher. When on her rare trips to the mall, she was accustomed to men ogling her, hitting on her, the elevator eyes undressing her inch by inch. Some men even followed her and smiled when their eyes met, hoping for a returned smile, an invitation. One never came from the dedicated career woman.

But a man who turned his eyes away when she looked at him, or turned in mid-step or ducked behind someone else was a concern. Julia felt pumped for aggressively confronting, going so far as to purchase a pair of running shoes and throwing her heeled shoes in the purchase bag. While dancing in high heels was possible, fighting in them was not. She picked her spot, and as her stalker approached the trap he thought better of the whole thing. There was another shadow. He was not following Julia. He was following her shadow. Both would report back to his superiors on her behavior. Her shadows would say the dame simply shopped. No clandestine meetings, passing of secret messages or packages. She carried a .22 Browning pistol in her purse, and as an expert shot, didn't need any more firepower or protection. She and Charlie would have to be careful when meeting, on the phone or even in their own homes. These antagonists were pros.

Chapter 28

AJ reluctantly rolled over in bed and grabbed his cell phone off the night stand. Back in Austin, time changes affected him more than most. The clock radio said 3:25 a.m. The caller's number was not in his address book. He expected silence or heavy breathing, a typical psychological trick used to intimate someone. AJ knew he was being tailed and was on high alert.

"Congressman Morales."

"AJ, I need help bad."

"Antonia? What's the matter?"

"I'm locked in a room. Four guys are playing poker for me. They ain't likeable guys."

"Have you called your father?"

"He won't pick up."

"What about your bodyguards?"

"My father pulled them. I think something big is up."

After receiving the address, AJ was in jeans, sneakers and sweatshirt and on the road in no time at all. The house Antonia was held captive in was in a seedy part of town. His black Caddy wouldn't work so he was on his black Triumph Street Triple, a black helmet providing anonymity. Cutting the lights and then the ignition he rolled onto the street to the address Antonia had given him. Three cars in the driveway, one car at the front curb, a teenager just opening the door. With some pizzas.

"Ah, there's my pizza. How much?"

"Twenty-eight fifty."

"Here's forty."

The grateful delivery boy drove off leaving the still-helmeted AJ with two large pizzas. Confidently walking up the driveway he rang the doorbell. A dog barked, but the loud music masked the sound of the bell. He pounded on the storm door, the dog barked louder and "Shut up" came from inside the house. AJ opened the storm door. The door opened. A big man, four-day beard, shoulder-less tee shirt, holding a Rottweiler back by its collar looked him in the eye and then at the pizzas.

"Wad I owe ya?"

AJ dropped the pizzas and pulled two Taser guns from his back pockets. Man and dog collapsed. AJ stepped over them and surprised three shaggy, heavily tattooed men, and fired at their chests. Knocking the CD player off the counter to silence it, he shouted Antonia's name.

"In here."

Unlocking the door then kicking it wide he saw Antonia, bottom lip twice its normal size and purple, her left eye swollen shut was tied to the bed post. He freed her, carried her over the sprawling bodies and in a few moments they were on his bike, headed to his place.

"Did you kill them all?"

"They'll be fine soon."

"Where are we going?"

"My place."

Her arms wrapped around his mid-section brought back memories of the passion and warmth they once had. At first it had been wonderful. It had been just the two of them. Then her obsessive behavior began to seep out until the dam burst and AJ beheld the mess that was Antonia Scozzari. The sex was extraordinary, but what newly bound couple could not say that? The "love is blind" syndrome faded quickly, and AJ realized he was engaged to a spoiled, Mafia boss's daughter who was both angry, pampered, and given the power her family wielded, could get her way every time. A daddy's girl on steroids.

The fact that Charlie had married her was shocking. AJ had left that melodramatic soap opera behind him when he enlisted. Memories of Antonia returned occasionally, fond moments in bed and out, plus the recurring feeling that he could have saved her, brought her into reality, into being grateful for life and love. But her family knew nothing of love or thankfulness, only of self-satisfaction, hatred and envy. The apple didn't fall far from the tree. For Antonia, the damage had been done.

"I can walk," Antonia said. "I'm not an invalid."

"Stubborn as always."

"I can take care of myself."

"Then why did you call me? What if I had said that to you on the phone and just hung up?"

"I—"

"And you are welcome for saving you."

"I am grateful. I—"

"Why didn't you call your father?"

"Better to have lived through what those ghouls had planned."

"Your mother, then?"

"She would have told me that I made my bed, so sleep in it."

"Your husband?"

"I've hurt him enough."

"That's peachy. 'Oh, I'll just call AJ. His feelings don't count.'"

"I didn't mean that."

"I'm a U.S. congressman, Antonia. I can't be zooming around D.C. punching out pimps and pushers and saving crack whores."

He saw that hurt her and cursed himself. "Go clean yourself up in the bathroom. We can go to the E.R. if something is really bad."

"My life is bad. Can the E.R. fix that?"

"Only you can fix that."

"Do you know what it's like living my life?"

"Do you know what it's like seeing your best friend's hairy ass on top of your fiancée?"

Silence. Two wounded souls each with unintended scars given and taken. When she returned from cleaning up, AJ pointed to the sofa and offered her a bottle of water. They sat together for a moment before he spoke.

"I'll take the couch. I didn't have time to make the bed, but it's yours."

"I know you were trying to save me ten years ago. It's all my fault, I know. And yet you are kind to me when no one else is."

"Perhaps my feelings go deeper for you than the other men in your life."

"Other men? All crooks, weaklings, sex addicts, men who want to dominate. All you men are the same. Even your father was just another corrupt politician."

"You know nothing of my father."

"Oh, I finally hit a nerve with you. Men are all the same. I've screwed a hundred of them. They'll say and do anything to get between a girl's legs."

"My father was schooled in a Jesuit seminary. Studied scripture, theology, and philosophy before he decided he belonged in the world of men. When I was young, my father walked into my room and caught me with a *Playboy*. This was when he was going through all of the shame from the lies Senator Cowel was telling about him to the media. The press wouldn't give him time to refute it, and it was difficult for him. So I thought I was seriously in for it. Instead, he unfolded the centerfold and gazed at it with a hint of a smile. 'She's beautiful, isn't she?' 'Yes,' I said. 'Desirable enough to drive you crazy. Me too.' I for sure did not know where this conversation was going. 'God sure put the perfect temptation in front of us. And with the help of our own imagination we created this unattainable symbol.' Dad wrote poetry as a hobby, always in Spanish because he said it was God's language, so he lectured us with sugar, as he called it—"

"And the point is..." Antonia squished her eyebrows together.

"He told me the picture was pure lust. Instant infatuation. Just what the American adolescent of any age wants. She wasn't a girl to me, but an object. He had felt it, too, he said. All of us are driven by sex. No one is immune. It's all tied up with life and death. We all want life. We all fear death. When we have sex we grapple with these things. There is a difference between intense sex and emotional intimacy. There are no shades of gray there. We live when we are coupled with this girl. The perfect woman. The perfect life. We conquer death. How? The possibility of a child, when sperm hits egg. If the girl happens to be a prostitute, you have paid her fee, so the illusion is complete – life, death and money. This is why prostitution is the oldest profession. Illusion. These are the base concerns of all men."

Antonia blinked a few times, took a sip of water. AJ didn't know if what he shared made any sense to her.

"But there is more. Imagine you have been blessed with finding the right girl, a real girl. Your initial lust and infatuation turn to love, to an intimacy."

"I believed in fairy tales once," Antonia said. "I was never truly princess material, but I did take some mighty big bites out of that enormous red poisoned apple. A couple hundred grand went into therapy for me. I was told my active sex life and over-the-top addictions to sexual fantasy were a result of emotional wounds I suffered. Even if that were true it didn't help. Then they prescribed drugs, and I went into the mother of all comas, for a decade. Where is the prince to kiss me and break the spell?"

"You're an expert at showing off your physical assets. Have you ever tried to show someone your inner beauty?"

"The egg and sperm that made me came from two monsters. Where the hell would I get inner beauty?"

"They were that bad?"

"From the earliest I can remember I was trained to do whatever he told me. As I got older and started getting willful, he would wrap a thick scarf around my neck and choke me with one hand until I almost fainted. I can still see his yellow teeth and that evil stare. And then I would do whatever he wanted. I still wet myself when he calls."

"What did your mother do?"

"She never knew. He told me that he would kill her and me if I told."

"Then it's time you talked to her."

"Mother and I are two peas in a pod, and we hate what we see in each other."

"Go see her, Antonia. Face to face. Tell her. This is no way for a human being to live. Your father is a monster. You had zero chance in growing up in a loving family. It's not your fault."

"Thank you for all your help, AJ. You are the only one who has ever seen something in me worth saving, but I will never go to my mother or father for help."

"Even if you could see that what your father has done to you he has also done to millions of men and women here? His drugs, his prostitutes, his dirty politics, his diseased mind makes others suffer as you do. And yet his is untouchable."

"Nobody should be untouchable. I might go to my mother on your behalf."

"Tell her what he has done to you and what he does to others. Just tell her the truth."

"There may be too much history for that."

"And let Charlie go, too. I think he has finally found the right girl."

"I never explained to you the how and why of when you walked in on Charlie and me. It goes back to my father, but those sins are still on me. Sit down."

Chapter 29

Julia appeared from around the hallway as the pizza delivery boy rang her doorbell. She had tracked him from the moment he pulled in front of her building and watched to see if anyone else followed him. She took the pizza with her left hand, her handgun behind her back, in her right. She closed her door and replaced the wooded 4x4 post against it. It would take a lot more than a door breaker to open it. As she began to eat, her cell phone rang, a picture of her mother popped up.

"Hi, Mom, how are you?"

"I'm more worried about you than us?"

"What's wrong?"

"This morning two men came to our door."

"What kind of men?"

"Younger men. In suits. Your father said military types."

"Oh, God. What happened?"

"They said they were FBI and would like to come in and talk about you. I asked them politely to come back later because my husband was not home. One looked at the driveway, saw the truck and Chet's car and then glared at me."

"Where was Dad?"

"Fortunately he was not at home. Chet was in the barn."

"The taller of the two yanked open the screen door, pointed a finger at me and told me that you were in danger and if you didn't keep your mouth shut it would go bad for you and us."

"Oh no!" Julia cried, tears wetting her cheeks.

"Chet shot him in the arm."

"What?"

"Julia, they weren't polite men. They scared me."

"What happened then?"

"Well, Chet kept firing, but at their feet, and they ran to their car and drove off."

"Oh, Mom, I am so sorry."

"Are you okay, honey?"

"Yes. I am involved in some nasty stuff here, but I never thought—"

"We are fine. I am calling to see if you are."

"I am protected. What is going to happen to Chet?"

"Chet called your father's cell, told the story and after some mean cussing, he congratulated Chet for doing the right thing."

"Mom, Chet shot someone. What if they were the real FBI?"

"Well, first, he only shot the man with his .22 so he can't be that hurt."

"Jesus."

"Then your father CB'd the description of the car and the plate numbers to all our friends. This isn't like the city. It's not easy to hide on the plains. Well as it turns out, that car drove right past Pappy Blackhall's place, and he put a bullet in two tires and called the police. They're towing the car now, and Pappy is just saying he saw a stalled car and called it in."

"Oh, Mom."

"Your father hasn't smiled like this for years. He's at Luke's Bar with Chet and the guys, talking their stuff, I'm sure."

"I'll get you some protection and quickly."

"We're worried about you, not ourselves. I doubt if anybody could get within five miles of us without being spotted by local friends. While we love our privacy and freedom, we want it for our neighbors, too. We have our minutemen on high alert."

"I'll call you back soon. Give my love to Dad and Chet."

Julia immediately called AJ who promised the FBI would be on it immediately.

Before she picked up her first slice of pizza, Charlie's face appeared on her buzzing cell phone.

"I have an eight p.m. meeting with Senator Cowel at the Iwo Jima Memorial tonight. I'll probably find out if I'm the new SMS CEO or I'll have to swear an oath never to breathe a word about

SMS, so help me God."

"Charlie, be careful."

"Julia, if my father is part of this group what would I have to fear?"

"What if he isn't? What if he is the good man you always knew and the man your mother fell in love with and still loves?"

"I guess I'll find out soon enough."

"I think my parents were threatened today, Charlie."

"I'll stop by after the meeting and we can compare notes, okay?"

Julia sat motionless, her mind engaged in what-if risk scenarios, probabilities, the motives of the enemies and finally she asked herself how she would act in this situation if she were an SMS kingpin.

Chapter 30

Charlie drove to Arlington, Virginia and followed the signs to the Marine Corps War Memorial, more familiarly called the Iwo Jima Memorial, just outside Arlington Cemetery. It was closed at this time, the parking lot deserted except for an official-looking government Lincoln. So the senator was there already.

While this famous monument of the Marines lifting the American flag on the Iwo hill was an American icon and was bustling with crowds every day, Charlie felt a bit spooked. The place was deserted and deathly quiet. No wind. No sound. Sort of a no man's land as he walked to the base of the memorial. A distinctive 'pop' made him whirl around to see a man in a hoodie collapsing twenty feet away. His eye caught movement and another 'pop' sent that man to the ground also. Charlie understood immediately that he was a sitting duck under the lights. Then he realized that the two men that were down were there to kill him. But somebody had taken them out. The fact that he was still alive gave him hope, so he ran, gimp leg and all, into the darkness and away from the monument, toward his car, expecting a bullet in the back with every breath.

The limo was still there. Nobody in it as before. He fumbled with his keys and drove toward Julia's apartment. He knew now it was thumbs down for him as CEO of SMS and that Senator Cowel's invitation was his planned execution. A lifelong family friend. A sitting U.S. senator.

"Julia, instead of the senator, two hit men were waiting for me at the memorial."

"What? Are you hurt?"

"No. Thanks to some invisible shooter. He took them both out. One shot each. I'm on my way to your place. I called just to tell you to be careful. Don't stand by any window or open your door to a stranger."

"Hi, Mom," Charlie said into his cell phone on way to Julia's.

"You sound upset."

"Tough day at work. Can I talk to Pop for a sec?"

"He's not home. He called yesterday and said he'd be incommunicado for a day or so. Something with work, I'm sure. He'll call when he's done with business and I'll tell him you called."

Charlie let the tears come, wiping them away with his sleeve only to see the road ahead as he drove to Julia's.

He was still white as a ghost when Julia opened her door. "You've looked better."

"I'm glad that you're safe."

Julia poured some bourbon for Charlie and a Merlot for herself. As she sat across from him Charlie chugged them both. "So I show up like a lamb to slaughter looking everywhere for Senator Cowel."

"And instead?"

"He sent two goons, walking up behind me, both armed with handguns. I didn't even hear them. I would have been turned off like a light switch and never would have known what hit me."

"Tell me exactly what happened."

"I heard a muffled pop from behind and to my left. I jumped. There was a groan behind me. As I turned, I heard another shot and watched a man about twenty feet behind me collapse. Then I noticed a body about ten feet behind me also down. Neither was moving, both had handguns lying next to their bodies. Then I just looked to where the shots came from, not knowing what to expect. Do you know what it is like expecting to be killed any moment?"

Julia's thoughts went back to Iraq. "A planned hit for sure. You didn't see the shooter?"

"No…I ran to my car, drove off like a wild man and thought every car behind me was following me. I drove until I was sure I was not being chased. Then I thought they might be after you, also. So I called and turned around, headed to your place. I thought of calling the police but what if they were in on it, or Agent Putney or Sampson?"

"You are safe, Charlie. I am armed, and we are both safe."

"Should we call somebody?"

"No. Let them call us. Both AJ and I are being tailed, so I suspect you were too. They've stepped up their game. You are lucky to be alive."

They hugged for a long moment. A marriage and estranged wife prevented any further outward emotion.

"If the FBI was trailing me, do you think they took out those two men?"

"That's what I'm hoping the explanation will be."

"So they should be calling me on my cell. Can I have another drink, Julia? This glass must have a leak."

"How you can maintain a sense of humor after a brush with death, I'll never understand."

"My way of handling stress. So SMS sent two of their thugs to kill me. I must have flunked the interview. What if my wife decided she suddenly wanted a divorce? She wouldn't go through the court system. What if one of them was from SMS and one from my wife?"

Julia put the refilled glasses on the table and sat. "Charlie, relax. We'll know soon."

"While I was driving away I was picturing myself dying – my own blood forming a bigger and bigger puddle all around me. I was getting cold, numb. Julia, I read that in Iraq you were hit, bleeding, yet you dragged another soldier to safety while still being shot at."

"It was war, and I was responsible for that team. Something like honor and personal integrity and even giving your word can be more valuable than your life."

"Then you rushed a machine-gun nest. I don't know if I could do that."

"You could and you would."

"How do you know that?"

"Because I've seen men crumble and others who fight. You're not one to crumble."

"I must look like a complete coward to you."

"Not at all, Charlie. The first time any of us comes close to dying, it affects us. In war, you can't afford to dwell on it. You have to focus on doing your job. Sometimes the job is killing them before they kill you or someone on your team."

"I wasn't even given a chance. I've known Senator Cowel all my life."

"The facts are showing we are being used by a cunning cold-blooded crook."

"Something my mother told me years ago makes sense. I can hear the song from *High Noon* in my head now."

"I think you need a drink."

"A double. I was nearly killed at the foot of the Iwo Jima Monument. A monument built for those who fought for our freedom. Just regular guys who rose up to fight the good fight. I've been wrong about America, about the people. They aren't slobs and self-serving dogs. They've been trusting, but led by the nose to become docile and dependent. And me, I've done nothing for my country except use it. Bred to rule and not to serve. Maybe it is time to pay the piper."

"Almost getting whacked agrees with you, Charlie. I am going to back AJ and his team one hundred percent."

"Count me in, too. Who do we kill?"

"Whoa, Tex. Time to lock and load. But just for protection. We fight for and with constitutional law. Ever shoot one of these," Julia said, pulling a pistol from her purse.

"Had one that size when I was seven. It shoots caps, right?"

"It's a Smith and Wesson .380 Bodyguard. Easy to conceal."

"Julia. I'm from Texas, remember. I won sporting clay championships with my Stoeger shotguns and own two .44 Magnums and a double holster. Do I need to get a handbag, too, to carry this plunker of yours?"

"It's a tool. You are the weapon. It holds seven shots. If you keep your calm and aim, it is highly effective at close range."

"*This nation will remain the land of the free, only so long as it is the home of the brave.* Elmer Davis," Charlie said. "*Where liberty dwells, there is my country.* Benjamin Franklin."

"*The only thing required for evil to triumph is for good men to do nothing,*" Julia replied.

"Don't mess with Texas and Remember the Alamo," Charlie said, "Gimme that popgun."

"I think you should stay here tonight."

"Maybe you're right. I've had too much to drink, plus I am wired."

"You can have the couch."

"Okay, but don't try anything sneaky. I am well-armed."

Charlie was still dealing with the facts of the last few hours and his vivid imagination when his cell phone rang.

"Agent Sampson," he said into the phone, "what a surprise."

"Where are you?"

"Safe."

"I can find you through GPS in no time."

"I'm at Julia Abbott's condo."

"Our tail lost you when a pickup truck hit it head on. We thought it to be an accident until we were notified of a shooting. We have two bodies near the Iwo Jima Monument. Neither with identification."

"I was there for a private meeting with Senator Cowel. Instead, those two tried to kill me, but were both shot by some unknown shooter. Since it wasn't you guys, it must be SMS."

"Did you see either assassin?"

"I was too busy shittin' my pants. And since you're calling it an assassination attempt and not an attempted murder, that must mean I am a somebody."

"Not the time for jokes, Charlie," Julia said, listening from beside the bedroom door.

"We did not know about the intended hit, sir, or we would have been better prepared. You should have alerted us to the meeting tonight. SMS is getting desperate. They know we have some serious documentation on their operation. Neither you, nor Ms. Abbott, nor Congressman Morales are safe. We will put agents around Ms. Abbott's house for now. Within a few hours you will both be officially in protective custody."

"Agent Sampson, I am in the apartment of a beautiful single woman, but she is fully armed. Now you tell me you are sending the FBI over for more support. What else can go wrong?"

"Back to the unknown shooter, funny man. Any chance it's your wife's connections keeping you safe?"

"I could see her in my mind's eye pulling the trigger, for sure, but not saving me. She didn't take well to my sense of humor either. But I am firmly in on doing whatever it takes to bring SMS down."

"You can make a huge contribution to our case and congressional hearings, Mr. Prendergast. Danger seems to bring out the tiger in all three of you."

"It is not danger. It is injustice. Count me in," Charlie said.

Charlie left Julia's condo at about seven a.m., accompanied by an agent. That afternoon, a delivery man knocked on Julia's door; instead of opening the door, she was behind him, accepted the package and watched the man depart. Back in her condo she opened a box with two dozen red roses and a card that read, *"Thank you for being who you are. I am reminded of the title song from the musical, Gigi, where Gaston sings, "When did your sparkle turn to fire and your warmth became desire, oh, what miracle has made you the way you are?" Love, Charlie.*

Chapter 31

Julia and Charlie were escorted to FBI headquarters. Four dark-suited men, each with the crinkled black wires hanging from their necks, scanned all for directions before opening the doors of one of those large black vehicles the movies like to show both the good guys and the bad guys driving. Escorted to an elevator, they were taken three floors down before the doors opened. Guided to a large conference room, they recognized AJ, a cup of coffee in his hand.

"You've looked better," AJ told Charlie.

"I almost got killed last night. What kind of government are you running, Morales?"

"What?"

"We are on top of this, Mr. Prendergast," Agent Putney said. "The limo was stolen; a decoy to make you believe the senator was there."

"You were shot at?" AJ's eyes widened.

"Two guys intended to shoot me, but someone else shot them first."

"Congressman, there was an attempted assassination on Mr. Prendergast's life late last night at the Iwo Monument. We did not suspect a hit, sir, or we would have been better prepared."

"Your ole pal, Senator Cowel asked me to meet him privately at the Iwo Monument, AJ. He's lower than a rat's ass."

"SMS is getting desperate," Agent Putney said. "That's an excellent sign. They know we have some serious evidence and key-witness testimony on the SMS operation. Neither you nor Ms. Abbott nor Congressman Morales are safe. You are all in protective custody as of this moment."

"Agent Putney," Julia asked. "While Charlie is still married to Scozzari's daughter, I would suspect it was a Mob hit."

"That's plausible, Ms. Abbott... Back to the unknown shooter.

Any chance it's your wife's connections keeping you safe?" Putney asked.

"I asked him that," Agent Sampson replied. "It is not a love match."

Chapter 32

Anna Alvarez's hands trembled on the steering wheel of her gunmetal BMW X1. She waved off the Texas Rangers escort with a smile. She was returning from a private meeting with former U.S. Senator William Kiddenly on his 70-foot custom yacht moored outside of Coopers Aly, directly across from the Corpus de Christi Yacht Club and marina. The senator had promised he owed her one after she promised not to follow up on a story about a pricey call girl who filed a police report of abuse following a meeting. While the story was buried and never followed up on, a snitch within the police department alerted Foremost 8 in Houston, part of the new Foremost Network and now the number 5 Network in the U.S. catering to English-speaking Hispanics with education and upward mobility.

Anna, being a newbie, a journalist major from the University of Monterey, Mexico, was given the story by her assignment manager. While knowing full well where the story would take Anna, the veteran reporter knew the Texas Rangers would stay mum on the story and that Kiddenly was famous for his choice of women, namely the willowy ice-princess type. Anna could have been the poster girl for the type. In fact, she wasn't hired for her impressive degree but for her pristine Latino beauty and her charming Spanish accent coupled with an articulate command of the English language.

When Anna returned to her office in Houston, and reported to her supervisor that she had no problem with the lack of interest from the police to investigate the abuse charge and classified the story as a dead end, her boss was pleased. Anna understood how the world worked, when to dig deeper, and when to stand down. An incident with a hooker and a powerful government patriarch would be forgiven, and not something a mainstream media source would feature. The fact that Anna only mentioned that she had met former Senator Kiddenly and that she and he had gotten on famously pleased her boss. Anna was not a blabber. She kept her cards close to her chest. Any kind of relationship with Kiddenly could blossom, and it was up to Anna to take it as far as she could to perhaps one day get a real zinger of a story. Not elaborating what went on with the senator was perceptive. Plausible deniability.

Anna worked behind the cameras mostly on investigative reporting for the Foremost O&O in Houston for eight months, virtually invisible, often underfoot and glared at by live TV face-time journalists. She learned her management liked dirt because the readership liked dirt. The more dirt, the more papers were sold; the happier the management. The buzz words, "bias is natural" were her mantra, so she imbued her work with a creative flair. She studied the media lobbyists who represented key players in the news business. They had the cash and clout to decide what story got attention and coverage. She dated a few – great meals at the best restaurants, where introductions helped grow her name. Her day-to-day involved fact-checking incoming press releases, looking for the wrong bias, exaggeration. These releases came by email, fax, and lately texts to her corporate cell phone, mostly from friends, like the car-dealership owner who gave her a terrific deal on the Beemer. Anna caught on quickly, could read intentions from body language and expressions. She had a fantastic job, was building a name for herself, but things were moving too slowly for her.

Then out of the blue came an invitation from former Senator Kiddenly. "I owe you one, Babe," he said. "Care to kick off an exclusive and watch from the front lines how I can send the entire political system of the strongest nation on earth into action?"

Anna pulled up in front of the senator's dock as quickly as the ultimate driving machine could get her there. Notebook, miniature recorder, and all the tools of her profession were on her person as the senator's security detail welcomed her aboard.

"It's been a while, Anna," the senator said.

"Yes it has, Senator. Almost a year."

"Well, good things take time. I told you I owe you one, and I've got a peach for you."

They sat next to each other in the plushy stateroom, on a long sofa, the yacht gently rocking in the afternoon waves. Anna clicked her voice recorder on Run and turned toward the senator.

"Now, Anna, I am going to help you enter an elite world. Are you ready?"

"Yes, sir?"

"After this your career will blossom. With the help of me and my friends, you will undoubtedly become a network anchor. Are you up for that?"

"That has been my dream since before leaving Mexico."

"Good. Before we go into the story, I'd like to get to know you. Sharing knowledge of global importance – information that can and will ruin political careers – cannot be done lightly."

"I understand. My background—"

"Drinks first. I need some bourbon to settle my nerves. This revelation is going to put me in the firing line. Can I get you something?"

"Well, I am a vodka martini girl."

Anna watched the senator waddle toward his bar and winced at the sight.

"Oh, this is perfect," she said, accepting her drink touching it to his tumbler. "Here's to the news."

"Rare Russian vodka. Costly, but the occasion warrants."

"Senator, is that your name on your glass?"

"It is. I confess to be a lifelong bourbon enthusiast. I have my own barrel soon to be opened. It will be a closed affair. The public does not wish to think of their senators as heavy drinkers, but I am retired, have too few years left in me, so I will indulge myself."

"How incredible. You do have the contacts, don't you?"

"Do you like horses, Anna?"

"With a passion. I took lessons for years."

"Then consider yourself invited to my horse farm outside of Taylorsville, Kentucky, close to Louisville. You can be my guest at the Derby."

"The Kentucky Derby?"

"Is there another? I'll introduce you to many of the most powerful men and women in the country. Think of what that will do to your contact list."

"I honestly can't thank you enough, Senator. I guess you are the one who is going to hand me my breakout story."

"Well, I need just one more refill. I apologize, Anna, but I'm known to hem and haw before I go public with revelations. Can I get you another?"

"I think not. This one has me a bit loopy. If I got stopped on the way home—"

"I'll get you a Texas Ranger escort. A fresh Russian vodka martini coming up."

Anna emptied her glass in one gulp and watched the senator return to the bar. She was not born yesterday and knew where she was going. The second martini would give her the courage she needed to go through with it.

I am not going to miss the chance of a lifetime by refusing a fifteen-minute afternoon delight indiscretion.

Anna gave a thumbs up to her boss as she entered the newsroom. He looked at her over the rims of his glasses. The gesture brought him to his feet. As Anna started her briefing she could see it took less than thirty seconds for him to realize – major political announcement, many opportunities for more digging and unfolding, a scoop. The news team Mobilized with the efficiency of a ghetto fire department crew. Shari was allowed to write the first draft copy while three assistants shouted possible follow-up spins on the story to each other. This was the heartbeat of the post-modern news room. U.S. senators, a censure, a whisper of treason and a minority congressman. All sound bites here. To hell with research. Let's quote the senator. Chop! Chop!

The polarized news media attracted and groomed a polarized audience as expected, and would seek out polarized stories to expand the audience and thereby increase profits, which increased salary and bonus in an ever-growing circle of polarization. The truth is what you can make the other fella believe.

Anna got goose bumps as she heard her introduction through her earpiece: "A breaking story from Foremost News. Here is Anna Alvarez live in Corpus Christi."

"Former Senate Majority Leader W.E. 'Billy' Kiddenly has just announced plans to contact the Texas Congressional delegation to assemble and discuss formal censure of a member of the U.S. House of Representatives, denouncing Congressman 'AJ' Morales, a Democrat representing Austin, Texas for treason against the People of the United States of America. In an exclusive interview with this reporter, the man known as the 'Father of the Lone Star GOP,' Senator Kiddenly, a six-term U.S. Senator from Texas promises to disclose information pertaining to treasonous activities pertaining to freshman congressman, AJ Morales, from his time in special operations while on active duty in Afghanistan. Senator Kiddenly will provide the Texas delegation with documents that have recently surfaced implicating the congressman in unauthorized meetings with high-level Al Qaeda terrorists. In addition to the documentation, Senator Kiddenly promises to produce testimony from an Afghani national who witnessed several meetings between Al Qaeda leaders and the congressman during his most recent tour of duty in country. The U.S. House of Representatives Ethics Committee is reviewing the allegations as we speak. Congressman Morales was unavailable for comment and did not respond to our inquiries."

More at 9 p.m. Back to you, Jessie."

"After the break," the perfectly coiffed Jessie said, "an in-depth analysis of the troubling growth of lip-synching as more and more celebrity singers begin to cheat their audiences with pre-recorded performances."

Chapter 33

"Benedetta?" Antonia asked over the phone.

"Who is this?"

"It's Antonia."

"What is it? And remember the phone may be tapped."

"Can I come and see you?"

"What have you done now?"

"I'm sick of my life. I hate my father."

"About time."

"I can't live like this anymore."

"That's good. Your father's warped you. To get at me."

"Do you hate me?"

"I never hated you. What I did hate once was that every time I looked at you it reminded me I actually let that monster inside my body. Two decades of therapy have cured me of that. But you wouldn't leave him."

"He threatened to kill me, and you too if I left him. I want to come home."

"Come."

Benedetta Scozzari, nee Calabrese, only child of a Mob don, looked out over her vineyard from the leafy balcony of her Texas Hill Country estate. This was Texas wine country. The dry, sunny climate and sandy loam soil atop limestone was ideal for Benedetta's production of the Cabernet Sauvignon grape. Her vineyard sat above the Ogallala Aquifer, so water was always available. The high elevation ensured the wind kept the mildew diseases from her vines. While Texas wine had been produced since the mid-sixteen hundreds by Spanish missionaries, it still came as a surprise to many to hear talk of 'Texas wine.' Benedetta aimed to change that, no matter how much it cost. But it took time, patience and countless efforts to assist nature to conform to what her taste buds desired. This harvest would come in early

August. These vines were Benedetta's real family. They had been cut from the family vineyard in Italy years ago. The call from her daughter had troubled her. Getting into a grudge match with Nicola was not an option. His SMS company was wildly successful, and both families profited. A war between two Mafioso families could turn these potent vines into ash.

While she had grown up used to getting her way, by easily provoking fear with a mere whisper of the threat of her family's power, her wine was superior, the business was legit, and she was respected for that – for her own efforts. Given away as the bride of a New York Mob Don to a groom who was the son of a Boston Don was a business merger. This was how kings and queens were married off for centuries. It was always business that came first. Her ex, Nicola, was given the reins of SMS, headquartered in Lexington, Kentucky. The move was required as more profits for ever-growing expansion of family members demanded their share. Nicola controlled the profits from SMS and all the other "initiatives" as they were called. Benedetta had to beg for money from day one. The allowance she received was a slap in the face. There was no love between them, only business. She was the broodmare, he was the underboss. A few years of respite, with the birth of Antonia, fed her maternal instincts, but Nicola was indifferent to her as a husband. A few messy affairs with chauffeurs and pool boys led to the divorce. Lust and infatuation were not the same as a warm and intimate relationship.

The families agreed they could part ways. Nicola's masterful revenge was his custody of Antonia. There was no public and nasty fight played out in the media. Not for Mob families. The dons decided. Nicola got SMS and Antonia. She got her vineyard. Even her own father decided that she was not a fit mother, so Antonia was led away by a sneering, reptilian snake of a man. Benedetta lost herself for a time in vodka and men, but began to fight back through her vineyard. She would produce the finest Cabs in Texas. She would gain respect on her own.

Antonia landed at the Austin-Bergstrom International Airport and on disembarking was greeted by her mother's chauffeur. Gino was in his late sixties, tall and lean, yet well-muscled, silver hair, eyes the color of robin's eggs. She once overheard another *soldato* – a Mob soldier – say that Gino was able to eat half a sandwich during lunch, wrap the rest carefully, leave it on the passenger seat, kill someone that Benedetta had put a hit on, and come back to finish his sandwich as if nothing had happened. He was Italian on his father's side, a necessity to be a Mob soldier, and Swedish on his mother's side, and favored her in coloring and build. If someone had called a hit on you, you looked for an Italian to come for you. One never expected Gino. He nodded to Antonia and took her overnight bag, looking into every face on the walk to the black 2011 Lincoln limo. In the unlikely event that someone tried to kill her for whatever reason, her blood would be on his hands.

She was ambivalent to being out of D.C. and back in Austin. Both towns had witnessed her turbulent lifestyle. Her name had appeared several times in the newspapers of both, whether it was a DUI, breaking and entering, assaulting a police officer, public nudity—she didn't care. When in Austin, Gino had come for her many times and drove her away to wherever. He also saw that she was never punished for anything. Any fines she incurred were handled under the table. The gates of her mother's estate swung wide as the guard and Gino nodded to each other. If either did not nod, it was a signal to the other that something was wrong. Guns would be drawn immediately to greet either hit men or the Feds.

Nobody got behind those gates unless invited. Nobody.

The winding drive along the ultra-manicured road gave Antonia a peek-a-boo view of the vineyards. Each tree, shrub and vine perfectly aligned with its neighbors. There was nothing haphazard about her mother. Anal retentive. Her pulse accelerated the closer she came to the entry portico. Her mouth was dry. Benedetta would not be at the door to greet her daughter. Gino would escort Antonia to wherever Benedetta was and then silently disappear. Today he led her to the tennis court.

"It's been quite some time, Benedetta."

"Yes," Benedetta said as she lay down her racquet.

"These clay courts are new."

"Three years ago," her mother replied.

Antonia took in her white cotton shirt and matching shorts, the lean tan legs and arms, the pert nipples jutting out against the shirt. Her mother's face seemed pulled back even tighter than the last time they were together. The wrinkles may have gone, but her mama's vanity blinded her to the obvious signs of plastic surgery. Her hair was blacker than black, her eyebrows penciled on in matching color.

"Sit," Benedetta said, pointing to the ice tea on the wrought iron antique table and removing her sunglasses as she also sat.

The women evaluated each other eye-to-eye.

"You've put on some weight in your face. That's from brown liquor, isn't it?"

"Bourbon was all I was allowed to drink besides water in Kentucky. Got used to it."

"Was it that bad?"

"Yes."

"I pictured you as the spoiled princess who had whatever she wanted. That's how I was raised."

"For me it was more like a wind-up doll who did exactly what she was told, or else."

"I know him. I got out. He's still pulling your strings, isn't he?"

"He broke this arm when I was eleven. It was set and cast at home – no hospital, no report, no apology."

"But you stayed."

"He told me he'd kill me if I left."

"Maybe he was bluffing."

"Was he bluffing when he beat you while I sat crying as a child?"

"Your marriage broke up."

"What the hell would I do with a good man?"

"What do you want from me?"

"I want a mother."

"I was a mother until you were taken away from me. My own father ruled against me. I had to learn to cope with that. I put it out of my mind. *My own father.*"

"And you are just as heartless as he was. It's business, right?"

"We cannot risk starting a war with the Boston Cosa Nostra."

"He'll know I came here. So now I just wait around to be killed. I wish I was never born."

"There might be another way to get you free of him."

Chapter 34

At a U.S. Justice Department safe house in rural Maryland's Eastern Shore, outside of Preston, a team, united in a desire to bring down a seemingly unbeatable foe, began to smell blood. Years of pent-up job frustration from "Do what I say or there's the door" career-oriented higher ups whose job was to keep their job and to hell with morality or quality or humanity began to focus on stripping the façade from a good-ole-boy network; on seeking justice. It was nearing the point of no return. Two tectonic plates were now vying for the upper hand.

"How is it that we are all over the news, and Julia is still unknown?" AJ asked Charlie as they watched TV.

"Never mind that, AJ. How you can go from a star running back to a damn Islamo-fascist and traitor to your country, I'll never know."

"Thanks, buddy. I'm pegged with treason, and you're telling jokes."

"AJ, this is like a nightmare to me. How is all of this possible? How is it that it has suddenly become visible to me?"

"I saw it first in Afghanistan, Charlie. It's like I had preset images in my head. My image of a politician was one of my father. A good man, honest, personal integrity. So if I saw or heard of someone in politics I superimposed my father's image, his very being, over them. Then I found that the man who destroyed my father was evil to the core and the image of a politician changed. Now it is an image of evil. I know there are reputable ones, and I force myself to see them. Same goes for the media. There has to be a few real journalists out there who strive to bring us an unbiased view of news instead of using it for career goals."

A new suit entered the main room. This one had tightly cropped curly blond hair. "Congressman?"

"Yes," AJ replied.

"My name is Agent Dell, CIA," he said, flashing his badge. "May we talk?"

"What can I do for you?"

"In private, sir."

"Charlie is a good friend."

"Yes," Charlie said. "He only gets bad-mouthed by senators. Me, I get shot at."

Agent Dell did not appreciate the comment. "Please, Congressman, this way."

AJ was led into another room where Agent Dell was joined by another agent.

"He's CIA, too?"

"State Department."

Agent Sampson joined.

"An Afghani native has contacted us on your behalf."

It took AJ a moment, but finally it hit him. "Mamadzai?"

"Yes."

"Good."

"Perhaps not, Congressman," Agent Sampson said.

"This Shapoor Mamadzai is affiliated with some of the nastiest stuff that has gone on in Afghanistan," Agent Dell said. "This is an odd friend to make."

"He is not my friend. I'm alive because of a tradition of his. I was his guest. Did you know many Afghanis hated Bin Laden, but gave him refuge for the same reason?"

Agent Sampson's brow furrowed. "This is the resource you spoke of, Congressman, in one of our briefings in your office?"

"Yes."

"You are aware that the Department of Justice has been asked by both senate and House leaders to bring you up on charges of treason?"

"Yes. If they show you proof, it is phony. Made up. Just like the proof they made up to use against my father."

"So it's the senate and House leadership's word against yours."

"No. It's the word of a U.S. Congressman, decorated U.S. veteran and American patriot against a group of powerful gangsters."

"Well said, AJ," Agent Sampson said.

AJ's nostrils were flared, his hands telling his thoughts along with his words.

"This Mamadzai is willing to fly to Montreal, meet with the U.S. State and Justice departments and show them proof of what they have on the lithium operation going on in Afghanistan and the collusion between our military, subcontractors and the American political system."

"Why Montreal?" AJ asked.

"The CIA is forbidden to conduct operations within the U.S. borders. At least officially. So they point the operation to Canada and then bring an Afghani into the U.S. where the FBI will take over."

"Excellent."

"At any time when you were in Afghanistan or here in the States did you work for or with Afghan insurgents?"

"I was taken on a tour of certain operations. At no time did I offer any assistance or divulge any sensitive information that would have been detrimental to my country. Keep in mind I was a prisoner. They let me go hoping I would share this information with the proper authorities. I have not found any and became a congressman to bring this information to the surface. Are you the proper authority to bring it out, make it public knowledge, Agent Dell? Are you a defender of the U.S. Constitution or just another bureaucrat living off the government dole?"

"I am a patriot, Congressman."

"But willing to avoid the mandate for the CIA to only work outside the U.S.?"

A small but telling smile appeared on Agent Dell's face. "Sir, over the last decade we have shit so much on our Constitution with things like the Patriot Act and others that my only concern is to help save America from political corruption. Once we do that I will go back to the strict rules we all should be following – a nation of laws, not men. So for right now, use me and my resources to bring these dogs down."

This admission was enough to convince AJ that this CIA man was a human being. An American human being.

Dell nodded, his eyes focused to the horizon. "It will take a certain amount of courage for Mamadzai to meet in a neutral place with representatives of our country. He is officially viewed as a terrorist."

"Meet with him. Listen to him. His depth of understanding of his country, ours, global politics, history and human nature will impress you. We need to stop the killing for immoral reasons. If our sons and daughters have to die, let them die for freedom and not to line some fat-cat asshole's pockets."

"Well, Franklin," Agent Dell said, turning to Agent Sampson, "I expected this to be another of your naive plans for saving the world. But with the information you have collected, what the congressman has, as well as the SMS VP in the other room, and if this Mamadzai character pans out, we've got the first real wedge into the so-called New World Order."

Agent Sampson just smiled.

"How so?" AJ asked.

"You can think of this as a body. Giant corporations, banks, government, insurance, petroleum and the Mob. They are the blood supply that brings money and profit to the heart and the brain. The mob is the capillaries, small but everywhere, doing the day to day. The government is the larger veins, the highways that connect the whole system together. The New World Order is the few families, the arteries that control the bulk of the blood supply, the money supply. Without them, the heart and brain dies."

"Are you telling me we need this garbage to survive?" AJ demanded.

"In a corrupt world, yes. It has always been the case. We have a hugely corrupt bureaucracy in place, and they dispense the profits, mostly our tax money, to their owners and favorite customers."

"I want to expose this. I want the American people to see what their apathy and indifference is doing to our nation, to our children."

"We are with you, Congressman."

"Good," AJ said. 'Time to kill something."

Chapter 35

An FBI spotter, outside with a walkie talkie, alerted the safe house of an approaching vehicle. A nondescript beige sedan pulled up the winding driveway of the safe house with fifty eyes watching its approach. It was yet another CIA agent. The FBI and CIA agents seemed to know each other, held the same views as servants of their country and not any specific ideology, but were extremely cautious.

"Good news and bad," she said as Agent Sampson asked for the news.

"Let's go with good first," AJ asked, hoping to sturdy himself for the bad news.

"Admiral Prendergast has called the president, and briefed him on what he knows of SMS."

Charlie breathed a sigh of relief.

"This is top secret. Not to be shared. Apparently your attempted assassination made your father face a difficult decision, Mr. Prendergast. SMS had threatened his family with death for years in return for helping him rise in command. Nicola Scozzari apparently made an uncharacteristic emotional decision to call a hit on you. That's quite surprising. Perhaps something to do with your estranged wife. The Admiral will turn state's evidence with complete immunity from the president and his personal involvement with SMS will never come to light."

"It's a great feeling to have my father back," Charlie said.

"Now for the bad news," Julia demanded.

"SMS wants a meeting."

"Who at SMS?" AJ asked.

"Senators Cowel, Ebers and Kiddenly."

"Satan, the false prophet and the antichrist?" Charlie said. "Why a meeting? The one I was invited to wasn't very friendly."

AJ was firm. "Those three are desperate by now. They cannot

be trusted. No bargains of immunity, no meeting."

"Both the FBI and the CIA leadership feel the meeting must be accepted."

"Bargaining for immunity?" Agent Putney asked. "In exchange for the names of some crooked captains and lieutenants? Are your directors afraid of being named as traitors? Congressman Morales here is not afraid?"

"The decision is unanimous right from the White House. You must go through with the meeting." The agent was adamant. Authority was in her voice.

"What are the demands?" Julia asked, as if she were back in her officer's uniform querying her troops.

"Mr. Prendergast and Congressman Morales are to present themselves for a discussion. It appears that you, Ms. Abbott, are no threat to them."

"Perhaps not yet, but I soon will be."

"Making threats against U.S. senators is not—"

"These are crooks, Agent," Agent Sampson said forcefully. "We know it. While I respect the office of these elected officials, the individuals holding these offices have tarnished them, let down the American people."

"They will choose the meeting location soon," she continued, unfazed. "And on short notice."

Putney spoke up. "That is a precaution against allowing our snipers time to set up. Our best guess is that it will be outside, at a remote location, with plenty of cover. You'll be electronically scanned and searched for any wires or recorders."

"They will have time for their snipers to set up," AJ said, "and with the two of us dead, there goes the case."

"We do have your father protected in a secluded location, Mr. Prendergast," the female CIA agent said. "His testimony coupled with our compiled research gives us enough concrete evidence to bring these three traitors to justice."

Agent Sampson shook his head, his lips pursed. "It is a given that Nicola Scozzari will undoubtedly go free, as always. He's too deep in the shadows to be trapped."

"Agent Sampson," AJ asked. "We are a nation of laws. We must obey them. We are not a nation of emotions or fashion. We must meet these men. What happens when we accept their invitation?"

"If you and Mr. Prendergast accept the meeting, Congressman, you both will be in significant danger. I can promise our best effort at protection, but there is a substantial risk to your lives. We suspect they will begin with intimidation – remind you of the power they collectively hold. They will threaten your family and friends. Then it might get ugly. Powerful men do not like to suddenly realize they are not so powerful."

AJ frowned. "But as you say, we do have enough evidence to prosecute now."

"True. But these boys have squirmed out of numerous incitements for years. Just like the Kennedy assassination over fifty years ago. Every corrupt official destroyed documentation, covered his tracks, lied under oath, spread rumors. Disinformation flowed."

"We need to know what their bargaining chip is, if any. Remember they control whole armies, loyal generals, the Mob. God knows what else."

"What about drones?" AJ asked.

Agent Dell locked eyes with AJ before answering. "No doubt it's a threat, Congressman. But we are in control of those facilities, not SMS."

"Tell me about drones," Charlie asked AJ.

"A drone is essentially a flying robot. It can find anything with the technology packed into it, and it is small enough to practically be invisible. Some can hover and spy on you with telescopic eyes better than an eagle. If SMS has control of drones, they could track us through our cell phones and launch a rocket into our car."

"And the new generation can travel with a small explosive or a biological weapon. If it hits you, you're dead."

"Unbelievable," Charlie said. "I could see using these things on drug czars, but we're using them on our own people. What the hell is going on in America?"

AJ answered. "The problem with America is everybody is expecting the other guy to do something. So nothing gets done."

"So three nasty senators want to meet us, and I wander into the scene to get chased by gizmos out of the *Matrix* movies."

"The first time I saw one in Afghanistan, all the wind went out of me," AJ replied. "It was a hovering thing. Like a hummingbird. You can't help but stop and stare at it like a child full of wonder. This one was about the size of a football helmet. It just hung there is space, perhaps fifty feet above me, looking right at me. Turns out we were testing new technology and I was one of the lucky guinea pigs."

Julia winced. "It's getting like none of us are safe anywhere."

AJ nodded. "When I saw that drone I realized that our country's biggest problem was not that wealth was accumulated in the hands of the few but that power was. We should be distributing power. Just like our Constitution lays it all out for us. The U.S. Constitution was based on God's laws, not those of flawed mankind. That is why greedy men try relentlessly to wrest our rights from us. They want to usurp God."

"Congressman," Agent Dell said. "I'll offer to ride with you. I'll bet my life we have you protected."

"Thank you, Agent, but you are needed to orchestrate the tactics for us. I'll put my life in your hands. Your word works for me."

"Count me in," Charlie said. "My ancestors fought the British on American soil, our own brothers in the Civil War on American soil and I can't wait to fight our own leaders on American soil."

"This is going to be a lot tougher than the Rose Bowl,

Charlie," AJ said, arm around his friend.

"I just hope it's your knee that gets blown out this time."

Julia shook her head. "You two are still at it. Like schoolboys, each daring the other. So what happens next?"

"A call will come in to us," Agent Putney replied. "The two of you will be asked to drive somewhere. After that, you'll most likely have your cell phones, GPS and any electronic communications blocked."

"Air support for us?" AJ asked.

"SMS will have some of their mercenaries out there with camouflaged handheld surface-to-air missiles and will threaten to shoot us out of the sky if we come near."

"So they are basically on their own," Julia said.

"Yep," Charlie replied. "But AJ and I will be taking no prisoners."

"We may only be messengers, Charlie. There is no telling."

"In past wars, the messengers' heads were often the only thing that returned."

"When will this all go down?" Julia asked.

"Probably tomorrow. Late afternoon," Dell said. "They were purposely vague if it is indeed intended to be a trap. It will be a place one of them knows well and not far from here."

Julia suddenly smiled wryly.

"What's the smile for, Julia?"

"It's not a smile, it's frustration."

"So we cannot be there with you initially," Agent Putney said, "but I doubt any gunplay with three senators on site. Do you gentlemen agree to this?"

Julia watched both boys give the "hook 'em horns" salute. She guessed it was their way of offering a thumbs-up to the meeting. Her stomach told her the whole thing was a plan for disaster.

Chapter 36

Two nondescript men turned their lights off and became one with the pitch black of the moonless night. Night-vision goggles lit their way as they rode slowly along a deer path for about 200 yards. Ditching their motorcycles into the heavily treed forest, each man removed his helmet and riding clothes, revealing camouflaged military garb. Oblong black bags from the side of their motorcycles opened to reveal unassembled hunting rifles. Once the rifles were fully operational, the men jogged silently to a preselected position, both cautiously scanning the surrounding area, their ears as valuable as their eyes. At the beginning of a clearing about one mile in diameter, they set up their rifles on tripods and the crickets resumed their chirping.

* * *

When the call came in to the FBI with the meeting location at 4 a.m. everyone at the safe house rose and became an interconnected machine. Computers connected to the Internet and onto secured access to both the DOJ and CIA internal sites, bringing up maps. Entire teams back at Langley, VA and FBI headquarters on Pennsylvania Ave in D.C. were already active. Several NASA satellites in orbit around the earth were commandeered, and their missions diverted to begin scanning a large radius of the earth surface – with the FBI safe house as the center point.

Just after dawn, Charlie, already on the road, received a first text of what road and what direction to take. A nervous AJ rode shotgun. He held Charlie's phone and stared at it, waiting. AJ's military instincts didn't like being pulled out into wilds of Maryland in a series of steps. The fifth text put them on a winding gravel road, which disoriented both men. The cell phone lost its signal as expected. All communications were being jammed by covert forces controlled by SMS. Within the FBI, CIA, DEA and other secretive organizations, those bought through bribes or threats vied against their fellow agents.

I have seen the enemy, and it is us.

Pulling out into the open clearing, driving through knee-high pasture grasses, surrounded by pines and maples, Charlie and AJ both scanned the area, looking for any movement. Charlie turned off the car. Both men waited impatiently, exposed and isolated. A black Lincoln limo entered the clearing driving from the opposite direction from where Charlie had. It moved slowly, headed directly at them. With sweaty palms, dry throats and beating hearts, the two former gridiron champions got out of their car, walked to the front of it and stood helpless.

The Lincoln stopped about thirty feet away. The driver emerged. Not as tall as Charlie, AJ noted, but almost as thick as he and AJ put together. A bull of a man. He frisked both men then returned to the limo, leaning back on the hood. Senator Cowel emerged, helping his retired mentor and symbol of the Old GOP, Senator Kiddenly. Cowel handed the portly old man his cane.

So weak, AJ thought, *and yet able to command so much power. What is power really? How can weak and flawed men attain so much? Do we follow them to be like them? Is it a herd instinct?*

Cowel waved Charlie and AJ to him as if calling a dog.

"Well, Charlie," Senator Cowel said. "I've known you since you were a young boy. Saw that you were malleable, and not too bright in the cunning kind of things. But I'd never figure you for having a conscience."

"Me neither, Parker. But here I am."

"And your pal here. He should remember what I did to his daddy when the beaner ran against my junior counterpart in the senate. With one phone call the media set the future of the election in stone. That's the power in my sails, boys."

"There's no wind out here."

Cowel's face turned dark. "Your mother is being picked up as we speak, Morales. She's illegal and will be back on her polluted native soil in no time."

"Just spoke with her. The FBI agents with her really like her coffee. Is that all you've got?"

Cowel's face reddened. Kiddenly dropped his head and shook it as if a sacrilege had just occurred. "Our man here, Fritzie, will kill your dad, Charlie. Strangle him. Tough way to go out. Helpless to the last and then you just give up. That's your final thought. You give up."

"You really think you can get away with that?"

"You might remember Fritzie, AJ," Kiddenly said. "He once drove a pickup truck into your car as your mother drove you home from school. Nothing personal. Merely a warning for your father."

AJ's stomach turned. So this was why, so many years ago, his father reacted so strongly to the accident. His father had been warned not to run for the U.S. senate. But after much soul searching, he did. He knew his country's sickness would only grow and eventually find his family anyway. So he ran for the office. *Good for you, Dad.*

"I recognized you back when Charlie here broke his leg at the Rose Bowl game. Great catch."

"Julia's parents and her brother will die in a house fire," Cowel said. "That chicken coop they live in won't even need an accelerant."

AJ responded in an even voice, almost casually. "We have all the evidence we need to try and convict both of you for defrauding America of billions of dollars."

"And loyal members of the FBI and CIA are on their way right now to arrest you bad boys," Charlie added.

"And they report to men who work for us who know we are here. Your obituaries are probably already written."

"AJ, I'm getting tired of this crap." Charlie raised his voice. "It's sounding like a bad episode of Dallas."

The wind picked up, and Cowel smiled. "Looks like I have the wind in my sails again, boys. An omen. Refuse to testify and you'll both be set free. You will save your families' lives. Go any further with this and you will see the power we wield."

"AJ, I'm for calling their bluff and just leaving now."

"Then it's plan B," Senator Kiddenly said, raising his cane in the air.

When nothing happened, both senators looked to the surrounding woods. The signal to shoot had been given. Cowel looked to Fritzie whose sardonic smile froze AJ and Charlie. From behind his back Fritzie pulled a sawed-off pistol grip shotgun and walked toward the unarmed men. As he began to raise the shortened barrel his head exploded, his body thrown backwards and onto the hood of the limo. The sound of a rifle shot echoed through the trees. Instinctively, Charlie and AJ turned and scanned the woods, looking for the source of the rifle shot. Turning back to the sound of Fritzie's shotgun being cocked, now in the hands of Senator Cowel, his red face contorted in rage. A red blotch mid chest, his clothes expanded with air, he crumpled to the ground.

AJ fell to his knees. Charlie covered his face with his open palms as if to blind himself to what had just occurred. As he recovered his senses and dropped his hands, he watched as Senator W.E. 'Billy' Kiddenly, eyes wide in disbelief, lost his balance and collapsed to the ground.

"Immunity. Immunity. Let me live and I'll talk."

AJ and Charlie watched incredulously as the man who was thought of as a venerable American patriot, elected six times as a U.S. senator by the good people of the U.S.A, squirm his way on hands and knees to the safety of the limo, pawing at the door handle until it opened, before crawling in for safety.

The expectation of being murdered along with Fritzie and Cowel weighed heavy on Charlie. He began to shake.

"We'd be dead already if that was the plan, Charlie. Chill out."

"Is it like this in war, AJ? When you're close to death do you feel like a disinterested party watching things in slow motion? Then does it hit you that you will be turned off like a light switch? No more awareness. No more nothing?"

"When I saw my first buddy hit with a bullet, and he fell dead, I couldn't believe how he was just there, moving, talking, and now he'll never move again."

"I need a drink," Charlie said, collapsing to his knees.

"I hear rotors. A helicopter. More than one. Wanna sit here and get a rocket zeroed in on you or make a run for the trees?"

It was like practices back at the University of Texas campus in Austin. Charlie Prendergast and his go-to receiver AJ Morales sprinted to the woods, each trying to pull ahead of the other. Halfway to the trees the amplified voice of FBI Agent Sampson filled the clearing.

"We'll take it from here, gentlemen."

Charlie and AJ slowed to a trot and then to a walk. Both bent over, hands on their knees, gasping for breath.

"You're out of shape, pardner," Charlie said.

"I was ahead of you."

"I was just about to start my sprint."

Two hulking helicopters skimmed the tops of the trees before landing in the clearing A third, smaller one, stayed high in the air, watching.

"That smaller one is an Apache attack copter. It's capable of taking out just about anything."

"Including us?" Charlie asked.

"These Sikorsky's are about to unload a whole bunch of our friends from the FBI and CIA. Any professional shooter will be long gone."

"So the Apache sneaks up from the other direction as the sound of the big helicopters' rotors cover its noise."

"You have a flair for this stuff, Charlie."

Before the large helicopters completed their landing, four

swat-team soldiers spilled out of the belly of each and ran toward Charlie and AJ, rifles at the ready. Agents Putney and Sampson followed, both dressed in camouflage, wearing bullet-proof vests. Another agent took snapshots, a fourth pointed a video camera.

"Thank God you two are ok," Putney said. "Is that body in front of the limo who I think it is?"

Charlie and AJ nodded.

"Someone assassinated a sitting U.S. senator!" Putney exclaimed. "Won't be able to keep this quiet. It's a media firestorm, for certain. What happened?"

"Speaking as the bait," Charlie said, "it beats the shit out of me."

"Kiddenly is in the limo," AJ said. "Stuff is coming out every orifice."

"He's hit?"

"No, he's just a spineless coward."

Putney waved an agent to the limo as well as the two cameramen. "It took a drone to find you. That's what took us so long. Somehow they were able to knock out electronic communications for ten square miles. We never saw that coming."

"We were offered terms as you expected," AJ said. "We refused, and the threats poured out of their mouths. Once they knew we weren't about to back down, Kiddenly raised his cane in some sort of a prearranged signal. When nothing happened he looked behind us. There."

Sampson shouted to several agents to explore the woods in the direction AJ pointed. "The only heat signature or motion we detected from the copter was a flock of pigeons and seagulls."

"Then be careful of those seagulls 'cuz one them is one hell of a shot," Charlie said.

A compact muscular agent with graying hair stooped to evaluate Senator Cowel's body and then that of Fritzie, the late chauffeur. Other agents pulled a reluctant sobbing Kiddenly out of the limo.

"What do you see, Piotrowski?" Putney asked the agent who was still kneeling by the chauffeur's body.

"Assuming the shooter was there in the woods," he pointed, to where AJ had also pointed, "I'd say a thirty caliber. Quite a shot. See how the wind is swaying the treetops off the harbor?"

"Congressman, how did all go down?" Sampson asked.

"When nothing happened from Kiddenly's signal, Cowel looked at Fritzie there who pulled out that shotgun, leveled it and then his head exploded, and his body fell backwards."

"Then," Charlie took over, "we looked back to where the shot came from, saw nothing, heard a growl-like sound, turned back and somehow Cowel had the shotgun and was about to pull the trigger when he was shot in the chest. That's when Kiddenly shit a brick and crawled into the car."

"Nobody shot at us, but we felt the woods were our best option for continued survival," AJ said. "Then you came."

"Wish I could have seen that," Sampson said before chuckling.

"Piotrowski," Putney said. "Why a difficult head shot to the driver and the easier chest shot with the senator?"

"The driver was wearing a bullet-proof vest. The senator wasn't. The shooter has an eye for detail. And that's 400 maybe 450 yards away if that's where he was sniping from."

The agent with the camera, a fresh-faced boy, probably still in his late twenties, pointed rangefinder binoculars at the sniper's suspected position. "426 yards to be exact, Agent Piotrowski."

The veteran agent glared at the boy. "You chair-born rangers are something else. Ever hear the saying, 'A fool with a tool is still a fool?'"

"Over here!" Someone shouted from the edge of the woods and curiosity took the best of everyone. Two men, both in camou-flaged clothing lay dead about twenty feet apart, their bodies lay just inside the cover of the trees and underbrush. "Crossbow bolt. There," Piotrowski pointed, "through the lung and into the heart. Bet the other guy has the same souvenir."

This proved to be true.

"Look at how both darts entered the bodies at the same spot. By the angle, the shooter was in a tree. Probably waiting for these two for most of the night. Two excellent and silent shots. Then the shooter was free to take out the driver and the guy in the monkey suit."

"That was a U.S. senator," the cameraman agent said.

"Not any more, you thumb sucker," Piotrowski replied.

"So until we get forensics reports, what happened, Ed?" Putney asked Piotrowski.

"Those two were pro shooters. You won't find IDs. If they still have fingerprints, you'll find them in the FBI print database. Take facial shots and send them to the CIA. They may be able to ID them by their mug shots. Unless they work for the CIA."

"No commentary. Stay with the facts," Sampson said.

"Whoever killed these two is a real mystery to me. Four perfect shots with different weapons. Probably ex-military. An experienced hunter for certain."

"Why a crossbow?" AJ asked. "Someone thinks he so good he's hot-dogging it and showing off?"

"If the shooter had taken out this sniper with a rifle, the other one would have immediately headed for cover. Then a gun battle would have ensued. A bolt shot into a body in that spot collapses the lung. You can't scream. It pierces the heart, and you die quickly; silently. Then our Robin Hood had all the time he wanted to cock his bow again, place another bolt and take aim at the second shooter. Two silent kills."

"He's not one of ours," Putney said to an unnamed CIA agent. "Yours?"

The CIA agent shook his head.

"It sure smells like the CIA," AJ said.

The agent glared at him.

"Knock it off, Congressman," Sampson said. "I'll vouch for

this agent. He's one of us."

"Well, whoever the shooter is," Piotrowski said, "I sure wouldn't want him coming after me."

"Any names come to mind from your past?" Putney asked Piotrowski.

"A few. Most in nursing homes. Doubt if one of the diaper generation could pull this off."

"We'll need them in your report. We have three murders and one assassination here."

"This wasn't murder," Piotrowski said. "It was garbage removal."

"Not a word on what went down here. By anyone. We will have to keep the senator's body on ice. The press will be all over us as it is. The politicians will start a damage-control project immediately, and their best spin doctors will be on this like flies on shit."

Chapter 37

Julia adjusted the volume on the TV with the remote button.

"Welcome to GNS Breaking News. I am Nancy Frasier in New York and we have Phil Karcher in Washington Harbor."

"Nancy, as this network's political analyst, give us your take on just what is going on in Washington lately with all these announcements?"

"Phil, not since Watergate or the IRS scandal have dominoes fallen so fast and so hard and with an indication of more to come. Since a Corpus Christie reporter supplied a confirmed statement from former Republican U.S. Senator Billy Kiddenly, saying he had evidence that Afghanistan veteran and war hero, U.S. Congressman AJ Morales was conspiring with Al Qaeda and contrary to America's interests when in Afghanistan, the dominoes began falling."

Julia's stomach rolled.

"Today, Democratic U.S. Senator Luis Vega, from New Mexico has verbally charged Kiddenly with an ethnic slur against Congressman Morales. Vega has called freshman U.S. Congressman Morales a war hero who spent three tours of duty as a special operations medic and was wounded twice. To call Morales a traitor to his country has infuriated many key players in the Latino community across the country."

What a country. Can't shake up people with facts of corruption, but they won't tolerate a racial slur. Julia realized at that moment much more work lay ahead of her.

"Demonstrations broke out within an hour in Austin, Texas and then in D.C. Crowd sizes are estimated to be more than ten thousand strong in some urban areas. To further fuel the fire, Kiddenly has since stated that Congressman Morales's mother is an illegal alien and should be deported. I have it on reliable authority that it has been confirmed that Mrs. Morales was naturalized over 30 years ago."

"Nancy, this seems like a Republican name-calling of sorts to discredit Congressman Morales and deflect the real issues."

"Less than an hour ago I learned from a source inside the U.S. House

that Congressman Morales is heading up a House subcommittee hearing concerning a company called Security Measures Services. The freshman congressman has recently subpoenaed a Washington lobbyist representing the SMS Company. While the CEO of SMS recently died of, get this, mysterious circumstances after also being subpoenaed, there is rumored to be a highly placed SMS resource who has promised to testify. SMS is being investigated for possible illegal operations in efforts to defraud the United States government through doubling billing, blatant payoffs, and collusion by powerful political factions here and in Afghanistan."

"Nancy, I could not help but question a possible link between former Senator Kiddenly's charges about the congressman's activities while in the military in Afghanistan and Morales' subcommittee hearing."

"That is an astute point, Phil. It appears that this review into the ethics of SMS operations in Afghanistan has been going on for some months. Resources from the U.S. State and Justice Departments are well-informed on this and are not talking as yet."

"Thank you, Nancy. As always, we will be following this story closely as it unfolds and keep you informed as we gather more breaking news. We'll have a complete update at 9. Join us then."

Chapter 38

Nicola Scozzari sat in his regal leather chair, watching his thoroughbreds graze in the twilight of the day. The rolling hills of his Kentucky estate looked more like a golf course than a natural setting. It had cost him a pretty penny to orchestrate his home office (he preferred "command center") view to make it just the way he wanted it. The goal was more to impress his view upon nature than to win a Home and Gardens award.

Things were not going well lately. But they would change. This had happened before. He would fix it all. Make it right. He always did. Congress was on his ass about SMS. Perhaps he had been a bit too avaricious about raising prices, double billing, and cost-added contracts. When the government bought a wrench for $250, Nicola expected the first $200 of it in his own pocket. Antonia was acting up again, slutting her way through Texas. Her husband was a weak-kneed disgrace with fear in his eyes and Nicola could smell it on him at their last meeting. Untrustworthy. So much for trying to merge his Scozzari empire with the East Coast blue bloods. While they thought they made presidents, it was Nicola that made the Congress. And when things got grim, they always came to him with their bargaining chips. He prided himself on being a shrewd bargainer.

Two of my own men taken out trying to kill Toni's husband. Who would stand against his orders? He would find the team and track them back to the source. He looked forward to just this kind of revenge. His orders would be fulfilled. It was inevitable. His two best snipers were in place to take out his son-in-law, this time for certain, and the troublesome congressman who he had steered his daughter away from years ago. A Latino in congress. That tightened his jaw. The call would come. He would answer it. The code words "chapter closed" would confirm the kills. Two problems crossed off quickly. This might end as a good week.

Why hadn't the dogs been released yet? By this time, they were usually chasing the damn deer off his property. The sheepdogs kept the geese from crapping by the pond, and his Dobermans took care of anyone stupid enough to crawl over his fence. He swiveled his chair and fired up his surveillance cameras. Nothing. Where the hell were his men? A button hidden under his heavy oak desk summoned his security center. He hit it again. This time he held it down and pushed harder as if that would make the signal louder. Nothing.

Alarms started going off, but they were the ones in his head. His imagination painted possibilities. The office was kept dark on his orders. He disliked bright lights and daytime in general.

As the king of all he surveyed stood to punish his subjects for their lack of instant attention, footsteps approached. No, not footsteps, but that of high heels on his marble floors. Reaching for his 9 mm Beretta, he laid it on his desk where no one entering could see it. The sight of his estranged wife, Benedetta, daughter of the New York Mob, turned his stomach.

"What could be worse than my ex-wife coming on an unexpected visit?"

"Long overdue, Nicola."

"Where are all my men?"

"They were never yours. Just on loan."

"I'm sending you truckloads of profits daily. The SMS scandal will never touch me. Why come here now?"

"Seems I've been reunited with my daughter."

"The apple never falls far from the tree."

"You tortured her."

"Why should you care now?"

A muffled sound came from the darkness behind Benedetta.

"I knew you would never come alone. Women are so pathetic."

Nicola Scozzari sneered at his ex-wife, Mafia princess, whispered *"what an artist dies in me,"* jammed the barrel of his

Beretta into his mouth and pulled the trigger.

Benedetta flicked away a spot of blood on her cheek and shook her head. "He always wanted the last word."

Chapter 39

The nondescript safe house, a typical farmhouse in need of a paint job, moss growing on the north face, and a sagging front porch had been skillfully turned into a mini-fort on the inside. The living room looked traditional, but further analysis would reveal the interior walls were lined in steel shielding. The basement was like a vault, capable of holding prisoners or as a safe room within a safe house in lieu of a breach during an attack. There was a decent-size conference room, a communications center to rival NASA and a kitchen staffed with a gourmet cook. Charlie and AJ sat in the kitchen, sipping coffee while agents sans suit coats, chest holsters visible, paced around in each room.

"My lawyer called last night," Charlie told his pal. "He received papers from Antonia in the mail. My divorce is final."

"Good news, buddy," AJ replied.

'Why the shit-eating grin?"

"I'm just happy for you."

"It was all legal and even included my signature, which I never signed, and it was witnessed by a notary public. Toni is done with me, and whether it was done legally or illegally, I accept it. I know you had something to do with it."

"Do tell," AJ replied, then flicked the newspaper he was glancing through on the table so Charlie could see the front-page picture.

Charlie smirked and shook his head. "I was proud of this picture, taken when the three of us thought we were on the top of the world. You, me, and Toni. I could hear Sinatra singing 'I've got the world on a string,' in my head. Turn the clock ahead a few years and it's back on Face Book, YouTube and anywhere else you look. Except everybody thinks I'm an executive at a corrupt multinational corporation and you were probably having tea with Osama Bin Laden when you were a POW. What the hell happened?"

"Did you ever stop to think you married into a merger between the Mob and a corrupt American political system?"

"Thanks for not sugarcoating it, buddy. But I deserve it. I've been just drifting through life up to now."

"No meaning to life, take it as it comes, no goals, no focus. Sounds empty."

"I was raised to confront problems on my own. Maybe some advice from Pop or close friends. It's my mother who kept prodding me to ask why, to go to the root cause of things. It bothered me then. Now I crave it. Is it the same in a Mexican-American political family?"

"No," AJ replied through a smirk. "My family would drown out the pain by practicing as a Mariachi band. I was on the trumpet and my mother played the guitarrón. I still have my sombrero."

"That's just how I imagined it," Charlie replied.

"Did you ever read Mark Twain, Charlie?"

"Some."

"As an elected official I am not particularly proud of my profession right now. Well, Twain once said, 'Suppose you were an idiot. And suppose you were a member of Congress. But then I repeat myself.'"

Charlie's cell rang, and he brushed past the agent who blocked the back door of the safe house. A call from his mother was something he did not want anybody else to hear.

"Hi, Mom. How's Pop?"

"Like two peas in a pod. He wanted me to call and ask the same about you. He's okay. How are you?"

"Fine, now that I know he's okay."

"He's up to his ears in political hearings and stuff like that but a delightful change has come over him. He's like the young man I married again."

"Mom, I thought for a time—"

"So did I, Charles. Your father has been threatened for years by men who promised to kill you and me and your sisters if he did not go along with their agenda. He swallowed his pride for all those years, on our behalf."

"Did you—"

"I always suspected."

"I don't know what to say."

"Once this all settles down he wants to talk with you. For now, he wants to let you know that he is always there for you."

"I guess I always knew that."

"He says he was especially with you on February 23, 1945."

"Mom, that doesn't make any sense."

"Doesn't it? Well, we'll all be together sooner than we know. You can ask him to explain then. Come home, son. We are all so proud of you."

On returning to the safe house, Charlie was summoned to the conference room where AJ and Julia were already there as well as the now-familiar faces of FBI agents Putney and Sampson, CIA agent Dell and several other men and women. With the room abuzz with several conversations before the official beginning of the meeting, Charlie turned to AJ and asked what the significance was of the date of February 23, 1945?

"It is the date of that iconic picture and the symbol for the WWII monument, Iwo Jima."

Charlie sat back and beamed.

"What's going on?" Julia asked.

"He was there."

"Who?"

"My Pop."

"At the monu—"

The friends shared a moment which only they could appreciate.

"I'll tell you all about it. That is, once I understand it myself."

"Brushes with death do wonders for you, Mr. Prendergast."

"Gee, thanks."

Charlie unintentionally jumpstarted the meeting with: "Can someone here tell me how the national media can get this can of worms we've all opened so wrong?"

"It may well be a proper place to start, Marcus, given the naivety of our freshman congressman and his companions," Agent Putney said.

Order, then control of the meeting went to the unknown Marcus, a stately looking fellow who seemed used to command. "A still-unraveling political situation of this magnitude is difficult to initially assess. The reasons are complex and diverse with many interdependencies to unravel. At a high level, remember we are a free nation, so free speech reigns. We have a hungry mass media feeding a hungry populace with a mixture of facts, gossip, speculation, and he said/she said. The competition for readers and viewers and whoever else is demanding the latest news is a cacophony of voices attempting to outshout each other. This evolving issue may take months to fully unravel."

"Great. Just great," Charlie said. "Kennedy was shot fifty some years ago, and we're still waiting for the truth from that conspiracy cover-up."

"I did not say 'truth' at any point, Mr. Prendergast," Marcus said. "At this very moment this room is being bombarded by electro-magnetic waves from audio, video, webcasting, broadcast, Internet, news carriers, subscription and pay-for-view services, all looking for a home to spew their data on us. We could control it all from one single point, but our Constitution prohibits that. So we must rely on the good intentions of those who write our stories and those who analyze and present them."

"I understand," Charlie replied.

"Bias and prejudice are natural and present in every emotion we ever feel. It's only with this politically correct horse crap where every opinion matters and every idea is equal that there is absolute equality."

"We get what you are saying, Marcus," AJ said.

"Thank you, Congressman. There was a time over a decade ago when I was in charge of illegal sports betting and prosecuting attempts to fix sporting events. It's an exceptionally lucrative business. I was afraid at one point I was going to have to cast serious shame one of the great moments in college football victories. I was following a possible one-hundred-thousand-dollar bribe to a running back to drop some critical passes. Turned out the wide receiver was a man of honor, and though almost broke, refused the bribe."

"Damn, Marcus," AJ said. "Lucky for that kid he made the right decision."

"Lucky for all of us he is still making right decisions. I happened to know the boy's father. He was a distinguished statesman and was cut off at the knees by a corrupt system. I've been following those perpetrators for a long time, and am beginning to see the light at the end of the tunnel that will allow me to get my hands on them."

"This is not the Inquisition, Congressman," Agent Putney said. "I know the FBI, CIA and their directors have gotten a bum rap from the media and the movies and the like, but everyone here is a red, white and blue American. We are proud to know you three, and we are here to serve and protect you."

"Does that satisfy you, Mr. Prendergast?" Agent Sampson asked.

"Actually I feel very ashamed for doubting you guys."

"Now to business," Marcus said, turning the meeting over to a nondescript man with a pointed finger.

"My name is John Bosworth. I am an associate attorney general for the U.S. Department of Justice. I will be working directly for you, Congressman Morales, on your subcommittee to investigate SMS and charges of corruption. My team and I will report directly to the president in this particular instance."

A knock came at the door, and Bosworth said, "Come in."

A CIA agent Charlie and AJ had seen before appeared.

"Sir, you said to interrupt when we were leaving?"

"Yes. Bring him in, Agent."

The agent waved another man into the room.

"Mamadzai?" AJ said, shocked and momentarily disoriented as his mind reeled from the present to memories of Afghanistan.

"Yes. Thank you for remembering me, AJ. Or I should say Congressman AJ."

"You are the bravest of men to come here and speak of what you know."

"My brother looks down at me from Paradise and smiles."

With that, Mamadzai was whisked away to who knows where.

"He will be treated fairly, Mr. Bosworth?"

"Yes. In exchange for his information on SMS we will actively work with him to remove the current Afghan dictator. What was his comment about his brother about?"

"Years ago, in Afghanistan, a PJ medic patched up some of our men in a Recon mission gone sour before they were flown to proper care. With a few moments on his hands, waiting for his time to board the chopper, he helped a wounded insurgent."

"And that insurgent was Mamadzai's brother?"

"Yes, sir. And he lived to tell the tale about the medical aid. Mamadzai let me live because of that single deed."

"This old marine was patched up twice by a PJ. 'That others may live,' right, Major?"

AJ nodded.

"So, barring any more interruptions," Bosworth said, "let's cover where we are with this."

"Senator Cowel is dead. He was assassinated in a rural area of Maryland. The media has not gotten word of this event as yet. Former Senator Kiddenly will not be charged, nor investigated by us. He has provided key information and has been granted immunity. All blame will be heaped on the late Senator Cowel and possibly, Senator Ebers."

"Dead men tell no tales," Charlie muttered.

"Nicola Scozzari, chairman of the board of SMS, will not be investigated either," Bosworth said, eyes looking at the table.

Charlie, AJ and Julia could only exchange frustrated expressions with one another.

"So where do we go from here, Mr. Bosworth?" AJ asked.

"Kiddenly will sit on his yacht, floating around the Gulf. He has been legally muzzled like a dog. None of his cronies will touch him with a ten-foot pole. He'll die a nasty and powerless old man. Most of the rats are leaving SMS as we speak. That's fine since you've cut off its head. Scozzari is in hot water with two Mob families now and is a diminished threat. While the investigation is active and guilt is being assigned, the media will be all over you three. Prepare yourselves for celebrity. So watch your mouths and get used to your newfound fame."

Another knock at the door and Bosworth gave permission to for an agent to enter yet again. The agent pointed to a cell phone and mouthed "important" to Bosworth who excused himself.

"So," Charlie said after a whistle, "talk about learning how to swim by being thrown into the deep end of the pool."

"I haven't seen you this animated in some time, Charlie," AJ said. "Surviving two assassination attempts suits you."

"Thanks. I've been reunited with my father and family. We see eye-to-eye on things. And," he winked at Julia, "I was just served with papers. Toni has finally agreed to a divorce."

"That's all great news," Julia said.

Bosworth entered, wearing a wide smile. "Gentlemen, with the demise of U.S. Senator Cowel, I have just been informed by Governor Bowie of the great state of Montana that he has selected a candidate to fill the vacant seat for the rest of the late senator's term. Let us all stand and applaud his choice. Congratulations Senator Abbott."

The roar in the room was immediate. Charlie watched Julia retain her cool, with head up, chin out.

"Senator, you have my departments and my personal pledge for complete support," Bosworth said.

"And the FBI," Sampson said.

"And the CIA," Dell said.

"Gentlemen," Julia said as she rose, "I know full well that your ongoing belief and tireless support of our Constitution has done much more for this country than the recent effort of us three, but thank you all."

"Congressman Morales," Agent Putney said, "please tell us that this butt-kicking trinity you have forged has no plans to stand down now."

It was only at that moment that AJ, Julia, and Charlie actually realized what they had accomplished as a team. They also realized this was not the end of something, only the beginning. None of them had any intention of backing down on political, military and corporate corruption.

Mr. Bosworth cleared his throat. "Before we all giggle and sing 'Yankee Doodle,' I'd like to inject some go-forward strategies here. What I have to say now is strictly confidential. Since all of you in this room have risked your lives and quite possibly those of your families, you deserve to know this. All of us have targets on our backs. There is a heartless and corrupt entity that has burrowed its way into the heart of America's political system, corporate America and our society. Collectively, they have been knocked to the mat this day, but they will rise again and with revenge on their minds. We will offer you three 24/7 protection, and we'll all be watching each other's backs, but I think all of you know this is not a guarantee that we are free and clear of retribution. As patriots, we did what was right and have accepted the consequences."

"Knowing this very well, Admiral Prendergast did not visit the president, tender his resignation and somehow bargain for immunity. This is just the cover story. The truth is that the president was invited, some say lured, to the Pentagon where he was confronted with not only Admiral Prendergast, the Chairman of the Joint Chiefs, but also his fellow service chiefs representing the U.S. Army, Navy, Air Force, the Marine Corps, and the National Guard, men and women appointed by the president through senate confirmation. The Secretary of Defense was also in attendance. The president met with this group in private for only thirty minutes. He came out of the room pale and deflated."

"Oh to have been a fly on the wall in that meeting," Agent Sampson said after a soft whistle.

"When you think about it," Agent Putney added, "it was Nicola Scozzari against the Admiral of the U.S. Navy. One could say we just lived through a showdown between the Mafia and the U.S.S. Enterprise."

Most laughed, all applauded.

"Best guess from our contacts on site," Bosworth continued, failing miserable at hiding a smile, "is that the strongest military organization on earth has been inspired by what Admiral Prendergast related to them and explained to the president that his military forces would support him as long as he kept his oath to defend the Constitution of the United States of America."

"Gentlemen, we have forged a team and have gained momentum now and must keep moving forward," Julia said. "As a sitting U.S. senator, I'd like to note that here sits a U.S. congressman, and there is the son of an American hero who has demonstrated we have the U.S. military with us, and here sit the U.S. Justice and State Department and their FBI and CIA agencies. I see a cohesive team of Untouchables. What we need now is to make the findings on SMS and its leaders as visible as possible. We now must move to help wake up the American people. And then that American Eagle will raise its magnificent wings and protect the land, talons outreached to protect the free and the home of the brave once again."

Nearly thirty men and women, once weary and ashamed government bureaucrats arose, renewed, teary-eyed, applauding, pledging their lives and spirits to fight, as patriots, for their country. Numerous conversations, handshakes and hugs ensued.

"AJ," Julia said, "despite our first disastrous meeting, you've become a second brother to me."

They embraced warmly.

"Never thought I'd ever hug a U.S. senator," AJ smiled. "Especially a Republican."

"And I hope a picture of me embracing a Democrat from the U.S. House never surfaces."

"Congratulations, Senator Abbott," Charlie said, holding out his hand, which Julia accepted.

AJ laughed, face to the ceiling. "Now doesn't that speak volumes about you two? I know you can throw a pass, Charlie Prendergast, but can you make one?"

Charlie felt the heat rise to his cheeks, and knew it spoke volumes.

"At least ask her out to dinner. She knows you are a single man again."

"Julia, will you—"

"Yes, Charlie."

Time Traveler

A view of today;
What might be of tomorrow…
Informing and prophesying;
A short glimpse of fate before it is too late
'to turn back time'.
Not making history nor predicting the future,
Alerting of the roads ahead,
A map and compass for the minds of man,
Traveling ahead, sprinting with time!
Sent with a message;
Ahead with a whisper
Waiting to be heard!

At Roundfire we publish great stories. We lean towards the spiritual and thought-provoking. But whether it's literary or popular, a gentle tale or a pulsating thriller, the connecting theme in all Roundfire fiction titles is that once you pick them up you won't want to put them down.